THE CAT, THE PROFESSOR AND THE POISON

The Cat, the Professor and the Poison

A Cats in Trouble Mystery

Leann Sweeney

AN OBSIDIAN MYSTERY

OBSIDIAN
Published by New American Library, a division of
Penguin Group (USA) Inc., 375 Hudson Street,
New York, New York 10014, USA
Penguin Group (Canada), 90 Eglinton Avenue East, Suite 700, Toronto,
Ontario M4P 2Y3, Canada (a division of Pearson Penguin Canada Inc.)
Penguin Books Ltd., 80 Strand, London WC2R 0RL, England
Penguin Ireland, 25 St. Stephen's Green, Dublin 2,
Ireland (a division of Penguin Books Ltd.)
Penguin Group (Australia), 250 Camberwell Road, Camberwell, Victoria 3124,
Australia (a division of Pearson Australia Group Pty. Ltd.)
Penguin Books India Pvt. Ltd., 11 Community Centre, Panchsheel Park,
New Delhi - 110 017, India
Penguin Group (NZ), 67 Apollo Drive, Rosedale, North Shore 0632,
New Zealand (a division of Pearson New Zealand Ltd.)
Penguin Books (South Africa) (Pty.) Ltd., 24 Sturdee Avenue,
Rosebank, Johannesburg 2196, South Africa

Penguin Books Ltd., Registered Offices:
80 Strand, London WC2R 0RL, England

First published by Obsidian, an imprint of New American Library,
a division of Penguin Group (USA) Inc.

ISBN: 978-1-61664-388-1

This book is dedicated to Lydia and Rufus,
the best friends in the world.
Thanks for always being there

Acknowledgments

I want to thank my husband for putting up with a writer who doesn't cook or even move away from her computer for months at a time. I love you. My three cats can't read, but I owe them so much for their inspiration. The dog, too, since she believes she's a cat on most days. And my sister for her encouragement. I know whom to turn to when the words won't come—my sister and my daughter. Jeffrey, Shawn, Allison and Maddie, you are wonderful and always in my thoughts. My writing group is amazing. Kay, Amy, Laura, Dean, Bob, Joe and Millie, and to my fellow bloggers on Writers Plot—Lorraine Bartlett, Sheila Connolly, Doranna Durgin, Kate Flora and Jeanne Bracken—your support and insights are always invaluable. Thanks, too, to Susie, Charlie, Isabella and Curry for your generosity and friendship. Lastly, my agent, Carol, and my editor, Claire. What would I do without your knowledge and support? Thank you, one and all, for everything.

Way down deep we are all motivated by the same urges.
Cats have the courage to live by them.

—JIM DAVIS, creator of *Garfield*

One

"'The smallest feline is a masterpiece,'" I said, using a trembling finger to gently stroke the newborn kitten curled in the palm of my hand. "And that's not me being brilliant. Those are Leonardo da Vinci's words."

"The *Mona Lisa* guy, right?" my friend Candace said.

"Yes, ma'am. An expert on masterpieces should know plenty about these wonderful babies," I said.

"Look at you," Candace said. "Your hand is shaking."

"This is a big responsibility," I said.

"You're doing fine with these itty-bitty ones," she said. "Better than I could do."

Tonight, here in the Mercy Animal Sanctuary's office, I definitely felt the full weight of the responsibility that shelter owner Shawn Cuddahee had bestowed on me. These four brown kittens entrusted to my care were preemies with a less-than-peppy mom. That meant tube feeding them every two hours, as well as caring for the weakened mama cat.

Though Shawn, who was spending all the daylight hours taking care of his shelter and these kittens, had taught me exactly what to do, I still feared I might make a mistake. That's why I'd asked Candace to spend the night shift with me—for moral support. She'd heard all the same instructions from Shawn and had taken notes, so she could help me make sure I did everything right. But as for hands-on assistance? Deputy Candace Carson of the Mercy, South

Carolina, PD performed better with an attitude and a gun than with a litter of kittens.

She said, "One more hour and we have to do another feeding. You did so good last time, Jillian."

"You're sure you don't want to give it a try?" I said.

"They all had nice fat bellies and fell right to sleep after you did the midnight feeding. Why mess with success?" Her right eye twitched, and her voice was strained by what had to be her unease. The thought that she might have to do a feeding obviously made her more nervous than when she'd stormed into my house last fall and taken a murderer into custody.

That week in October, when my Abyssinian was cat-napped and I came face-to-face with a murderer, had changed me forever—and in ways I never would've imagined. I'd moved to Mercy with my husband, John, who'd been fourteen years older than I was, when he wanted to retire. But he died of a heart attack not long after we arrived. Now I made my living sewing little quilts for cats, a mostly online business and a very quiet job. I'd thought my life was over when my husband died. But then I'd gotten involved in a mystery and a murder, and by the end of it I'd realized I had made new friends and was beginning a different life for myself.

Once the fireworks of the murder investigation ended, I began receiving e-mails from all over the country. Seems the story had reached the major news outlets. For some reason, folks have decided I can solve any mystery involving cats. So not true. I may be as curious as a cat, but I have no investigative training whatsoever. I responded to every e-mail to tell these desperate cat and dog lovers as much, but some remained persistent and have kept me updated about their lost animals. And of course they keep insisting that I can help them.

Putting those thoughts aside—the stories did tug at my heart—I said, "You're nervous about the feedings; I get that. I promise you don't have to do a thing except make sure we have enough coffee to keep us awake until six a.m.

And I am running low." I lifted my Belle's Beans travel cup. The last time I'd stayed up all night on purpose was to cram for a college exam about twenty years ago.

Candace smiled with obvious relief. "I can do coffee. That antique Mr. Coffee machine Allison insists on keeping has met its match. I will serve you awesome java."

Allison is Shawn's wife and one of the sweetest people I have ever met. But Candace was right about the coffee-maker. I knew what to get them for their next anniversary.

Candace reached into her backpack and pulled out a small purple bag labeled STELLAR BREW. "This is from the Organic Coffee Company. Bought it online." She stood and tiptoed over to the small table where the pot sat.

I set the sleeping kitten I'd been holding next to its mother's tummy, and he never stirred. Though the office was small, the space heater did a less-than-adequate job of heating the place, and I didn't want him to get chilled. Despite the gorgeous spring day, the night had turned cool, and I was glad I'd worn a sweatshirt. I'd also brought a couple of cat quilts along, hoping to finish hand binding them, but the lighting was too poor for sewing. So both Candace and I had added to our own warmth by sitting on the quilts instead.

The kittens, of course, with their heated pallet and their mother's body, would be fine, temperature-wise. But the mama couldn't lick her kittens enough—Shawn wasn't sure why she was so weak—and every so often I stroked each one to keep its blood circulation adequate. I also had to rub their tummies with tissue after feeding to stimulate urination, another task the poor cat couldn't do regularly enough. She didn't seem to mind my help, but still, the babies looked so fragile, so breakable. I vowed not to make any errors tonight.

As Candace filled the Mr. Coffee with bottled water, Snug—that's Shawn and Allison's African Gray parrot—said, "Put on the pot, Allison. Put on the pot."

Candace turned and stared up at his cage, which sat on a shelf close to the ceiling. "I'm not Allison, and I'm not sure

I like being ordered around by a bird. Shawn needs to have a talk with you about the word *please*, Mr. Snug."

"Shawn should have a talk with himself if that's how he speaks to Allison," I said with a laugh.

She pointed at me. "That's a better idea."

The mother cat mewed pathetically, and I reached into the box and stroked her head. "This sweetheart was fortunate to have been dropped at Shawn's doorstep right before she delivered."

"Lucky?" Candace sat back down to the grumbling tune of the old coffeepot as it worked its magic. "I'd say someone knew what they were doing—knew how amazing Shawn is with animals. Course, that might just be the cop in me, because I don't believe in luck and I don't believe in coincidences. No, ma'am, not me."

"Tell me something I don't know," I said. "But you're probably right. Luck had nothing to do with it. Shawn has told me before how people are always dropping off dogs and cats in the dead of night. I could never do what he and Allison do. I'd be too furious with the people who'd abandoned the animals to think straight."

"Not everyone believes that cats are the most wonderful creatures on earth," Candace said.

"Wonderful? That reminds me." I took my phone from my jeans pocket and pulled up the live feed on my personal "cat cam." I laughed out loud at what I saw going on in my living room across town. My three cats, Chablis, Syrah and Merlot, were tearing apart a roll of toilet paper. Syrah was sitting like a king in his own special shredded pile. I handed the phone to Candace. "Check this out."

Her blue eyes widened, and she grinned. "I think they want you to know exactly how mad they are that you left them alone all night."

"This shredding thing is nothing new. I might have to put a child safety lock on the bathroom cabinet. Both Syrah and Merlot can open anything, though. They'd figure it out eventually."

Candace handed the phone back. "Knowing your cats,

I'd place bets on that. But exactly why did you volunteer for night duty here? I know you're a sweetheart and when Shawn asked you couldn't say no—just like I couldn't say no to keeping you company—but you've never done this before, have you?" She stood as the wonderful aroma of freshly brewed coffee filled the office. The pot was sputtering and beckoning now.

"No, but with Allison driving to Clemson a couple days a week for classes, she needs her sleep. And leaving the kittens at the vet was too expensive. Contributions to the shelter are way down."

"I forgot about her starting school," Candace said. "What's she studying, again?"

"Preveterinary medicine." I took the cup of steaming brew that Candace offered. "In a few years they won't need to pay the vet. She'll *be* the vet."

"Wow. She'll make a great veterinarian," Candace said, sounding wistful.

I'd met Candace last year during the murder investigation, and ever since, we'd become closer and closer friends. In some ways I felt motherly, but really more like her good friend. Despite our twenty-year age difference, we seemed alike in many ways. She was obsessed with becoming a better cop, and I was obsessed with my cats and my one-woman job. There'd been a time when my old job had consumed me, so I guess I understood Candace on that level. I'd traveled the world buying fabric for a large company, but that hectic life was over. I'd met John, the financial adviser for said company, and when he was ready to retire to go fishing and sit by the lake, I discovered I wanted to return to my first love—the simplicity and peace of handwork. If only we'd had more time sitting together looking out on Mercy Lake. If only.

Knowing that Candace wanted desperately to go back to school herself and become a crime-scene investigator or even an FBI forensics expert, I decided that talking about Allison's new venture wouldn't work. Since Candace helped her mother with her bills, money was tight and the topic of school made her depressed. Time to change the subject.

"Cards?" I said.

"Double solitaire?"

"Sure, just don't injure my hands when you slap down those cards. I have kittens to feed," I said.

"So you want an advantage? Guess I have to go along with that this one time," she answered with a smile.

We sipped coffee, chatted and played cards for the next several hours, stopping for the scheduled tube feedings. Candace was too afraid to even pick up the kittens, saying she was scared she might injure one. Both of us handling them probably wasn't a good idea, anyway.

Snug had finally tucked one leg close to his body and went blissfully to sleep while Candace and I kept each other awake. But at four a.m., both of us were having a hard time keeping our eyes open, much less shuffling the cards. The only thing that helped me stay halfway alert was the tarantula that Shawn kept in the glass case across the room. I don't mind spiders, but a big hairy one that might climb out of that tank and wander my way gave me the creeps.

We both started when Candace's phone jangled "Sweet Thing," a Keith Urban song she adored.

"Must be the job calling at this hour," she mumbled before she answered. But she didn't even get to say hello before I heard a frantic female voice on the other end. Candace listened, rolled her eyes, listened some more. Finally she said, "Robin, calm yourself. I understand this is important to you, so I assume you've called the station?"

Robin's voice bordered on shrieky when she started up again. I heard Candace inhale deeply and let the air out slowly. After she listened again for several seconds, she said, "What you were told is true. The night-duty crew has the whole town to cover, and if they say they can't get there—"

More agitation spewed from Candace's phone, and she held it away from her ear. After she let Robin go on for another fifteen seconds or so, Candace said, "How's this? I'll come by a little after six. That's as soon as I can get there. We'll have plenty of time to figure this out before little Jack leaves for school."

When Robin spoke this time, she must have been relieved by this offer, because I couldn't hear her response. Seconds later, Candace closed her phone.

"You could leave now if someone needs you," I said. "I've got a handle on the kittens."

She held up one finger, her jaw tight. "First off, the last thing I want to do is deal with this now." Another finger went up. "Second problem. I don't have a ride because a certain someone by the name of Jillian Hart wouldn't let me do the driving tonight."

"Oh. I forgot about that," I said. Candace drove like she and Danica Patrick were sisters, so I do the driving when we go anywhere together. "Who's Robin?"

"Robin is the most overprotective mother in Mercy. Don't get me wrong; she's got a great heart and loves her boy, but I guess since I'm the only female on the police force, they turned her over to me after all the 911 calls."

"I'm not following," I said.

"Robin was calling 911 for everything from Jack's splinters to when he'd come down with the flu. So now, instead of calling 911, she calls me."

"Everything is okay, then?" I said.

"It's no emergency, but since you insisted on doing the driving, I'll let you go with me to her place when we leave here. Then you can see for yourself."

I could hardly refuse, considering that Candace had agreed to stay up all night before her day off to keep me company here. "Can I have a hint what this is about?"

"We're gonna see a woman about a cow."

Two

The drive to Robin's house took longer than I thought, considering that every destination I knew of in Mercy was about five minutes from every other destination I knew of in Mercy. But we traveled over a country road I was unfamiliar with. The sunrise in front of us was muted by a flimsy fog, so no sunglasses were required. Candace kept me on a mostly southeastward track away from Mercy. Since I'd moved to South Carolina from Houston only a little more than a year ago, I shouldn't have been surprised that there were rural parts of town I'd never explored.

Shawn had arrived from home to take over kitten duty at six a.m. on the dot, but the man was cranky and there had been little conversation. If he lived inside the shelter he'd probably be even more of a grouch. Everyone needed their sleep, Shawn included. He said he had a new volunteer, a tech who worked for the veterinarian, Dr. Jensen. She would handle the next night shift. Allison would take over for the weekend and beyond since her spring break was coming up next week. I felt a little sad that I wouldn't be seeing the kittens again for a while. I could already tell them apart and had named each one before the dawn broke: Binky, who tried to suck the thin feeding tube; Pokey, whose little paws moved in slow-motion; Sleepy, the one who didn't like waking up; and Lovebug, the one who enjoyed nestling into my palm the most. Their beautiful mackerel tabby mother, whom Shawn called Clara after his grandmother, was precious and lovable. But she was weaker than her offspring, and when she wouldn't eat on her own, I'd had to give her a bottle of watered-down baby-food meat.

After twenty minutes, Candace directed me to turn left onto a long dirt driveway. The battered mailbox we passed bore the name West. The sun shed pale streaks of light across the fertile green fields on either side of the drive. Ahead I saw a small blue clapboard house and behind that a dilapidated red barn.

"Robin's husband left her about five years ago—just up and took off," Candace said. "This used to be her parents' home, so at least he didn't leave her with a mortgage. But raising a kid like Jack alone? That's been tough."

"A kid like Jack?" I said.

"Little genius. Mercy Elementary has its hands full trying to teach him anything he doesn't already know. And he's sensitive, too. To the food, to the smells, even to what fabrics touch his skin. Never knew smart kids could be as tough to deal with as the ones without as much gray matter."

As we approached, a black cat slunk out from behind the house and sat on the walkway as if waiting to greet us.

"What a beautiful baby," I said as I parked behind a white Chevy truck.

"Did you ever meet a cat that wasn't beautiful?" Candace asked.

"I definitely have not." I killed the engine, got out and knelt near my van. I reached out, and the cat didn't hesitate. It came straight to me to be petted.

"That's Lucy, the barn cat. If you have a barn, you have mice. Lucy has important duties," Candace said.

Lucy was purring up a storm, her green eyes narrowed to slits.

"Hi, Miss Candace," I heard a young voice say.

I looked up to see a dark-haired boy wearing Spider-Man pajamas. I guessed his age at about eight or nine.

"And who've you brought with you today?" he added.

Candace climbed the two porch steps and gave him

a hug before saying, "This here is my friend Miss Jillian Hart."

"Not 'this here,' Miss Candace. Just 'this' is all you need to say," Jack said. He smiled at me. "Pleased to meet you, Miss Jillian."

"Back at ya. And that's a colloquialism, by the way," I said with a grin.

"I know. And 'this here' is a regionalism. But people often look down on Southerners because of their grammar, and we can—"

"Jack, what do you think you're doing?" The woman who spoke sounded irritated. She must have come around from the barn. Her dark brown hair was the exact same shade as Jack's, and she wore pressed, immaculate blue jeans that contrasted sharply with her muddy but brightly flowered Wellington-style boots.

"Greeting our visitors, Mom. And before you get started, I know I'm wearing my pajamas outdoors. I happen to like them."

Robin West sighed heavily. "Your teacher will not applaud your choice of clothing if you go to school like that, Son. Please go get dressed."

Jack hung his head. "I'd prefer to stay home today, but if you insist." He turned and went into the house.

"He wants to stay home because I'm freaked-out about the cow. He thinks he has to take care of me," Robin said.

From what I'd overheard on the phone earlier, she was indeed freaked-out about the cow, the one Candace had told me was missing. That left her poor kid with a job—taking care of Mom. But though I only thought these things, Candace had no trouble saying them out loud.

"And who exactly made him decide he had to take care of you? You are putting a burden on that boy, Robin," Candace said.

Robin stared at her boots. "You're right. You're always right, Candy."

"Don't go all wimpy on me, girl. I'm just stating the truth, and you can take it. Invite us in so I can find out what happened to Harriett." Candace glanced at me. "Harriett is the milk cow."

"Ah," I said, as if this explained everything.

Robin removed her Wellies and placed them beside the door. We followed her inside the house, with Robin making sure Lucy didn't sneak in with us. We walked through her small and supremely tidy living room into a spotless kitchen. She offered us coffee, but I couldn't have drunk another cup if someone had put a funnel in my mouth and poured. Candace must have felt the same way, because we both opted for water.

Robin made herself a cup of tea in the microwave, a ritual that would have taken me two minutes. But Robin, it was becoming apparent, had a little OCD problem. She took her time lining up the tea bags in their box, each one as close to the next as possible. Then she wiped down the microwave, even though all she'd done was boil water. After that, she measured out a quarter cup of milk and stirred it into her tea. I almost dozed off as she washed the spoon, dried it carefully and put in the dishwasher. Finally she joined us at the round kitchen table.

"There," she said with a sad smile. "And now please help me find Harriett."

"I'll do what I can." Candace took a small notebook from her back jeans pocket. "How far do you think a cow can wander overnight?"

"I don't know," Robin said, her voice rising. "She's never run off before. She hardly comes out of the barn. And now Jack won't have his raw milk before school, and—"

Candace placed a hand on Robin's forearm to hopefully control this escalation of emotion. "I know that's what's troubling you. But one day without raw milk will be—"

"Wonderful," came Jack's voice from the kitchen entry. "I dislike raw milk immensely."

He was dressed in khaki shorts and a short-sleeved blue polo. I noticed his freckles for the first time—just a sprinkle over his nose, not the hundreds I'd had when I was his age.

Robin checked her watch. "You have your wish. There

will be no raw milk today. The school bus will be here soon, so if you will excuse us, I'll walk Jack down the driveway."

I stood. "You talk to Candace about your cow. Jack and I can find that bus."

Robin's eyes widened, and she half rose. "But—"

"Mom. Please do not embarrass me. I like Miss Jillian. She is Miss Candace's friend, so you can trust her. She and I can handle a walk down the driveway."

"But sometimes the bus drives up so close, and—"

Jack had walked over to me and now took my hand. "Let's go. And, Miss Candace, give Mom a chill pill if you have one handy."

Before we even made it out the door, Jack's questions began. "What do you do for a living?"

I turned to give him a smile and said, "I make quilts for cats. And I do charity work making quilts for soldiers' children—kids whose dads or moms have gone to war," I said.

"I've read a little about the conflicts in the Middle East. The United States needed a better understanding of the-ocracies before they went to war, wouldn't you agree?" He kicked a stone at the beginning of the drive as we made our way toward the road.

"Um . . . yes. I think you're right. What's your favorite subject, Jack?"

"All of them." He was continuing to chase the rock, and I smiled. At least something about this little guy was childlike.

"Why are you with Miss Candace if you make quilts?" he said. "I thought you were a new police officer in training, though you appear older than her. Starting police work at your age is unusual, I would imagine."

Thanks, I thought. I explained about the premature kittens and our night at the shelter, and by then we'd reached the end of the drive. And right on time, too, because the bus rumbled to a stop next to us a minute later. Jack waved and said we had more to "discuss" about "the infant cats" before the bus doors closed and he was gone.

Even though I was no expert on children—I'd never had any of my own—I knew this was one unusual boy.

"Jillian," Candace called as I was walking back toward the house. "Come check this out."

I picked up my pace and soon was standing next to her and Robin in front of the barn.

Candace said, "Robin was right to be concerned. See that padlock?" She pointed at the barn doors.

I stepped closer for a better look and saw immediately that the lock had been cut apart, though the edges of the curve had been placed close together so the damage wouldn't be quickly noticed. "Someone stole the cow?"

Robin had her arms wrapped around herself. "I just saw the door ajar. I didn't realize the lock was cut. Unbelievable. I want Harriett back, and I want to know who would do this to my Jack."

To Jack? That didn't make sense at first, but then I got it. "Maybe they didn't know about Jack and his raw milk," I said gently. "Maybe they simply wanted a cow."

"That's a problem, too," she said. "How did they know I even had a cow? Did they come sneaking around here in the dead of night? I mean, I have a precious child. What if they'd taken him instead of Harriett?"

I pictured a black-clad stranger standing between the barn and the house thinking, "Cow or kid? Hmmmm . . . guess I'll go for the cow." Then I immediately admonished myself for being so insensitive. Robin was upset, and for good reason.

Candace said, "You know how people talk in this town. The fact that you have a cow is well-known."

Very true. I'd learned that everyone knew everything about everyone's business in Mercy. Just then I was distracted by a glimpse of Lucy streaking from the barn. She kept running down the driveway. That cat was definitely on a mission.

Candace, meanwhile, was trying to calm Robin down. "I'll look into this, Robin. But first I need some sleep."

I was still watching Lucy, and then I saw why she'd been in such a hurry. "What color is Harriett?"

"She's a black-and-white Jersey," Robin said.

I pointed down the driveway. "Like that?"

Robin's hands flew to her lips before she took off running toward the lumbering cow. The poor cow looked as tired as I felt.

We all met up with Harriett in the driveway, and Candace lifted a piece of a rope dangling from the cow's neck. "This what you use to tie her up?"

Robin shook her head. "She doesn't need to be tethered. She never wanders farther than the fields."

"Looks like she escaped from whoever took her, then." Candace carefully removed the rope remnant from Harriett's neck with a smile. "And the thief left me a piece of evidence."

Oh no, I thought, managing to keep myself from groaning. I'd seen that gleam in Candace's eyes before. Anything that she considers evidence is a treasure. She had a bovine mystery this time, and for some reason, I had a sinking feeling I'd be involved in her quest for answers.

Three

I had never worked the graveyard shift, but I shouldn't have been surprised to learn that there is nothing my three cats like better than my spending the day in bed. Even Merlot, my twenty-pound red Maine coon, had stretched out beside me. He rarely joins me for sleep, so I was surprised he chose to hunker down on the bed. Chablis, the Himalayan, planted herself on my chest, and Syrah, my Abyssinian, used my legs for a bed.

Robin's cow was back home, and all was well with the world. Okay, *her* world, not Candace's. My friend had been extra quiet during the drive to her house, tightly clutching the paper lunch bag where she'd stowed the piece of rope. As my threesome's purring lulled me to sleep, I wondered whether Police Chief Mike Baca would let her work a case if the stolen "item"—not the best word for a cow, I admit—was no longer stolen. Somehow I didn't think so.

I awoke at about three o'clock in the afternoon. My cats may have been used to sleeping away most of the daylight hours, but I wasn't. I felt groggy, which I decided was due to a serious coffee hangover. I stumbled into the shower for a wake-up call, and when I came back into the bedroom, I saw all three cats circled around a bug on the floor. On closer inspection I saw it was a dead spider. They'd made quick work of the poor thing, and before one of them ate it, I grabbed a tissue from the bedside stand and tossed the spider in the trash.

The disappointed trio wandered in the direction of the kitchen while I made the bed. The quilt, which was large enough to cover the entire bed, had been a favorite of my late husband, John. I'd completed it for him before we'd married—a bear-paw design made from plaids I'd bought during a trip to Lancaster, Pennsylvania. Having something he loved close to me while I slept made the nights easier—and it *was* getting easier now that more than a year had passed. Grief was a fickle friend—embracing me at times and abandoning me at others. I supposed that was better than the constant companion it had been during the six months right after John died.

As soon as I'd smoothed out the quilt and propped the sham-covered pillows against the headboard, Chablis appeared and jumped back on the bed to settle down for another snooze.

Merlot was waiting for me in the kitchen. He'd changed into even more of a watch-cat than before. After all, last fall his best buddy, Syrah, had been nabbed, and then I'd allowed a murderer into our home—albeit unknowingly. Yes, Merlot had been in hypervigilant mode ever since, his usual warbly meow all but disappeared. His vocals were deeper, almost as if he felt he needed to sound strong. Every bedroom door had to be open, every noise attended to.

I fed Merlot and Syrah—Chablis enjoyed her naps too much to appear right now—and was making a fresh gallon of sweet tea when I heard Candace's familiar *rappity-rap-rap* on my back door. Merlot sat down by the door, staring at the knob. I called to her that it was unlocked as I squeezed the tea bags over the big pitcher and threw them in the trash can under the sink.

"Hey there," she said as she entered, bending to pet Merlot. He didn't stay around, just sort of hopped playfully and took off to a new hiding place, one never far from me.

Candace looked so fresh, so wide awake, so . . . *young.* Boy, how I missed bouncing back awake like that.

"I can't believe I didn't have sweet tea ready for this awful afternoon awakening," I said.

"Sweet tea can fix anything." She wore blue jeans and a pink T-shirt, and her blond hair was loose on her shoulders. I considered her pretty even without makeup. Especially when her eyes still glittered as much as when we'd parted this morning.

This visit had to be about her piece of evidence. Candace is enamored of evidence, is engaged in a constant love affair with all things criminal. "Grab some ice, would you?" I poured liquid cane sugar into the hot tea while Candace scooped out a handful from the ice maker.

As she plopped the cubes into the pitcher, she said, "I have an idea. But I think you should have tea first."

She was right about that, because Candace obviously had an agenda. I put two glasses on the counter, and she poured. I added more ice to our drinks, and we went around the counter, past the dining room table and into my connecting living room.

Candace settled onto the sofa and got right to it. "I'm staking out Robin's barn tonight, hoping the thief will come back. That cow got away, and I'm betting someone wants it back. Care to join me?"

"Um, I am not exactly a police officer," I said. Another night shift? I might not survive.

"Doesn't matter. I've gotten permission for you to do a ride-along. Citizens pay the bills, and they're entitled to see how we officers spend our time."

"Your boss, Mike Baca, gave you permission to take me with you?" That seemed impossible considering how we'd gone nose to nose last year and the chief of police was sure I'd been wrong about . . . well, just about almost everything.

"The chief is on vacation. Did you know he has a daughter from his first marriage? He's gone to see her in Florida for spring break."

"I didn't know." It made me realize that Candace didn't know about Kara, John's daughter—and my stepdaughter—either. Talking about Kara was difficult for me, but I did miss hearing from her. In fact, I hadn't heard from her since her dad's funeral, but I figured she'd call when she was ready. "So you don't exactly have permission for this stakeout? I'm not sure I—"

"Morris Ebeling, my once and future partner, is in charge since he's the senior officer. When I told him about the missing cow and the possible break-in, he said I could investigate all I wanted. He laughed about a missing cow and said that a ride-along was fine since he wouldn't be the one with me." Her lips thinned almost into a sneer. "You know what he's like. That man is as lazy as a lobster."

"Lobsters are lazy?" I said.

"I don't know. My mother always says that. Anyway, you stayed up last night, so your brain's in night-shift mode anyway."

"I feel drugged, if that's what you mean. But don't you think Mike Baca would take issue with me being involved in anything police related, even while he's on vacation?"

"He is so over you getting involved with that whole murder thing last year. After all, you did help figure things out at the Pink House."

The Pink House is a Mercy landmark and now under new ownership as a bed-and-breakfast. "Mike Baca is over what happened? I can't believe that, Candace. He looks the other way every time we pass each other at the Piggly Wiggly."

"That's because he's embarrassed about everything that happened. I've heard him say you're one of the smartest women he's ever met. Says you have good instincts. And I agree with him." She smiled. "Come on. The second night shift is always easier; you'll see. We'll bring a giant bag of Cheetos and pick up peanuts from Harvey Weatherstone's roadside stand."

I polished off half my drink, wondering how I could get out of this one. "You sound like we're heading for the Cinema Ten in Greenwood. Should we stash Cokes in our purses, too?"

"This particular *movie* will probably be boring as all heck. That's why I need you with me, so you can nudge me awake every so often. Come on. I stayed up with you last night, didn't I?"

She had me there. "Okay," I said wearily. "What time do we leave?"

My cats were confused when I left late Thursday for another night shift. But then, I'd slept most of the day, so maybe they thought I'd finally turned into a cat and was ready for fun in the dark, as they always seemed to be. I'd made sure to take a headache medicine that contained caffeine—because, boy, did I have a headache. I did feel more awake, but a dull throb lingered at the back of my skull. My IOU to Candace would be paid in full after this second and *last* overnighter.

Unfortunately, she was driving this time since this was police business. Not her squad car, since any potential thief wouldn't be dumb enough to raid a barn with one of those in the driveway. We went in the only unmarked car Mercy owned—a Taurus that smelled like someone had spilled beer on the carpet about ten years ago.

I was wide awake when we reached Robin's house. Candace's driving—which was like that Wild Mouse ride they used to have at amusement parks when I was growing up—jangled my nerves big-time. I'd given up asking her why she had to take every corner with squealing tires. I could tell by her smile that she loved speed—simple as that.

Robin was expecting us and came outside to direct the car around the back of the house, where we'd have a good view of both the barn and the driveway. Harriett, Candace had postulated from the tire treads, was taken away in a trailer last night, and if the thief returned to take her again, that truck would probably return.

Robin wore a terry-cloth robe and held it tightly against the night chill. The temperature had dropped from pleasant seventies this afternoon to around fifty now. She held out a key to Candace. "This is for the back door. There's a powder room right past the washer and dryer in the kitchen. Just try to be quiet. Jack needs his sleep. Poor Harriett had no milk after her ordeal, so Jack's a little run-down without his daily fix."

Isn't raw milk bad for you? I wondered. I'd heard something about people saying it was good for you again, and I guess if you owned a cow and drank it right after it was milked it might be. Certainly, people drank milk like that for years before Pasteur came around, but I wouldn't be asking for any samples. We thanked Robin for letting us use the facilities, and she went inside.

We climbed back in the car. I'd brought my pillow and now tried to position myself so I wouldn't end up feeling like I'd slept on the ground after this little adventure ended. The headache was returning in force, so I added a Coke to help with the tension headache pills I'd taken earlier. Enough caffeine, I decided, to keep an entire police force awake.

We were parked in the shadow of a huge pecan tree to make the car a little more difficult to spot, but Candace told me to recline my seat just in case we were visible. She did the same.

The promised Cheetos appeared, as well as the peanuts. Eating all that salt made for two thirsty women. It was the four Cokes we consumed between us that did us both in. I had to sneak into the house at about one a.m., but Candace managed to hold on until about three before she needed to relieve herself.

Wouldn't you know, as soon as she left, I saw a dark-clad figure skulking around the driveway curve, a pair of what looked like bolt cutters in his or her left gloved hand.

My heart started thumping in my chest as I focused hard on the intruder. There was something else in the other hand, but I couldn't tell what it was . . . Then I caught a glint as it swung by the trespasser's side. A gun? *God, please not a gun.*

My heart sped up so much, I could feel it pounding in my throat now. But curiosity wouldn't let me hide under the dash. I saw the person set down the shiny thing—a pail, I realized with relief. He or she needed only one quick snap of the tool on the replaced padlock, and the barn door swung open.

Candace, hurry. Please.

But she wasn't hurrying . . . or maybe time had simply stopped. I thought about heading for the house now that the thief was in the barn. Candace needed to get out here fast.

My fear intensified when I spotted Lucy the cat creeping toward the open barn.

No. Not the kitty. Please not the kitty.

I was about ready to try to distract Lucy when Candace opened the car door. I swallowed my surprise before it came out as a screech. "Someone's here," I whispered harshly. "In the barn. Right now."

"Gosh darn it, wouldn't you know." Candace reached beneath her seat and pulled out her gun. The gun I hadn't known was there.

I swallowed what little saliva I had left. "You brought your gun?"

"Duh, yeah. I'm on duty. Stay put. I'll take care of this." She was out the door without another word and edging toward the barn door as quietly as Lucy had.

I was afraid for her—scared stupid, to put it bluntly. What if that . . . that *horrible person* had a gun I hadn't seen? What if there was a shoot-out and Candace was injured . . . or worse? No, I couldn't think like that. She was smart, a good cop. She knew what she was doing.

Though I couldn't and shouldn't follow, at least I could listen, so I rolled down the window.

A few seconds passed before I heard Candace's angry voice say, "*Professor?* What in hell do you think you're doing?"

Four

A few seconds passed before Candace and the man she'd called *professor* appeared outside the barn.

I sighed with relief and wondered whether *Gilligan's Island*'s Mary Ann might not be far behind the professor. But this was no old TV rerun. Candace had the man by the elbow and was pulling him toward the house. Lucy, tail in the air, scurried eagerly beside them. Her curiosity had been satisfied, and all was well with the world—or so it would seem. I do tend to interpret for my own cats, so why not Lucy, too?

I felt safe enough now to get out of the Taurus and was glad I'd again worn a sweatshirt. I shivered in this dead-of-night chill.

Candace tossed me the house key. "Wake up Robin so she can meet her trespasser. But be as quiet as you can. Jack doesn't need to be a part of this."

Turned out I didn't have to wake Robin. She met me at the back door and said, "I heard voices. What happened?"

"Do you have a back-porch light?" I asked.

She flicked two switches by the door, and suddenly the Taurus and the dirt driveway were illuminated. And so were Candace and the professor. Candace's prisoner, I saw, was in handcuffs.

The man's head was down, and the black knit hat he'd been wearing was gone, revealing a mop of chin-length salt-and-pepper hair.

"Here's your thief, Robin," Candace said. "This time he decided not to steal the cow. Easier to steal the milk, I guess. Reminds me of a very bad joke."

Robin marched up to the man. "Look at me."

He slowly raised his head, and their eyes met.

"I-I-I'm s-s-sorry," he managed.

"You frightened me to death. Just who are you?" Robin asked.

"This is Professor Hubert VanKleet," Candace said. "Teaches biology at Denman College. Isn't that what you told me when we met at Belle's Beans?"

He cast his gaze downward again. "Th-that would be correct."

Robin bent and tilted her head so she could see his face again. Her tone was gentle when she said, "I would have given you milk if you'd asked. Why go to all this trouble?"

"You would have?" With his raised eyebrows and wide eyes, he seemed genuinely surprised.

Candace said, "That's the way we do things here in Mercy. Folks need something, all they have to do is ask. Guess you haven't lived here long enough to figure that out."

"What do you need the milk for?" Robin said. "Do you have children?"

"In a way," he said. "It's for my pets. I l-lost my own cow last week. She was old and she died. The cats need f-food, and I'm rather short on c-cash since taking a sabbatical from my job."

Exactly how many cats did this man have? I wondered.

"A sabbatical means you're not working, Professor. I didn't know that." Candace had backed off with the stern tone. Concern seemed to have taken over. She turned to Robin. "Do you have any No Trespassing signs posted?"

"No. I didn't think I needed them," she said.

"Only reason I ask," Candace said, "is that I can only arrest the professor for trespassing if you've got a sign posted. Course, now that he's been warned he *will* go to jail if there's a next time. Unless you want me to charge him for destroying your padlock."

"Wait a minute," I said, not feeling as nice as a Mercy-ite should. "What about stealing Harriett? Isn't that a crime?" For some reason I didn't feel a great deal of sympathy for this man, maybe because I was concerned about cats drinking only cow's milk. That wouldn't be good for them at all. Didn't this obviously intelligent person know that most adult cats are lactose intolerant? Or maybe he was simply desperate for anything to fill their tummies.

"Did you steal that cow, Professor?" Candace said.

"I—I *borrowed* her; that's all." Something in his tone, or perhaps it was the way he averted his eyes, told me this wasn't the whole story. And if he'd had an old cow, he wouldn't have been getting any milk from that source. This wasn't adding up.

Meanwhile, Lucy had taken a devoted interest in the professor's pant legs, sniffing them from calf to ankle.

"You want to press charges about the cow, Robin?" Candace asked. She seemed tired, perhaps deflated by her cow thief turning out to be a nerdy man with dark shadows under his eyes and a defeated stoop to his shoulders.

Robin again addressed Professor VanKleet. "You won't do this again, will you?"

His small, hazel eyes livened with hope. "N-no. I promise. P-please let me go. I have cats to care for. They need me."

Okay, he finally had me feeling sympathetic, too.

"Don't set foot on my property without an invite. Are we clear?" Robin said.

"R-right. I promise."

Seconds later, he was free of the handcuffs, and Candace again warned him that the next time he came near Robin's barn it would result in a stint in the town jail. "I can't hold you for anything tonight since Robin is being generous, but I hope you understand the trespassing laws now, Professor."

He ignored Candace and said, "Th-thank you so much, Ms. West. Th-thank you." VanKleet turned and started off down the road, his body no longer hunched over in shame or remorse or whatever emotion had a hold on him earlier. He'd been acting, I decided. He wasn't the least bit sorry.

"Wait a minute," I called. "How did you know her name?"

He swiveled back around—quite spritely, I might add—and offered a lopsided grin. "It's on the mailbox."

No stutter, a spring in his step. And as he walked away, I felt a small chill race up both arms. Cat owner or not, I didn't like the guy—not one bit.

My daytime sleep on Friday was cut short by cell-phone noise. I'd set my phone to vibrate, but apparently it pulsated enough to fall off the nightstand and clunk onto the hardwood floor. This woke Syrah, too, and he bounced onto my stomach before heading for the floor to attack it in case it was a living creature. Still groggy, I leaned over the side of the bed and watched through sleepy eyes as he pawed at the phone. Then I spoiled his fun and picked it up.

Shawn interrupted my "hello" with "I'm sorry, but I really could use your help again." He was speaking in a rushed whisper.

I sat up and blinked several times. Chablis stood and stretched, her lovely afternoon sleep ended. "Sure. What do you need?"

"Allison can't get back from Clemson until after supper. Some group project. And I've got this woman here, and she will not leave me alone. Allison would take care of this problem in a flash, but I got to thinking you could do just as well."

That was kind of a backhanded compliment, I thought, but instead said, "What woman? Has Lydia the stalker set her sights on you now?" Lydia Monk, the deputy county coroner, was obsessed with a good friend of mine, Tom Stewart. I'd met Tom when he installed the security system and set up my wonderful cat cam. But I knew Tom didn't think much of Lydia, so maybe she'd turned her sights on Shawn, married or not.

"No, not that nutcase Lydia. Can you come to the shelter? You'll see what I'm talking about."

"Do I have time to pick up coffee at Belle's Beans?" I wouldn't be functional without some java.

"No. I'll make some." He hung up.

Shawn may not have the best social skills with people, but his heart is pure gold. If he needed help from me, then help he would get.

Sans even lipstick, I arrived at the Mercy Animal Sanctuary in less than thirty minutes. My hair was still wet from the quick shower that had helped clear the cobwebs.

I smelled the coffee before I even got to the office door. Strong coffee. Guess that's what I needed, but I had a feeling it might resemble sludge if Shawn had made it.

When I entered the office, I saw Shawn looking less than genial, seated behind his small desk. A woman I did not recognize was parked in the lawn chair across from him. She was about my age, maybe mid-forties, with sandy hair and dark brown eyes. I noticed her muddy plaid boots, similar to what Robin had been wearing yesterday. Was it yesterday or the day before? I'd lost track of what day it was after these night shifts.

Shawn stood when I came in. "Thanks for coming, Jillian. I might have to cut you a paycheck. This here is Ruth Schultz." He came around the desk and quickly poured me a mug of coffee.

I smiled at Ruth and then took a swig of the worst lukewarm liquid I'd ever tasted. But I needed caffeine so desperately, I drank half before setting down the mug on Shawn's desk. I held out my hand to Ruth. "Jillian Hart."

As we shook hands, I caught her expression. Eyes downcast, she said, "Nice to meet you."

"Ruth has come with an admission," Shawn said. "That mama cat and her litter you helped me with? She left them at my door."

Ruth's cheeks flushed. "And I am so sorry, but I knew something was wrong with that mother cat. The way my business is going, I couldn't afford to take her to the vet,

and I'd heard about Shawn, and I am so sorry, but I thought
I was—"

"It's okay." Shawn rested a hand on her shoulder. "The
mama and litter are being cared for. Tell Jillian about the
other problem."

Ruth took a deep breath, and her exhale was shaky.
"Other cats have been coming to my barn. A new one arrived this morning, and by her swollen teats, I can tell she's
just given birth. What am I going to do with all these cats?
And where are her kittens?"

Shawn shook his head, looking frustrated. "I can't go
check this out right now, and I refuse to call that useless
animal control officer."

The one who has the restraining order against you? I said
to myself. Shawn thought the officer was lazy and uncaring,
which had resulted in a shoving match last year and subse-
quent legal action.

"What do you need me to do?" I asked.

"You're good with cats," Shawn said. "From what Ruth
has explained, they don't sound feral."

Shawn had explained to me more than once that all fe-
rals are strays, but not all strays are feral. I looked at her.
"They come up to you, then?"

"One of them does, and I can tell the others want to, but
they're skittish," Ruth said.

Shawn said, "Could you assess the situation, Jillian? Tell
me what we're dealing with? I can start networking with
other no-kill shelters to take on these cats if need be, but
that will take some time. I got my hands full here or I'd go
myself. Someone has to feed those newborns, and a man
called to say he's bringing me a dog he found."

"Okay. Assess the cats how?" I said.

"Take a cat count, see what, if any, health problems are
obvious. Fleas, ticks, abscessed teeth, wounds from catfights.
I'll load up your van with food from my donation box. Ruth
here has come on hard times, like so many small farmers."

I turned to Ruth. "You're a farmer?"

"I own several acres. I do small stuff," she answered.

"Tomatoes, okra, corn, beans, peaches and berries. I have a stand in the summer, canned fruits and veggies in the winter. But the Whole Foods in Greenville doesn't buy as much corn or okra from me as they used to, and money's tight. Either feed what tuna I've got to the cats or feed it to me. Right now we're sharing, and the supply is running short." Her eyes glistened, and she blinked hard to fight back tears. "This is so embarrassing."

I took both her hands in mine and squeezed. "I understand. My grandfather was a farmer, and he knew hard times, too. Let's get this problem taken care of right now."

She said, "That mama cat . . . her kittens. I feel so awful about what I did, and—"

"Don't worry," I said. "You brought her to the right place." I turned to Shawn. "Now, where's that cat food?"

Minutes later Shawn had loaded two twenty-pound bags of dry cat food in the back of my minivan and then went to his storage shed for a couple of crates and a pair of leather gloves, in case any of the cats needed transport for medical care. Meanwhile, I showed Ruth my cat cam. Only Merlot was in the living area, his long, red fur shimmery as he crouched in a patch of sun on the living room floor. He was swishing his tail. What was he stalking now? More spiders?

"He's so big," Ruth said with wide eyes. "And so pretty."

"And strong. My ninja warrior. This cat saved my life—in fact, all three of mine have done that in more ways than one. But that's a story for another day. I'll follow you."

Soon I was trailing her pickup, taking the same route Candace and I had used to reach the West place, but we turned off before we reached Robin's land and went through a gate and over a cattle grate. We then traveled a good distance on the narrow road. Hearty green kudzu invaded every foot of fence along the way.

She parked her vehicle near a tiny house with a screened porch, the porch probably equal to the square footage of the house. I parked behind her. On the porch I saw a bookcase lined with canning jars—jars filled with peaches and green beans. Maybe I could buy some to take home with me later. Her barn, painted a gorgeous rusty red, was in much better shape than Robin's.

A calico cat peeked from behind the side of that barn, and when I slipped out of the van and knelt down, she came toward me but stopped short. Ruth came up alongside me, and I asked, "This is the one that just delivered?"

"Yes," she whispered. "She's still hungry, is my guess."

"Let's fix that," I said.

After Ruth fetched a large plastic bowl from the porch, I said, "Do you have a paper plate? Plastic bowls can give cats little ulcers and abscesses in their mouths."

"Oh, I didn't know," she said. "Is glass okay?"

"Yup. Cats have smart immune systems. They react to toxins quicker than humans, but glass is fine."

Soon we'd filled several large Pyrex pans with dry food, set them about halfway between the house and the barn and then retreated to the porch to watch how many cats would come for supper. Since their sense of smell is so acute, I figured it wouldn't take long. A minute later, four cats were chowing down—the calico, two tabbies and a sleek black cat that tried to push aside the other three without success. They were all too hungry to tolerate top-cat shenanigans.

Ruth, her arms wrapped around her, said, "Those are the only ones I've seen—unless there are more tiger cats and I can't tell one from the other."

"Have you been able to pet them?" I said.

"The calico and the black one. Blackie seemed healthy, has a beautiful coat. Very friendly."

"Let me see if I can get closer," I said.

I stepped out through the screen door and down three steps. I moved toward the cats, and this did not go unnoticed. The black one was the first to respond to my outstretched hand and quiet calls.

He was soon rubbing against me, and with a little gentle probing I learned that he was a neutered male and that he loved to have his head scratched. The mackerel tabbies took note that their friend or leader was getting attention they might like as well. Soon they came over, too—these cats had obviously been around people—and I discovered they were a boy and a girl. One had horrible ear mites, and they all had fleas, but from what I could tell, they seemed otherwise healthy.

Mother Calico had at first continued to eat but by now was finished and sat grooming herself. Would she take off to find her litter? I guessed yes, and sure enough she started to wander off, but not without a backward look. She almost seemed to be beckoning me. That raised a flag immediately. New mothers like to hide their litters, and yet I was certain she wanted me to follow her.

I patted the black cat's head one last time. "These three are probably not going anywhere now that they know you'll feed them," I said. "I'll follow Miss Calico. My bet is she hasn't traveled far in search of food."

"Thank you, Jillian. These cats deserve better than what I can give them right now."

"They wouldn't have found you if they didn't think you were the right person to help them. It isn't all about the food, you know."

I took off, but following the calico proved far more difficult than I'd imagined. It wasn't that she disappeared. No, she kept meowing, and her mostly white coat offered little camouflage in the verdant landscape. Yup, she *wanted* me to follow, but the terrain wasn't exactly friendly. Brambles and bugs and blackberry vines with prickly stems attacked me along the way. My shins below my capris looked as if I'd shaved my legs for the very first time when we finally reached a barbed-wire fence. Our journey had taken about twenty minutes.

Miss Calico slipped underneath the fence, but I stopped dead. When I didn't follow her, she turned, sat and offered a wide-mouthed and very loud meow.

"You did a great Lassie imitation, but this is tricky, little mom." I glanced right, checking the fence, which seemed to extend forever. It was also covered with that damn kudzu vine, which was as tough as the barbed wire and entwined every inch of the fence. And it hid the barbs that lurked beneath the lush and tricky green vines.

But to my left, the fence turned a corner. I walked that way, and when I reached a post, I wiggled it. It gave enough for me to know that the wood might have rotted some at the bottom—this part of the fence was rusted and old, and not quite as obscured by strangling vines. I used both hands to loosen the post even more, and it didn't take much for the thing to lean away from me, taking down a section of fence with it.

Being careful not to get stuck by rusted metal, I stretched one leg as far as I could. The fence was still not flat enough, so I used even more force to loosen the post.

Who's trespassing now, Jillian? I thought. But I hadn't seen any POSTED notice like Candace had mentioned yesterday. I wondered whether that meant I'd be warned and not arrested if caught by the property owner, or whether a fence was enough to get me in trouble. This time, using the post to hang on to, I extended my leg just past the fallen barbed wire, though I was practically doing the splits. And I don't think I'd ever done the splits before.

I quickly learned that I'm no yoga goddess. Maybe if I had been, I wouldn't have fallen.

I yelped in pain as a barb tore through my cotton pants and punctured my flesh. I carefully crawled off the fence, adding new scratches to the ones I'd already sustained in my trek.

"This better be worth it, Miss Calico," I said to the cat sitting patiently waiting for me to get my act together. "Because now I might need a tetanus shot."

Checking the back of my thigh where I'd ripped my pants, I saw a small, widening bloodstain. *First aid later, Jillian. Let's find out what this cat is trying to show you.*

We traveled over a small hill wild with Carolina jasmine and goldenrod—a beautiful yellow sea. Miss Calico picked up her pace and headed toward more fences. I squinted, trying to make sense of what I saw.

Seconds later I stopped in shock. "Oh my God," I whispered.

I saw a long, cream-colored metal shed and shiny new galvanized steel fences that looked like the dog runs at the shelter. Bordering these compartmentalized spaces were long sand trenches. They looked like outdoor litter boxes. And not well cared for, either. Very smelly.

They were for the cats.

So many cats.

Five

I had no time to consider exactly what Miss Calico had led me to because just then the shed door squeaked open. I dropped to the ground, the sweet fragrance of jasmine engulfing me and the goldenrod hiding part of me, or at least I hoped so.

I pressed my hand over my mouth to stifle my surprise when I saw him. That darn trespassing professor with the funny name had come through the shed to the cat runs, a notebook in his hand. His long gray hair was tamer than before, and he wore a baggy blue suit and a red bow tie. He looked ready to teach a class at the college.

Somehow I didn't think the cats would be interested in anything he had to say. From the cries and mournful meows rising into the late-afternoon air, I could tell they were hungry. Very hungry. The sound upset me so much, it nearly brought tears to my eyes.

I resisted the urge to stand up and shout out a few hard questions. The bad vibes coming from that man, the isolation this place offered and the fact that I had no idea what was happening here stopped me. *Watch and learn*, I told myself. *And then get help.*

The professor moved to the far end of the runs and took notes as he stopped at each caged enclosure. I raised my head a tad, hoping to see how many cats were imprisoned here. I saw tiger-striped ears, orange faces, torties, black cats—maybe five or six in each cage. Those poor kitties must hate every minute of this. Didn't he know cats needed their own space? Obviously he didn't care, because he seemed to have no problem ignoring their cries. But it was tearing me up inside.

After he'd taken his notes at each enclosure, he went back inside the shed. I hated leaving the cats here, but this problem was too big for me to deal with alone. I was about to turn and crawl back the way I'd come when he appeared again, dragging a huge bag of kibble. I was relieved to see him begin to fill cat dishes, but when he stopped halfway down the cement walkway and took the food back inside the shed, anger boiled up into my throat. *What about the rest of them?*

I wanted to march down to those runs and give him what he had coming, but he appeared again before I could even move, this time carrying a gallon-size jar. He fed the rest of the cats a slimy, red, nasty-looking concoction from the jar, using what looked like a half-cup measure. The cats quieted, and when I wiped the few tears that had escaped from the corners of my eyes, I noticed long red marks on my shaking hand. Apparently I'd scratched myself on the fence, but I felt nothing but the pain of seeing those poor cats having their meager meal rationed out to them. It made me ill.

I lay in the jasmine vines for several minutes after the professor finished his task and had disappeared into the shed again. I could see Miss Calico, her back to me, lying down in one of the jails closest to me. She must have dug under the fence to get in and out. At least she seemed to be housed without other cats that might have harmed her kittens. Since she was on this end, she'd gotten the red slop for her meal. No wonder she'd been out scrounging for food. And she'd arrived back just in time, or who knew what would have happened to the kittens I assumed she was now feeding?

The goldenrod finally pushed me into action. When I started sneezing, lots of surprised cat faces turned my way. One particular tabby locked eyes with mine. He had the biggest, most gorgeous ears, but those eyes—I wouldn't forget them. I whispered, "I'll come back for you," before the next sneeze hit.

I reluctantly crawled away until I was out of sight of that shed, trying hard to keep what was now nonstop sneezes as quiet as possible. I'd paid no attention to what other buildings might be on the property. A barn? A house? I'd been completely focused on the cats. But by now I feared the professor might spot me or hear me any minute.

I clambered over and down the wildflower hill, but not without stumbling on two more unpleasant surprises: dead rats. I wondered whether this was the work of the cats who'd managed to escape and make it to Ruth Schultz's place. I stepped over them, swiping at my dripping nose. My eyes felt like they were on fire as I started back the way I'd come.

I glanced ahead in the direction of that wicked fence. Surely I could make my retreat without further injury and get back to the sanctuary. I had to tell Shawn about this. Maybe he could help me figure out what was going on with those cats.

The trek back to Ruth Schultz's farm was taking longer than the trip out, without a calico cat to guide me. It wasn't like I had any real path to follow. Turned out the lack of a path was the way I was supposed to walk after all. I'd stopped sneezing long enough to hear the weak sounds of a cat meowing.

I turned, thinking Miss Calico had followed me, but no, these mews were persistent, soft and up ahead to my right. I stepped slowly in the direction of the sound and soon found the source: a thin gray cat lying in trampled grass. Another escapee from the professor's farm? Probably.

The gray made no attempt to move as I knelt and extended a hand. The mews stopped, and sunken green eyes looked up at me. Unlike the other cats I'd been close to, this one definitely needed help. I reached a hand out and gently ran my fingers along the side of the gray's face. A minute later, he was in my arms and we were on our way without so much as a protest from the cat. He was weak, possibly dehydrated and far too thin for his frame.

I found Ruth in the field tending her tomato plants.

Since she was kneeling, she saw my nicked and scratched shins first. She looked up, her eyes wide. "What happened to you?" She rose. "And what happened to this one?"

"I found out where the cats are coming from, so I'm heading back to get this one to Shawn. This gray needs help."

"But you need those cuts cleaned up first," she said. "And your eyes—why are they so puffy?"

"Allergies. Really, I'm fine," I said, shrugging off her offer and heading for my van. "Do you know your neighbor, the professor?"

She walked alongside me. "*Professor?* Who are you talking about?"

"There's property about a twenty-minute walk from here. Do you know the man who owns it?"

Her eyebrows knitted in confusion. "Someone bought that place?" She shook her head. "I get so involved in planting this time of year, I literally have my head in the sand. That old farm has been vacant for years. Most of them in this area are abandoned. Small farms are nearly extinct around here."

"It's not vacant anymore. Can you open the front passenger door?"

Ruth did so, and then I had her grab an old cat quilt from the back. She spread it on the passenger seat, and I laid the gray down. He meowed but made no effort to move.

I scratched an itch on my left arm. Geez. The bug bites from slithering on the ground were almost as itchy as my nose.

"All my new friends belong to this professor, then?" She nodded toward her barn, rubbing dirty hands on the front of her jeans.

"Probably—but it doesn't seem like they're his pets. When I met him, that's what he called them—*pets*. What a liar."

"You talked to him?" Her gaze traveled back and forth between the cat and my cuts and scratches.

"Not at his place. I'll explain later. This cat needs help now. Since you have cat food now, will you be okay with a few extra mouths to feed?"

She smiled. "Certainly. I do want to help."

We said our good-byes, and she reminded me once more to get first aid as soon as possible. *Sweet lady*, I thought as my van rumbled down the back roads of Mercy toward the sanctuary.

When I walked back into Shawn's office fifteen minutes later, his gaze immediately went to the limp cat in my arms.

"Looks like you've been in combat, Jillian," he said. "But I get the feeling it wasn't with this cat. Give him here."

I eased the gray into Shawn's arms and then followed as he took him through the office and into the part of the sanctuary where he had a stainless-steel examination table. The gray didn't like this much, tried to get up, but didn't have the strength to resist Shawn's firm hold. Shawn lifted the cat's right cheek to expose the gums and pressed a finger above the upper gum. He then ran his big hands over the gray's body, all the while murmuring that everything would be fine.

"Dehydrated," Shawn finally said. "I'll give him some IV fluids under his skin." Shawn looked me up and down. "Did any of the cats scratch you?"

I held out my hands, glanced down at my legs. "These? No, these are from sneaking around in the country on my belly. Mother Nature bites sometimes. We have a situation that needs immediate attention—but I don't know where to start."

I gave him a hurried summary of what I'd seen, where I'd found the gray cat and how I knew about this professor.

Shawn's reaction was instantaneous anger. "I've got to see this for myself. Can you stay with this guy after I give him fluids?"

"Hang on. There's too many cats—at least fifty by my quick count. You can't handle fifty cats alone."

He took a deep breath, the tips of his ears scarlet. "But I have to do something."

"I feel the same way," I said gently, hoping my tone would transfer an air of calmness to him, even though I felt less than calm myself. "But we need help."

"If this professor has a cattery license and those cats aren't being properly fed, he's in big trouble." Shawn walked over to a cabinet and retrieved a clear plastic bag of what I assumed were the fluids the gray needed. "But that means we have to go through the animal control officer. Last thing I want to do is call that dumbass Chester. I'll go over to that farm and see what's what first."

I'd left the door to the office open, and Snug took the opportunity to pipe in with "Chester's a dumbass. Chester's a dumbass." I guessed the parrot had heard that refrain plenty of times.

"Not a good idea to go there alone, Shawn," I said. He'd been suspected of murdering a catnapper last year thanks to the combination of his quick temper and his passion for the well-being of animals. I wasn't sure he could be trusted to keep his anger in check once he saw what I'd witnessed.

He threw up his free hand. "You're the one who came back with this poor animal asking for help, and now you don't want me to do anything?"

"I didn't say that. Listen, Candace did the stakeout at the West place, where we caught that professor red-handed. She's already warned this man about his questionable behavior. If he's doing something illegal, she can step in. Meanwhile, you start calling volunteers to be ready to take in cats. I'll gladly take the calico and her litter."

"I don't have a long enough list of volunteers around here to handle fifty cats. So you're right. We do need a plan." He paused, scratched his head. "I have friends in other parts of the state who'll help. The cats might have to stay at this idiot's so-called farm until volunteers can get here."

"You sure you can't call on Chester? I mean, how will we get around him?" I asked.

"Chester's a dumbass," Snug called.

I had to smile.

Shawn sighed. "I probably can't keep him out of this, but I sure as hell wish I could. Okay, phone Candace. Meanwhile, I'll make some calls, check the state licensing board online about new catteries—'cause I sure haven't heard a peep about any new ones around here. If there's no license, well, seems to me this professor's in big trouble every which way you look. This poor guy is evidence of mistreatment if he came from that farm—and I'm sure he did."

While Shawn tended to the gray cat, I went outside to call Candace. A late-afternoon breeze helped me feel a little less grungy. Seeing all those cats locked up had me thinking of my own three. All of them had stayed in shelters after Katrina, and that's no life for a cat, even when the animals are surrounded by loving volunteers. Before I called Candace, I checked my cat cam.

My three weren't sleeping as I'd expected. Chablis and Merlot were crouched nose to nose, staring down at something between them—what, I couldn't tell. Syrah circled them, he, too, intent on whatever they'd captured this time. Maybe that spider had given birth before they killed it and my house was now infested. Sheesh. I didn't need this right now.

I disconnected from the feed and speed-dialed Candace. She sounded tired when she answered—I remembered then that she'd told me she had to go in on the evening shift this afternoon. She told me she was at Belle's Beans getting a coffee fix. No criminal activity was happening in Mercy at the present time, and she was having a hard time keeping her eyes open. Man, I envied her that coffee.

When I told her about the professor and what I'd seen, she said, "That's horrible. I'll call this in to county animal control right now. I can't promise they'll move quickly, though. They've got one guy."

"Chester, right?" I said. "Shawn won't be happy."

"Shawn knows there are steps we have to follow," she answered, sounding more than a little irritated.

"Can't you tell Chester this is an emergency? Because those cats sounded miserable."

"You think that will make a difference to him?" she said. "Don't repeat this, but my opinion of Chester matches Shawn's."

"Okay, tell Chester I'm about to call the *Mercy Messenger*. Animal stories like this one draw lots of media attention, and—"

"Jillian. Are you resorting to extortion?" She was definitely tired, and I'd pressed the wrong button.

"I won't really do it," I said quickly. "But you could tell him I will."

"Oh. So *I* deliver the extortion message?" She sighed wearily. "All right. I'll call you back."

And she did. Seems Chester succumbed easily to threats of bad publicity. He would be meeting her at the property, which she'd already located on her police cruiser computer.

"Can I come with you?" I asked. "I promise I won't get in your way."

"Only if you stay in the car," she said.

"Yes. Absolutely," I answered.

"Pick you up in five," she said.

She arrived at the sanctuary several minutes later, and she'd brought me a big cup of rich, dark coffee. I almost kissed her.

She gave me the once-over. "You look like you fell in a thicket."

"Nothing a shower and a little Neosporin can't fix." I took the lid off the coffee so it would cool quicker, while Candace went inside the sanctuary to talk to Shawn.

I climbed into the passenger seat of the green and white squad car. When Candace returned and slid behind the wheel, she said she'd told Shawn to stay here and wait for a call from her or from Chester.

"Bet he liked that." I sipped at my coffee. *Man, I needed this*, I thought.

"He did a quick computer check, and no cattery or kennel licenses have been issued for these parts in years. Looks like we do have cats in trouble. Again."

We took off and ended up on a different road from the one leading to the other farms we'd been to in the last two days. I was grateful that Candace was driving more carefully. I could actually drink my hot coffee instead of wear it.

Chester had not yet arrived when we pulled up to a mailbox that bore the number 911. *Prophetic*, I thought. We might need a special 911 emergency number for cats in a little while.

Candace said, "We'll wait on Chester. He gets paid to deal with these situations." She parked the cruiser on the side of the road next to a driveway similar to Ruth's and left the engine running.

No cow grate, I thought. That's why Harriett had been able to leave and wander on home. "You mean situations that might be considered animal neglect?" I said.

"Right. Kinda makes me sick even to think about," she said.

"My stomach's been churning since I saw what's going on here. Dirty outdoor runs. Unhappy cats. And some that might be in bad shape like the gray." I checked my watch. Almost seven p.m., with the sun hanging below the tree line and painting the sky blood orange.

We waited in silence, the tension in the car as steady as the loud purr of the engine.

When Chester hadn't arrived by seven twenty and he wasn't answering his phone or his page, Candace finally spoke. "For pity's sake, I can't sit here forever waiting on this man."

I felt the same way—anxious and worried.

Before Candace got out of the car, she pointed a finger at me. "I know you. You want to see if those cats are okay.

But stay put. If the animal control wagon arrives, tell Chester I've gone to check this place out."

"I've got a bad vibe, Candace. Let me go with you. My gut told me from the minute I met him that he's got serious issues, and—"

She patted the weapon on her hip. "I have help right here." Then Candace slipped from behind the wheel.

I called, "Be careful," before she slammed the door.

Once she was out of sight, I shut off the air-conditioning and rolled down the window. The evening's muggy warmth and the smell of jasmine engulfed me. On another day and another occasion, that combination might have been soothing. Not today.

I poured what was left of my coffee into the dirt. The coffee seemed only to have made my stomach feel worse. Candace had been thoughtful to bring me the boost I needed, but I would have preferred a purring Chablis in my lap. A purring cat helps me through any tough time.

I told myself that with Candace on the job, the cats would be taken care of. I should just calm down.

A mere thirty seconds passed before I realized I *couldn't* calm down and was too restless to remain in the car. I turned off the engine, took the keys and began to pace at the end of the driveway. I heard the rumbling sound of an engine and looked out on the road. A white panel van sputtered by, and the driver waved his hand out the window as he passed. I waved back—that's what you did in Mercy. But I was distracted by the situation at hand. I began to gnaw on my index fingernail. I was listening for cat cries. But I heard nothing. Maybe they were happier than the last time I'd been here—which seemed like a hundred years ago.

Or perhaps the breeze was carrying their pleading voices in the other direction. I ventured several steps down the curving, hedge-lined gravel driveway, hoping I could hear something—anything. Soon the peaked house came into view. White clapboard—or used to be white. More like gray now.

Still hearing nothing, of either the cat or the human variety, I edged closer to get a full view of the house.

And that's when Candace bolted out through the front door, pressing the walkie-talkie she usually wore on her shoulder close to her mouth.

Her already pale skin was sickly white, and suddenly she dropped the walkie-talkie and fell to her knees.

She began to retch.

Six

I ran to Candace and knelt beside her. "What's wrong? Are there . . . d-dead cats?" I rubbed circles on her back, noting that sweat now dampened her brown and green uniform shirt.

She took a deep breath. "No. A dead professor. I've called for backup."

My hand covered my mouth in shock, and I mumbled, "Oh no. Is it awful?"

"Yup. Pretty darn awful. But that's not what made me sick. It's all the raw meat. Looked like a hind quarter of beef on the counter."

"Deep breath," I said. "You're hyperventilating."

She closed her eyes and took in a huge breath, let it out slowly. "This is so stupid. But when I was a kid, my daddy used to make me lend a hand dressing the deer he shot. The last time he forced me into helping, I threw up on his shoes. That was the end of that."

"I have some Pepto chewables in my purse," I said.

She swiped at her mouth. "Nope. I'm fine. Got to get myself together before all the boys show up. Don't want to hear them say I'm acting like a little girl."

"Are you sure the professor's dead?" I said.

"Oh yeah. He was all twisted up, and his eyes were bugging out. I couldn't find a pulse." She took another deep breath before she stood.

I stood as well. "He was alive a little more than an

hour ago," I said. "You think he had a seizure or some-thing?"

"Maybe, but that was one hell of a seizure, if you ask me." She stared down at the pool of coffee she'd vomited up. "Damn, I wish I hadn't done that."

"You're human," I said.

She started walking away from the house, her eyes trained on the ground. "If a crime's been committed, we have to preserve any evidence we can, so we'll walk back to my patrol car exactly the way we came and wait for backup."

Follow exactly the way we came? Seemed impossible, considering I had no idea where I'd walked, but Candace needed the comfort of trying to preserve evidence, so I kept my mouth shut.

Unfortunately, the backup came in the form of one Morris Ebeling, who arrived in his own SUV wearing street clothes—cargo-style khaki shorts and an orange Hooters T-shirt stretched over his generous paunch.

"What's going on, Candy? You're as white as my new Reeboks," he said.

"What are you doing here, Morris? You're off duty," Candace said.

She had to be rattled, because she didn't bother to correct him when he called her "Candy."

"Who's the acting chief?" he said.

"You are," she mumbled.

"Then you got your answer. We got a suspicious death here? Or natural causes?" He started to walk past Candace, and she grabbed his arm.

"I'm not sure, so wait until I get my evidence kit and some crime-scene tape before you go traipsing down to the house. Is anyone else responding?" Her color was return-ing, thanks to Morris. He usually did bother the heck out of Candace.

"Fire truck and paramedics should be here any minute." Morris turned to me. "Why are you here, Citizen Hart? An-other *ride-along*?"

He sounded so sarcastic, I nearly bit my tongue holding back some sarcasm of my own. He wouldn't get to me. Not today. "There's a situation here concerning the possible neglect of cats. We came because I brought this to Candace's attention. She agreed to check it out, and I . . . well . . . I had to show her where the cats were."

"Really? She couldn't find her way over here alone?" he said.

"You know me. Couldn't get that map thingie on the computer to work," Candace said quickly. "But Jillian had a good idea where the house was."

"And then Candy happens to find another dead person right after you've been here?" He shook his head. "This is sounding way too familiar. After all, you are the one who discovered the last dead body we had here last year."

"She never went inside the house today, Morris," Candace said. "And you know she didn't kill anyone last year."

"All I can say is that some folks in Mercy might be wishing you'd take yourself back to Houston once they hear about this, Ms. Hart."

"And you'd be one of them?" I couldn't stop myself this time.

His face relaxed. "Actually, no. Much as an old coot like me hates to admit it, I like you. But I'd sure be happier if you'd quit seeing dead people."

"I haven't seen any dead people today," I said.

"My mistake. Just more cats you have to help. I'm slow, but I'm beginning to understand."

The wail of a siren drew our attention. The bright red fire truck was speeding toward us so fast, I almost ducked for cover behind the patrol car.

Billy Cranor, a muscled hunk Candace had a crush on, was the first to jump off the truck after it halted behind Morris's Ford Explorer.

Billy said, "Paramedics are right behind. But we all know CPR, so if you need me—"

"CPR won't do any good here," Candace said. "But you can help me string crime-scene tape."

"Did you hear me say we need crime-scene tape, Candy?" Morris's short-lived patience had expired.

"Sorry, *sir*. Seems to make sense we treat a suspicious death with the utmost care." Candace's tone was calm, but I could tell by the way her blue eyes had darkened that she was seething.

"And we will. Billy, you and the boys string tape across this driveway so no idiots drive right up to the house. Plenty of trees on either side to attach it to."

The "boys" were four other volunteer firemen who had gathered around us, their eyes alive with curiosity. Anything out of the ordinary grabs people's interest in Mercy—something I'd learned firsthand.

"Heard on the scanner there's a dead guy, Candy," one of them said.

"It's *Candace*," she said through gritted teeth.

The knot in my stomach relaxed a tad. She was back to her old self.

Another patrol car and the paramedics arrived as the firemen were stretching the tape. Candace instructed me to stay in her cruiser yet again, as she, Morris and two uniformed police officers started up the driveway toward the house.

In my heart I understood a sudden death was important, but my thoughts returned to the cats. Were they okay? And exactly where was Chester? I sure as heck didn't know how to get in touch with him. Since I hadn't been instructed to keep my mouth shut, I took my phone from my pocket and called Shawn—a better option than Chester any day.

When he answered, I said, "The professor is dead. Right now, I don't know about the cats, but do you have volunteers yet? And crates? You'll need plenty of crates."

"What happened?" he said.

"I don't know. They won't let me near the house, and Chester hasn't shown his face."

"Surprise, surprise. Allison is on her way to man the fort here, and then I'll come. But where exactly are you?"

I remembered a few road names and the turns we'd

made getting here. When I offered these to Shawn, he said, "The old Taylor place? Didn't know anyone moved in. Hang on, Jillian. I'll be there as soon as I can."

Afternoon had given way to dusk and brought cooler air. I waited for what seemed like hours, though when I checked the time on my cell phone, only about forty minutes had passed. It was now eight p.m. and totally dark, on this, one of the longest days of my life.

I saw headlights in Candace's passenger-side mirror. Thank goodness Shawn was finally here. Or maybe it was Chester, whom I'd never met and didn't exactly want to meet. I was already stressed to the max. I opened the door and got out.

But it wasn't Shawn or even the dog catcher.

"What in the holy hell are *you* doing here, you little man-eater?" Deputy Coroner Lydia Monk said when she spotted me.

Oh brother. Here we go. "Waiting," I said. *Keep it simple, Jillian. Best not to get her any more riled than she already is at the mere sight of you.*

"For Tom Stewart? What's he doing here?" She was looking me up and down, her disdain obvious.

"He's *not* here," I said.

"Guess I'll find out how big a liar you are once I get inside. But as a reminder, you know he belongs to me, Miss Prissy. I've told you more than once to keep your distance from him."

This woman, with her teased blond hair, 38D implants and low-cut spangled T-shirt, was delusional when it came to my friend Tom Stewart. Who *was* just a friend and *not* my lover as she kept insisting.

"As I said, Tom's not here, Lydia. But the dead man I believe you came to see is," I said.

We both turned in the direction of the driveway when Candace called, "Lydia? Is that you?"

"Yeah," Lydia said. "Just assessing the scene out here."

"Hurry and come see this. The body is changing. Something's happening," Candace said. "And, Jillian, there are sick cats in the house. Can you come, too?"

I ran in the direction of Candace's voice, but since Lydia wore her usual spike heels, she was forced to take her time. I didn't want to be within three feet of her anyway, so this worked out for the best.

Once I reached Candace, who was waiting about half-way up the drive, she took my elbow and led me to the front door.

When we stepped across the threshold, Candace said, "Try not to look. It's ugly."

I wasn't sure whether she was referring to the body or to the raw meat—which I could smell now. Not the freshest meat from the market, if I were to guess.

Problem is, if someone tells you not to look, of course you have to. And I did as she guided me through a shabby living area toward a hall to my right. The professor's body lay in the entrance to the kitchen on the left. He was so con-torted, he reminded me of a bow ready to release an arrow. His back was arched so badly that the crown of his head and his twisted legs touched the floor, but not his spine.

What would do that to a person?

I paused, transfixed, and touched trembling fingers to my lips. "Oh my God. You can't call that a natural death, can you?"

"Shh, we'll talk later," Candace whispered.

The hall was well lit, unlike the living room, and just as we entered a bathroom, I heard Lydia say, "I never thought I'd see the day. Look at that man, would you? And all you macho police people never thought to put on a mask?"

Panic gripped me. "Mask? We need masks?"

"I'd be dead by now if we did," Candace said. "That's Lydia being Lydia. We need to worry about these two crit-ters." She pointed at the bathtub.

A skinny long-haired orange cat and a small brown and gray tabby lay curled together at one end of the chipped and filthy bathtub. A disposable litter box sat at the other end of the tub. It must have been brand-new, because neither cat seemed to have used it. These two looked to be in a condition similar to that of the gray cat I'd found earlier.

I knelt and put my hand out so the cats could sniff me. Their rheumy, sad eyes stared up, and the tabby squeaked out a meow. I rested fingers against its face, and he or she rubbed against them. Then I did the same with the orange tiger. Neither made any effort to move. *What had that professor done to these poor animals?* I bit my lip, fought back tears.

"I called Shawn," I said, my voice shaky. "Told him to bring crates. But we'll need a vet for these two. Unless the animal control guy takes them. And where in heck *is* this Chester person?"

"His wife called me. She said he tried to impound a dog before he came here, and the owner took a shotgun to the dog-catcher wagon's tires. Chester is being treated for shock at some emergency clinic."

"Oh. Not a good day in Mercy for anyone," I said.

"You got that right. Back to these cats. They need the vet, but they didn't get all stiffened up and die like the professor. So what's wrong with them?"

I said, "The one I found earlier was dehydrated, but look how skinny the bigger one is. Maybe malnutrition, too?"

Candace stayed in the bathroom entry. "I don't see any cat food dishes, so maybe you're right."

"The meat you talked about could be spoiled or—"

"Do not even mention meat. Can you watch them until Shawn gets here? They don't look all that mobile, but they could mess up evidence if they decide to get out of the tub," Candace said.

"You didn't want to close the door and leave them alone, did you?" I said.

She smiled sadly. "You know me too well. That's why I brought you inside. See, one of them—don't know which— was meowing something pitiful. But you've fixed that. They feel safer already."

She left to do her job, and I sat cross-legged on the grimy

vinyl floor next to the tub. My fear, the nerves and the panic all gave way to rage. When an animal is mistreated, that speaks to the dark side of human nature. And these two cats—not to mention the fifty or so outside—confirmed what I'd felt about the professor from the minute we'd met. Not a good man. Not good at all.

I took several deep breaths, working hard to quell the anger. Transferring my negative emotions to these helpless cats wouldn't help them. They needed loving care right now. I leaned over the edge of the tub and stroked the tabby and then the orange guy—probably a male, since most orange cats are boys. He was big enough to be a Maine coon like my Merlot but so thin I couldn't tell. Maine coons usually weigh in at about twenty pounds, but this one was nowhere near that heavy. I alternated the petting, and soon they were both purring.

Meanwhile, I kept hearing snatches of what Lydia was saying. She does tend to yell. She was saying something about coroner school and a textbook death. But the words that came next made my own spine straighten, made me recall the dead rodents I'd nearly walked on in the field when I was returning to Ruth Schultz's farm earlier in the day. Her words?

Rat poison.

Seven

When I heard "rat poison," my focus immediately returned to the cats in the bathtub. I swallowed hard. Had they been poisoned, too? Was it only a matter of time before their muscles starting going rigid? And what about the cats outside?

But from what I knew of rat poison, which wasn't much, it was a blood thinner, not something that would turn a person into a grotesque human sculpture. Bile rose in my throat as the image of the professor with his arched back and stiffened limbs flashed through my mind. *Stop. Think about these cats right now. They're alive. They need help.*

Where was that vet? Where was Shawn?

But I couldn't quit thinking about poison. Maybe there was more than one kind of rat poison and these cats had been harmed with a different substance. They were limp and lethargic. Is that what the kind of blood-thinner rat poison found in the grocery store did to animals before they died?

I bent and looked more closely at them—sure, like that would tell me something—and noticed they both wore thin collars. I lifted the tabby's chin and saw a white paper tag attached to the buckle. Written in ballpoint ink was TRIXIE.

The orange cat had a similar tag. His said VLAD.

"Hey, Vlad. Hey, Trixie," I said. "I promise you'll get help soon."

When I heard Candace say, "My friend the cat whis-perer," I nearly jumped out of my skin.

I'd been so focused, I hadn't heard her come back. "You scared me," I said.

"This is a scary place. Shawn's here with volunteers, and Dr. Jensen's not far behind. An officer will bring the vet in here when he arrives."

I sighed with relief. "Good. I'm even afraid to offer them water. Maybe they'd start—"

"I don't want to know what might happen. Anyway, there's no light out back beyond that shed, but the sheriff's department has arrived with portable halogens. It'll proba-bly freak out those cats when we turn the lights on, huh?"

"You bet it will. As if they're not freaked-out enough," I said.

"Can you help outside? Like I said, the vet will be here any second."

I stood, my worried stare on my two new friends. "Of course."

As I followed her back out into the hall, she said, "Please stay on my heels and don't touch anything."

"Can't we go around the shed?" I said. "Maybe there's a gate or—"

"No gate. To get inside the cat runs, you gotta go through that shed."

Cat runs. Thoughts of what I'd seen earlier made my an-ger resurface. The man who did this to them had died a horrible death, and though I wouldn't wish that on anyone, I was still mad at what he'd done.

When I heard Lydia's loud voice, I said, "Is she okay with me ... um ... *participating*?"

"Oh, perfectly happy now that she's checked every nook and cranny to make sure Tom Stewart isn't here and won't be called upon to help out," Candace said. "Why does the county designate someone like her to be in charge of suspi-cious deaths, anyway? It makes no sense."

"You think the government is supposed to have com-mon sense?" I said.

"I'd say 'how true' except I am part of the government," she reminded me.

I smiled and said, "But back to Tom. Why would you call in a security expert for something like this?" I said.

"I wouldn't. But you know Lydia. She believes if Jillian Hart's around, well, Tom must be lurking, too, ready to jump your bones right in front of her," Candace said.

A blush warmed both my cheeks. "She is so frickin' crazy, it's ridiculous."

"For now, she's in charge. Try to ignore her, okay? In her defense, she does seem to have some knowledge about the cause of death." Candace stopped at the end of the hall, where it made a hard right turn. "We'll pass quickly through the kitchen and out the back door. Stay right behind me."

"I'd love to ignore her, but she's the one—"

"Forget about her, Jillian," Candace whispered harshly. "Frightened cats need you right now."

Lydia Monk and Morris Ebeling were in the kitchen, a room that could have traveled through time from the set of *Father Knows Best* with fifty years of dirt added. The meat that had so upset Candace was spread out on a dirty countertop, and an old-fashioned grinder was clamped to the counter's edge. Professor VanKleet had obviously been making food for the cats, but in a place the FDA would have shut down in a nanosecond.

A gloved Lydia knelt by the body in the other entrance to the kitchen, the one that led to the living area. She said, "The contractions caused by the strychnine are wearing off, Morris. That's why the body is relaxing. I told you this was no rigor mortis you were seeing when—" She stopped talking and smiled up at me as if nothing had happened between us earlier. "Glad you're here to help with the animals, Jillian. Mercy has such concerned citizens. Truly heartwarming."

"Thanks," I mumbled, as Candace practically dragged me past the meat-covered counter to the back door.

"This is the worst suspicious death I have ever worked,"

Candace said once we were outside. "And before you say anything, I'm not calling it murder until we know for sure. Maybe the guy overdosed. Sometimes dealers use tiny amounts of strychnine to cut cocaine. Could be the professor's supplier slipped him bad stuff."

"You're thinking he was on drugs?" I said.

"If his thinking was impaired, it could explain his doing crazy stuff like stealing cows and grinding meat," she answered. "But that's just a wild guess. And I shouldn't be guessing."

"Is strychnine what they sell in the feed store to kill rats? Because I thought they used something else," I said.

"Lydia told us it used to be a standard rat killer. Not so much anymore," Candace said. "Dangerous, and as I explained, used to cut illegal drugs."

I inhaled the fresh night air and felt my shoulders relax. "But if the poison is off the market, then—"

"I can't say any more about the evidence, okay?" she said.

"Got it. Sorry," I said.

The shed stood maybe ten feet ahead, and we walked toward it down a stone path. Before Candace opened the flimsy screen door, she said, "This is where you have to be especially careful. We haven't searched this building thoroughly yet."

As Candace led the way, I didn't even bother to glance around. We were through the shed and out to the cat runs in seconds. Two county sheriffs were setting up their halogens, though I couldn't see much more than their silhouettes. And still, no cat cries. *God, please don't let them be dead like the professor.*

To our right, Shawn and a man and woman I'd never met stood waiting for the lights to come on. Meager reinforcements for fifty cats . . . but of course if the cats were—no. The cats were alive when I'd seen them earlier.

"Hi, Shawn. Hi, Shawn's friends." I offered a small wave, noting the stack of crates that had been broken down and brought outside on a flatbed dolly. Bet that trip through the possibly evidence-laden shed had given Candace night-mares.

Their smiles were grim when they nodded my way. They had no idea what they were about to see, and the fact that it was so darned quiet out here made goose bumps rise on my arms.

The bright blast when the lights came on made me shut my eyes reflexively, and when I opened them, I was not prepared for what I saw.

Shawn said, "What in hell happened here?"

We did not see fifty cats. Instead, we saw that the chain-link fence had been cut open at the bottom of each small jail cell.

And the cats were gone.

"Where did they go?" I said. "They were here. I saw them."

"You saw them?" It was Lydia, who, unfortunately, had decided to join us.

"Yes," I said. "That's why I called Candace. That's how she found the body . . . because I told her that cats were possibly being mistreated here, and—"

"You can explain all that later," Candace cut in. "I think I see a few cats in those end runs."

"Oh my gosh. You're right." I started in that direction.

Candace grabbed my arm. "You, Shawn and the others need to wait. I have to photograph this place, look for evidence. Then we'll see about the cats."

"But—"

"No buts, Jillian. The cats will be okay for a few minutes."

"She's right." Lydia looked at Candace. "You've got this covered, though I believe Jillian and I need to talk later about what she saw and when she saw it." She smiled, turned and went back through the shed.

We stood there for more than thirty minutes, not the few that had been promised, as Candace did her job. Meanwhile, Shawn introduced me to the volunteers. Sam Howard was a retired veterinarian with snowy hair and a warm smile. Jane Haden, a soft-spoken black woman, had intelligent dark eyes and beautiful posture that exuded an air of authority. Since she was a school principal, that authority was probably put to good use.

I explained my presence, and the three of us ended up sharing photographs of our beloved pets. Sam Howard laughed at the cat cam, but Jane was intrigued and asked lots of questions. I was afraid to tell her that Tom Stewart had set it up for me for fear that if I mentioned his name Lydia would come running out in psychotic mode again.

A county deputy was showing Candace how to lift a footprint off the walkway with what looked like giant Scotch tape. From the adoring look she gave the guy, I knew he'd just made her day. She had *evidence*. Then both county officers helped reposition the lights so Candace could photograph each enclosure. She used her flashlight to closely examine the fence areas that had been cut away. I'm no police person, but it sure didn't look like fingerprint territory to me. Then Candace began photographing each enclosure and the cement path that allowed access to them.

As we waited, we decided to put together three large crates to take away the remaining cats when Candace was finished.

Doc Howard, who was kneeling next to me as we worked, said, "I've dealt with some pretty radical animal rights groups, but killing someone has never been in their bag of dirty tricks."

"As Candace would say, there's no evidence yet that whoever removed these cats killed the man," I said. "We don't even know if he was murdered."

"You got me there. I *am* jumping to conclusions," he said. "I've just seen way too many people go off the deep end and act foolishly when it comes to domesticated animals. Let's hope whoever took the cats was on the animal *welfare* side."

"More like us, you mean," Jane said as she stood. She had her crate put together. "I was at a cat show once when a protestor made a scene. She'd drawn whiskers on her face with a Sharpie. How does that kind of behavior help anyone?"

"I sell quilts at cat shows, and I've seen the same sort of thing a couple times," I said. "But I like what you said. Animal welfare versus animal activism? I'll take welfare every time."

I'd finished my crate, and so had Doc Howard. A few minutes later we were allowed to walk down the path to the last three little jail cells: two black cats in the first we came to, two white cats in the second and my calico angel and her kittens in the last. Only the calico remained calm. The other four cats had their backs up and were hissing and spitting at the invasion, first by the police and now by us. I didn't blame them for being upset.

Shawn said, "Doc, can you take the whites?"

"I'll do a cursory check for deafness back in my van," Howard said, pulling on long leather gloves.

"Do they have blue eyes?" I asked.

Howard looked surprised. "Can't tell until I get up close. But how did you know that blue eyes might indicate deafness in whites?"

I tapped my temple. "Crazy lover of cat trivia."

He smiled and dragged a crate toward their cage.

"Jane, black cats for you," Shawn said.

"I adore black cats," she said with a smile. "Works for me."

Shawn took a cream-colored instrument off the dolly. It looked like the scanner they used to price giant bags of kibble. But then I realized what it was. I'd recently had microchips implanted near the shoulder blades of all my cats. Dr. Jensen had used a tool exactly like that to show me how the system worked. He'd held it over the shoulder area after each cat had had its chip put in, and the chip number came up on the device's screen. Their unique embedded chip numbers are now in a database in case any of them ever get lost again.

"You think these cats have chips?" I said.

"That would be too good to be true, but South Carolina

law says any rescued cat must be scanned for microchips. And I'll look for tattoos," Shawn said. "Some folks used tattoos to identify their pets before the microchip age."

"Scanning is the law? I had no idea. Might be a challenge to scan them the way they're acting right now." I took my crate to the last enclosure. "I assume you're taking me up on my offer to foster the calico and her kittens?"

"Do you mind? That litter I've already got is a handful," he said. "Mom's getting healthier, but we're still tube feeding."

"Don't mind taking them, but Syrah, Chablis and Merlot might," I said.

Doc Howard said, "I brought vaccines and will examine all the cats before we take off. But until their feline AIDS and parasite tests come back, these cats must be kept away from your pets."

"I have plenty of room, so no problem. Do you do this often? Help out like this?" I said.

He knelt and offered a hand to the white cats cowering in the corner. "All over the state. Terrible cat and dog stray problems, especially in rural areas like this."

His attention was fully focused on the cats now, and I had a job to do, too.

The calico almost looked like she was smiling up at me as I pulled the crate into her prison. Her kittens were feeding—two mackerel tabbies, a bicolor orange and white, and a calico baby that had less white than mama cat. I squatted near them and talked soothingly for a few minutes, noting that she and the kittens lay on straw. That professor hadn't even given them a blanket. I'd just finished about a hundred cat quilts for a future craft festival in Atlanta, and one of those little quilts would soon be put to good use.

I opened the crate door, thinking that would help Miss Calico get used to it, but she amazed me once again. She stood, washed her babies' faces and licked all their bellies. Then she proceeded to lift each by the scruff and carry them one by one into the crate. Once she'd carried the last one in, she stayed in there with them.

Meanwhile, Shawn was having an awful time scanning the other cats, but he finally finished.

He walked over to my jail cell, wiping sweat off his brow with a forearm. "Cats never like to be told what to do." At least he was smiling. "Seems you had no problems."

"She put her litter in the crate all by herself," I said.

"No way." He came around and bent down to look at them. "Pretty bunch. But she's not in a position where I can get a good scan. We'll take care of that later. Let's get out of here. This is a bad, bad place."

Shawn carried my crate, and when we passed Candace on the way out, I said, "You look deep in thought."

She blinked and met my gaze. "I am."

"About evidence you found?" I said.

"No, I'm thinking about the why of what we found here. Seems like someone came and rescued most of the cats and may have killed the professor. That conjures up plenty of suspects of the animal-activist kind—people who thought these cats weren't being treated as they should."

I nodded. "Makes sense. Sort of."

"What do you mean, *sort of*?" She brushed a stray blond hair off her furrowed brow.

"They left cats behind," I said. "No true animal lover would leave even one behind. Not in a million years."

Eight

After Shawn, Doc Howard and Jane took the cats out to what Howard called his "portable vet clinic" for examination, Lydia instructed me to wait in the living room so she could question me. If I hadn't been such a mess from my encounter with barbed wire and fields of jasmine and goldenrod, I wouldn't have wanted to sit on one of Professor VanKleet's grubby armchairs. The original color was long lost in a layer of filth. But I was probably dirtier than the chair. I sat, my scratched-up hands clenched on my knees

Our Mercy vet, Dr. Jensen, arrived carrying a crate less than a minute after I sat down. I said hello and started to rise, ready to lead him to the cats in the bathroom. But Candace came in right behind him and gestured for me to stay put. Minutes later, he passed back through the living room carrying the orange and the tabby in the crate. I'd known him long enough to detect both his urgency and his concern when he departed. *Please, oh please, let them be okay*, I thought.

Lydia, to her credit, kept me waiting for only ten minutes and brought along Morris Ebeling as her designated note taker. He sat in the equally dirty chair opposite me. After Lydia considered her option—a torn-up, stained Victorianesque sofa—she remained standing, her manicured hands on her hips.

"Tell me about this adventure of yours this afternoon.

Candy filled me in for the most part, but I'd like to hear your version," she said.

I didn't trust her gentle and reasonable tone for one instant. I wanted to say, "You are one crazy quilt, Lydia," but instead I kept my voice even when I said, "Are you worried I may have somehow managed to pour this poison—what was it, strychnine?—down Professor Van-Kleet's throat?"

"Well, I never thought of that, Jillian. You have opened my eyes to a whole new realm of possibilities. I know how much you love cats. Is that motive enough to kill a man you thought was mistreating them?" Her syrupy smile made me want to vomit.

Morris cleared his throat. "Um, Lydia. Do you really think—"

"Morris, you're here to take notes," she said.

"But I am the acting chief, and—"

"Which you've told me a hundred times. Sorry, but Jillian has brought a crime theory to our attention, and I hope you've written her words down for our report." She focused on me again. "Now. Tell me what happened today."

I did. If I wanted Lydia to leave me alone, I needed to relate everything as dispassionately as possible—just the facts, ma'am—and so I recited what had gone on since Wednesday night, including the premature kittens and the missing cow.

"Good. That matches what Candy told me. You can go," Lydia said abruptly. She waved in the direction of the door. "If you were trespassing here, I figure that's Candy's business."

"My business, too," Morris said. "And from what you've told me about this poison and when the rigidity wears off, Ms. Hart was probably with Shawn Cuddahee at the time the man died."

"And you're discussing this in front of her?" Lydia whispered to him out of the side of her mouth.

Morris reddened. "She's no suspect in my book, but as for the cats—"

"Who cares about the cats? You can leave, Jillian," Lydia said. "There's no compelling evidence that you had anything to do with this death." So she believed me just like Morris did? Thanks to what I guessed was a recent Botox treatment on her forehead, it was hard to read her.

I said, "I'd love to go, but I don't have a ride."

"That's right. You've been playing policewoman with your pal Candy again. Don't go calling up Tom and pleading for him to come and pick you up. Morris will find you a ride." She returned to the kitchen, and all I could do was give the palms-up "I don't get it" gesture to Morris.

But once he walked me outside in search of a ride from fireman Billy Cranor or a paramedic who might still be hanging around, we found Shawn pacing at the end of the driveway.

He said, "Been waiting for you. Need a lift back to the sanctuary?"

How could I have forgotten that I'd agreed to take the calico and her litter home? Stress, I decided.

I believed Morris was more grateful than I was for Shawn's presence. He thanked Shawn and headed back toward the house.

The crated litter and their mom—her white tag read DAME WIGGINS—were in the backseat of Shawn's extended-cab truck, and they made no sound. Sleeping, no doubt. What a long, awful day for everyone. On the way back to the sanctuary, Shawn told me that Dr. Jensen believed the most pressing issue with the cats from the bathroom was dehydration. Dame Wiggins was in amazingly good shape, but then she'd found a way out of her cell in search of food, probably more than once.

I shook my head, feeling terrible about what the cats had endured. "What was wrong with that professor?"

"Whatever it was, he paid in spades. Man, the way his body was all twisted up was the nastiest thing I've ever seen. The other cats seem a little malnourished, but not nearly as bad as those two Dr. J. took to his hospital."

"Thanks to Dame Wiggins and her escapist ways, we

probably saved some cats today. I never would have found out what was going on if not for her," I said.

I arrived home close to midnight, and after I disabled the alarm, I took Dame Wiggins and her family into the house through the door below the deck. This entrance led to the basement game room, which had an attached unfurnished bedroom. I set up my foster cats with fresh water, food and a disposable litter box. This "basement apartment" had a fully stocked pantry and a bathroom—for the guests that so far I hadn't had yet.

There was a guest room upstairs, but John had made sure we'd finished the basement for the grandchildren my late husband hoped to have. I couldn't have kids, but John did have his daughter Kara from his first marriage. She'd never even got a chance to visit us in South Carolina. The last time I'd seen her was at John's funeral in Houston, where she still lived. We had never been close, and John's death hadn't changed that. How I wished that were different.

"Dame Wiggins," I said before I went upstairs, "I bequeath this empty room to you and promise to bring a comfy quilt after I visit with my friends upstairs." I opened the crate for her and then left, closing the bedroom door behind me.

I'd also closed the door to the upstairs so three curious friends wouldn't come down to check out what I was doing. Syrah, Chablis and Merlot might not appreciate feline visitors, although I'd occasionally kept a few lost cats and they hadn't minded too much. But kittens? Nope, I'd never brought home kittens, so I had no idea how they would respond.

I climbed the stairs and opened the door, leaving it ajar now that Dame Wiggins was safely sequestered. Cats hate closed doors.

When I flipped on the kitchen lights, three loving feline faces stared up at me—and they had been waiting with a gift.

A dead mouse lay in front of them.

Syrah tapped the lifeless body toward me, as proud as punch. Sheesh. Another dead body. Tiny but still dead. But it wasn't like they hadn't made offerings like this before.

I said, "I've eaten, thanks. But nice work, you three." I recalled the stalking behavior I'd witnessed on the cat cam. They'd been chasing bigger prey than spiders in my absence. I took a wide path around the poor dead thing—didn't want to hurt the cats' feelings and dispose of their prize too soon. That might seem ungrateful.

Once we were all in the living room and far from the dead animal, I sat on the floor and bestowed plenty of love on my best friends. But my cats were less interested in petting and playing than they were in sniffing me from head to toe. Merlot even put his Swiffer duster paws on my chest and met me nose to nose. He recognized the scent of a foreign cat and wanted to drink it in completely.

A few minutes later, they grew tired of me. After all, I hardly ever came in through the basement, so I was sure they felt something must be explored down there. And I was also sure they were hoping there would be other invaders that needed to be stalked, trapped and killed.

As they hurried down the stairs, I followed as far as the kitchen, ready to dispose of the dead mouse. I pulled a few paper towels off the roll, realizing I felt more compassion for this creature than for the professor. Did that make me a good recruit for animal activism? No, not yet, I decided, as I headed out the back door for the trash can to dispose of the mouse. Whoever released or captured those cats today had probably tackled more barbed wire in their pursuits than I ever wanted to see again.

Right before I lifted the trash can's lid, I had a thought.

I could call an exterminator tomorrow. I'd seen a dead spider earlier today, and now this mouse. Just the kind of things exterminators live for. Not that I actually wanted to exterminate anything. No, I wanted an expert opinion.

As I'd waited those ten minutes in the professor's disgusting living room earlier, I'd thought about his note taking, the way he fed half the animals dry food and the other half that repulsive concoction from the jar. Was that why he was on sabbatical? To develop some new kind of cat food?

But before he could complete whatever he was doing with the meat on the counter or the red mixture in the jar, the professor had died. The question remained—had he been done in by his stupidity or by another's hand?

Maybe someone not quite as nice as Ruth Schultz got angry about cats wandering on their property. A few cats had managed to escape from the professor's prison and ended up with her, after all. Could someone else have tracked down the professor and decided to gather all the cats and dispose of them at the same time they got rid of the source of the problem—the instigating professor?

That could mean the missing cats were victims, too. Now they were who knew where, maybe some as sick as the gray, or the orange cat and the tabby Dr. Jensen took away. Though it wasn't my business to investigate anything aside from how well certain fabrics complemented one another, I felt compelled to help in any way possible. Cats were involved. Lots of cats. Since Mercy has experts on everything from quilting thread to coffee beans, why not rodent poisons—and, sadly, possible cat poisons?

Yes. I needed to talk to an expert first thing tomorrow. And with that thought I pushed down the little voice that said, "What are you getting yourself into now, Jillian?"

Nine

I finally got to sleep at a reasonably normal time on Friday night and woke up the following morning feeling almost myself again. First thing, I contacted Rufus Bowen, the owner of What's Bugging You? The choice of an exterminator was easy, considering only one company was listed in the thin Mercy yellow pages.

I tried questioning him over the phone, but Rufus cut me off, said he knew where I lived and would stop by on his way to an appointment. Then he hung up.

He knew where I lived? Guess I shouldn't be surprised. Everyone knew everything about everyone in Mercy.

When I answered the front door a half hour later, my gaze was drawn past his tall, broad and muscled body. I was looking at his truck parked in my driveway. A giant cockroach does catch your eye, and this one was painted on the side of the pickup. The customizing was beautifully done, but I still stifled a "yuck." Spiders and mice I could handle. Cockroaches made me shudder.

Syrah and Merlot entered the foyer when I greeted Rufus. One whiff and they hightailed it to parts unknown. Since cats have a sense of smell hundreds of times more acute than that of humans, I figured they probably detected the "odor-free" chemicals clinging to Rufus Bowen. All I smelled was perspiration.

Chablis didn't bother to show her face, unusual since she enjoys greeting visitors. She'd been downstairs when

I went to feed Dame Wiggins early this morning, and my educated guess was that she was still there, parked outside the bedroom door.

"So you got yourself a vermin problem?" Rufus said.

"Not exactly," I said. "Can we talk for a minute?"

He glanced at his watch. "Sure, but I don't do snakes if that's—"

"No snakes. Come into the kitchen."

I led him through the living room, and when we sat at the kitchen counter he removed his Atlanta Braves baseball cap to reveal thinning, greasy brown hair.

"Would you like coffee? Or sweet tea?" I asked.

"No, ma'am. I just need to know the problem."

"Here's the deal. My cats killed a mouse yesterday, which got me thinking that exterminators would probably know plenty about any chemicals that kill animals."

"You'd be correct, ma'am. But are you saying there's more than one mouse hanging around your house?" His glance swept the kitchen floor. He was doing a "Candace." Looking for evidence of infestation.

"Perhaps there are more mice, but that's not—"

"If so, you got two better exterminators than this old boy. Nothing prettier than watching a cat pounce on a rodent." His lopsided smile indicated genuine admiration for cats, and I liked that.

I said, "What if the mouse was, say, *poisoned*, and one of my cats ate it. Would that make him sick?"

"Did they?"

"Did they what?" I said.

"Eat it?"

"Oh no, but I'm just asking what if. See, I saw some dead rats close to where several cats were being . . . *imprisoned* is the only word to describe it," I said.

He squinted at me. "I think I know where this is going, but quit throwing curveballs and pitch one right down the middle of the plate. What do you want?"

"A consultation—which I am happy to pay for," I said.

"You don't need to pay me for talkin'. Glad to assist you, ma'am."

I smiled gratefully. "Here's a couple of questions: What would be your first choice to kill a mouse if I didn't have my own personal exterminators? And what might be the danger to the person handling the poison?"

Rufus nodded and for the first time seemed a tad uncomfortable. "This is about that peculiar professor getting poisoned, ain't it? Read the cop column in the *Messenger* this morning, and when I stopped at Belle's for coffee I heard a bunch of cats got sprung from that setup he had at the old Taylor farm. And you're interested, huh?"

"Very. That's why I called you for an expert's knowledge. But you said 'peculiar' professor. You knew him? Because I sure didn't."

"Nah. He wasn't here long enough, but I saw him around town. Man needed a regular haircut. Dressed and talked funny. Heard he once took all the coins out of that cup sittin' by Belle's register. You know, the one where they have change if you're a few cents short?"

I nodded. *And he stole a woman's cow, too.* That did qualify as weird . . . or desperate. "Would you say he was hard up, then?"

Rufus looked down at the chunky hands resting on his thighs. "Yeah, and I shouldn't be calling him peculiar. My mama heard me speak unkindly of the dead, she'd slap me upside the head."

"Promise I won't tell," I said. "Back to my original question. What's the best product for killing . . . anything?"

He said, "Nuclear bomb, I guess. Seriously, though, it's all about how much poison. Anything can be considered deadly in the right dose. Even plain old table salt or water."

"Everyday items from the kitchen aren't the problem in this case. I was at the professor's place last night, and—"

"You was there?" He grew more alert, and did I detect a wariness in his eyes?

I nodded. "Yes, I was there."

"Yowee. Folks are gonna start crossin' to the other side of the street, they see you comin', Ms. Hart. That's two bodies you've been up close and personal with in the last year."

"Not how I want to be remembered. Anyway, the deputy coroner said the professor was poisoned with strychnine. Do you ever use that for killing rodents? Because, as I said earlier, I noticed a few dead rats on the property before they found the professor's body."

Rufus said, "You sure Lydia said strychnine?"

"Yes. She said that considering the condition of the body, the way he was all . . . *contorted*, that it had to be strychnine," I said.

Sweat beads popped out on Rufus's forehead. He averted his gaze and didn't respond.

"Was she right?" I asked.

"Oh, she's right. Might be the first time ever for that woman. Meanwhile, I got to be going." He slid off the stool, his demeanor totally different now. He seemed eager to get the heck out of my house as soon as possible.

He was halfway through the living room before I even left my stool, and I had to hurry after him. *What just happened?*

I said, "What's wrong? You seem upset."

"Not bothered any which way, but my next customer might be if I don't get there lickety-split. Nice to meet you, and if you ever have a real problem with bugs or varmints—"

I touched his arm and said, "Wait. I have more questions."

He looked none too happy when he faced me. "I don't think I can help you."

"Just one more. Would strychnine be something you'd supply for killing rats?" I asked.

"Nope. Don't need anything that strong for rats. Better and kinder ways to get rid of them. Thank you, ma'am, but I can find my way out."

He was done with me; that much was certain. And I surely didn't want to keep Rufus from a paying customer. I watched him leave, still puzzled by his abrupt reaction to the mention of strychnine. I wished I could have asked him about the sick cats and whether he thought they could have been poisoned with something different. Perhaps another day.

My cell phone rang, and I pulled it from my pants pocket. It was Shawn.

"Heard from Doc Jensen," he said without a hello.

Merlot and Syrah reappeared and meowed several times. They started toward the kitchen, and I knew from their "feed me now" cries that I'd better pay attention or they'd get even louder. They *are* the boss of me, that's for sure.

"What about the gray? And are the bathroom cats, Trixie and Vlad, okay?" I asked as I followed them.

"Doing much better. Too thin, dehydrated, but all of them are eating and drinking this morning," he said. "They'll be just fine."

I sighed with relief. "That's great news. They weren't poisoned, then?"

"Doc doesn't think so. No microchips on them, though. Three more strays that'll need loving homes after they're neutered. Same with the other four we took. They weren't spayed or neutered neither. The vet'll take care of all of them soon. You willing to donate anything toward the cause?"

"My quilt business has picked up since all that publicity after the murder last year, so sure, I can help out," I said.

"Bags of pet food would be great, which reminds me. How's your hungry little bunch of fur this morning?" he said.

"You mean the ones yowling at me this minute or the rescues?" I said with a laugh.

"Them and the visitors you took in, but it sounds like you'd better do right by your best friends," he said.

I opened the pantry, looking for a flavor of wet food they

hadn't eaten recently. "The mama cat and kittens are doing fine," I said. "But Chablis wants to visit them. Can she?"

"Yup. Leukemia, parasite and FIV tests were negative on the mother. Doc used a flea comb on our Dame Wiggins, but I'd check those kittens for any fleas or ear mites before you let your three anywhere near them. You got any ear-mite medicine?"

"I do." I breathed a sigh of relief. Fleas and mites I could handle, but unlike humans, cats can transmit leukemia to one another, and FIV stands for feline immunodeficiency virus, another deadly and transmittable illness. "Do you have any clue about who might have taken the other cats?" I asked.

"No such luck. Candace asked me to check with rescue groups, seeing as how they're the most likely folks to stage a raid, but I got nothing. Problem is, since there's been a death and all, I doubt I'll hear anything."

I picked a can of chopped grill, and Syrah nearly tripped me by winding in and out of my legs as I left the pantry. Merlot plopped down beside the empty cat dish. He was doing the half-tweet, half-purr call that said, "If you don't hurry, I might eat you, my human servant."

I said, "No chance the people who cut the fence just set those cats loose?"

"If an activist did it, no way. Heard tell Candace and Morris were headed back over to that professor's place this morning to look for any evidence outside the runs. They needed daylight to see if someone dropped something or left footprints at the spots where the fence was cut. Maybe they'll get a lead or clue—anything to make Candace's day."

I put the phone on speaker and set it on the counter. Then I popped the can and squatted by the cat dish. *Chopped grill* sounded so haute cuisine, but was merely a brown smelly blob of who knew what.

Syrah was on the food so fast, you'd have thought I never fed him in his life. Merlot quieted, waiting for his turn. He might be bigger, but Syrah was first in line when it came to food.

"Did you hear if there are any suspects in the professor's death?" I asked Shawn. I stood and opened the fridge. Time for sweet tea.

"Suspects? Are you thinking he was murdered?" he said.

"I understand he could have killed himself, or maybe his death was even an accident, but the fact that those cats disappeared says someone wasn't happy with the professor," I said, pouring myself a glass.

"His house was salmonella waiting to happen," Shawn said. "I'm thinking he did himself in. Besides, all I care about are the feline victims. Not sure I care diddly-squat about this professor. And professor of what? Evil?"

"That's like one of the worst lines ever from a B movie, Shawn. And no one deserves to die such a miserable death," I said.

"You sticking up for the guy?" he said.

"No. But sometimes you say things I don't think you mean. You never even met the man."

A short pause followed, and then he said, "I get hot when people do ugly stuff to animals; that's all." He went on to tell me I could visit the gray, Vlad and Trixie at the veterinary hospital. Then he said an abrupt good-bye.

Shawn will be Shawn, and he'd have forgotten about this less-than-pleasant end to our conversation the next time we spoke. But he did have me thinking.

Professor of more than just biology?

Ten

Syrah and Merlot gave up on their food when they saw me head for the hallway. They thought I was about to start working on quilt orders, since it was that time of the morning. But rather than enter the sewing room, I went to my office and booted up the computer. They sat next to my desk chair and looked up at me as if to say, "You're in the wrong room, staff person." Though the computer was fun because that meant I stayed in one place, the days I spent quilting were heaven for all of us. Yes, they loved fabric almost more than I did. Syrah had even been known to sit on a three-inch square of fabric if that's all that was available.

But I wanted to learn about the professor, seeing as how I knew next to nothing, except that he liked to dress up like a cat burglar and steal cows. I remembered he'd been on the faculty of Denman College, and I brought up the school's Web site first. Not much to learn, I soon discovered. They offered degrees in general studies, biomedical engineering, mathematics, nutrition and biology. Not big on the arts, but the school was small. No profile page for him when I clicked on the button for faculty.

Next, I Googled Professor VanKleet, and that yielded better results. I found a ten-year-old photo of him and his wife, Sarah, at a fund-raising event. No long hair, and he seemed genuinely happy, his arm around his wife's waist. But her expression seemed tense, and her hands gripped a rhinestone bag so tightly that her knuckles were white. I printed out that picture and veered back onto the Internet highway. I learned that the professor had dual PhDs, one in animal nutrition and one in biology. At least he'd told the truth about teaching biology. There was a link to a profile page at Denman College, but all I discovered was a message saying that the page no longer existed. The few abstracts for academic papers I was able to locate indicated that he had researched commercial pet food. This was confirmation of what I'd thought yesterday, so no surprise there.

Science was never my strong point in college—my degree was in fiber art—thus, the few summaries I dug up on his papers made my eyes glaze over. Though I didn't understand all the talk about amino acids and vitamin content, I at least felt more confident that the man might have been researching cat diets in that grubby farmhouse kitchen.

When I sat back in the chair, processing this information, Syrah jumped up on the desk. He stared intently at me.

"Do you like what I feed you, sweet boy?" I said.

He meowed in response to the distress he must have heard in my voice. If what I'd seen in the professor's kitchen had anything to do with the breakfast I'd just fed my cats, well . . . I didn't want to know that much about cat food.

I was set to resume my quest for more personal information on the professor—including wife Sarah—but I was interrupted by the doorbell.

I checked my watch and discovered it was already noon. *That's what the computer is—a giant time suck.* Syrah and Merlot were joined by Chablis by the time we reached the foyer. All three sat several feet from the door as usual, not too close, but they of course wanted to see who might be calling this time.

My eyes widened in disbelief when I looked through the peephole. John's daughter, Kara, stood on the front stoop. I hadn't spoken to her in so long, I couldn't imagine why she was visiting.

"Hey there," I said, after opening the door. I saw right away that dark circles under her eyes marred her complexion. Her shiny brunette hair drooped over her right shoulder in a braid. Although Kara looked tired, she was still one of the most attractive young women I'd ever met. I opened my arms for a hug.

She embraced me briefly and then rolled her suitcase past me and into the foyer. "Hope you don't mind, but I need a place to crash." Her tone was brusque, and her brown eyes avoided mine.

"Um, no problem. Sure," I said. "Been a long time." I swallowed hard. Gosh, she looked like her father—that is, when John had been dog tired.

Kara dropped her shoulder bag, released her hold on her suitcase and glanced in the direction of the living room. She put her hands on her slim blue-jeaned hips. "So this is the house that Daddy built."

The house your daddy and I built, I thought. But this was Kara. I'd so wanted her to warm to me, but that had never happened. She was here now, and no matter what, she was part of John and that made her special.

"Are you thirsty? Hungry?" I said.

"Nope. Why don't you show me the house? I've been driving for hours and would rather walk off the stiffness." She started down the hall that led to my office, the sewing room and the bedrooms.

I noticed that all three cats were gone. A cold wind *will* make a cat run for cover. Kara was out of sight now, and I rolled her suitcase behind me down the hallway toward my bedroom. When I caught up, I said, "Let's drop this off, and then I'll give you the tour." We walked on to the last room on the right, and while I put her suitcase in the guest room closet, she stopped at the four-poster bed and rested a hand on the quilt. It was one of my favorites, a monkey-wrench pattern in pinks and browns.

"Nice," Kara said.

I mumbled a thank-you. Did she realize I'd made the quilt? Surely she must. I pointed out the bathroom before we walked back down the hall. We stopped in my office, and her gaze settled on the bookshelves. I noticed her swallow and close her eyes briefly. She recognized many of those books. They'd belonged to her father.

She blinked several times and said, "What else is in this hall?"

I led her to my sewing room.

Though I went in, Kara stood in the entry. "This is where you run your little business, huh? How's that going?"

She did remember what I do, and her tone hinted at interest rather than the indifference she'd shown in the past.

I said, "Better than I ever imagined. I can hardly keep up with the orders."

"I suppose all that publicity after you became the hometown hero didn't hurt," she said.

"I wasn't a hero," I said quietly. "But I guess that means you read about what happened here."

"Duh. I worked for a newspaper."

She'd gone snarky on me, something I was familiar with since the day we'd first met. She'd been a freshman at the University of Texas. Her mother had died of cancer a decade before. At that first meeting, it seemed obvious to me that she still hadn't gotten over her mother's death. *Sullen* didn't begin to describe her attitude back then. And nothing much changed over the ten years John and I were married.

I hadn't missed her use of the past tense when she'd said *worked*. "Newspapers are going through tough times," I said. "I don't want to pry, but I do care, and—"

"Yes, I lost my job. And no, I don't want to talk about it. Show me the rest of this place. Daddy talked so much about the plans, the lake, and . . . *you*. Since I have nothing but free time now, I thought I'd find out about his life before he died."

I heard the catch in her voice, and it dawned on me that though my grief over losing John had begun to ease, hers might only now be kicking in.

She turned and pointed across the hall. "Is this your bedroom?"

"Yes," I said.

In the master bedroom, all three cats lay on the king-size bed. This time, they didn't run off.

Kara stopped a few steps into the room and whispered, "How Daddy loved those cats." She approached them and held out her hand. Merlot stood and arched his back to stretch and then sniffed her fingers. He rubbed his head along the side of her hand. Cats know when a person needs comfort, and Merlot was great at offering affection whenever I was upset or troubled. He was doing the same for Kara now.

She petted him for a few seconds, but then the photograph on my bureau caught her eye—the last picture of John and me, taken on one wedding anniversary when we'd visited Ireland.

She walked around the bed and picked up the photo. Though her back was to me, I heard her say, "I don't have this picture."

She lowered her head, and her shoulders began to shake with sobs.

I went over and rested a hand on her shoulder. She stiffened and continued to hold the framed picture tightly. At least she didn't step away from my touch.

My search for information concerning the professor was forgotten. For the first time since I'd married John, Kara and I talked about him—for two solid hours. But she was still as standoffish as she'd been during every holiday or vacation we'd shared together while she was in college and after. Plus I was stuck with my original assessment that she had only begun to grieve her enormous loss. She'd worshipped John and had trouble with my marrying him from the beginning. I tried over and over again to befriend her, made her gifts, called her, sent her cards, but I could never break through the wall she'd built between us. But that didn't mean I stopped trying. Oops. Except for the last year and a half. Yes, I'd allowed my own grief to consume me, had cut myself off from the world.

During our conversation, I'd managed to get Kara to eat a tuna sandwich. I didn't ask, just made us both one and put hers in front of her. When she would come home for college semester breaks, usually with two or three friends, I could put anything to eat in front of her and it would be gone in fifteen minutes.

Now, between bites, words poured out of her like a stream that had been dammed up since her father's death. But she never made eye contact with me. That wall remained between us.

When she finally seemed to be finished talking, at least for the time being, I asked whether she'd like to visit my new foster children. One thing I was certain about Kara— she did love animals. She'd had a little mutt for a while but had to find him a home when she moved to a place where pets weren't allowed.

Soon we were down in the basement sitting next to where Dame Wiggins and her brood lay on the quilt I'd brought down last night. And since I left the door open, Chablis joined us. Her wish to visit these strangers had finally come true.

I told Kara about the suspicious death and what had led up to it, but she was so taken with the kittens, I wasn't sure she heard a word. And though I expected a hissing face-off between Wiggins and Chablis, it didn't happen. Chablis took her time getting close, and just as I finished my story about the events of the last three days, my cat did something that totally amazed me. She curled up on a corner of the quilt near Wiggins's tail and began to groom her newfound friend.

"This shouldn't happen," I said.

"What do you mean?" Kara stroked Wiggins's head.

"Not so much as a hint of a catfight—but then Dame Wiggins is probably the most unusual cat I've encountered, and Chablis is as gentle as Mercy Lake at dawn. Dame Wiggins did lead me to her litter, while most cats would have done just the opposite. This pretty calico seems to have a keen sense of what's safe and what's not."

"Dame Wiggins? What a funny name. She obviously understands that Chablis is no threat," Kara said. "But I could have told her that right away. Chablis is a sweetheart."

I smiled. "She is that."

My cell phone rang for the second time today, and I saw Tom Stewart's caller ID after I dug it out of my pocket. I answered with "Hey there. What's up?"

"What's up is that I'm at your front door, but no one's home. I wanted to talk to you about last night, and I even brought coffee," he said. "Where the heck are you?"

"I'm home, just didn't hear the doorbell. I'll be right there." I closed the phone and looked at Kara. "A friend of mine is here. Do you mind if we visit?"

She never took her eyes off the cats. "No problem. If you don't mind, I'd like to stay here with the kittens."

I smiled at Kara and went upstairs. A minute later, I let Tom in, and as he handed me a latte from Belle's Beans, he said, "Whose car is that in your drive?"

"Kara Hart. John's daughter," I said.

"Oh. He had kids?" Tom said.

"Just Kara," I answered. I didn't talk about John with Tom, didn't really talk about him or Kara with anyone.

Merlot and Syrah appeared, and they sauntered up to Tom and began sniffing his jeans for traces of Tom's own cat, Dashiell.

He handed me his coffee and knelt to pet them. "Kara came loaded, that's for sure."

"What are you talking about?" I said.

"Her car is packed to the roof with stuff," he said.

"Really? Maybe Mercy is on the way to wherever she's headed," I said.

"Mercy isn't on the way to anywhere, Jillian. It's a destination." He rose and took his coffee. "Let's talk about last night. I want to hear all about this latest mess you're involved in straight from the horse's mouth."

We went to the living room, but I was still processing that one little sentence.

It's a destination.

Eleven

Tom Stewart sat across from me in my living room while I related yet again all that had happened in the past few days. Tom is a great listener. Maybe working in security and doing PI work helped him hone those attentive skills, or maybe it was his former job as a police officer—the job he refused to talk about. I can't fault him there, since I'm tight-lipped on certain subjects myself.

But I was surprised when I finished telling my story. He didn't start questioning me about the professor but rather said, "What's with the daughter?"

"Kara? She lost her job. She's a reporter, and I guess no one is reading the newspaper anymore," I said. "But what about the professor and—"

"What newspaper?" he said.

"The *Houston Press*."

"How old is she?" he asked.

"Twenty-eight. No, twenty-nine. Seems I lost track of a year there," I said. Had I even sent Kara a birthday card the year John died?

"You were a stepmother to someone only twelve or thirteen years younger than you? How did that work out?" he said.

No one, not even John, ever asked me that. "Kara was a challenge. I tried. I'm still trying." But was I a lot like Kara? In protection mode? I had kept Tom at a friendly distance after we'd met last fall. I knew he wanted our relationship to be more than platonic, but I wasn't ready then. And what about now? I still wasn't sure.

"So Kara is—"

"Right here. What about me?" Kara said.

I wondered how long she'd been standing behind the breakfast bar that separated the living room and kitchen.

He turned her way. "Tom Stewart. Nice to meet you."

I thought she was about to smile, but she contained herself. "Hi. You obviously know my name already." She looked at me. "He's got great eyes. Nice catch, Jillian."

"It's not like that," I said. Maybe not yet, anyway.

Tom broke the awkward tension by saying, "Jillian was telling me you lost your job. Sorry to hear that."

Kara's eyes narrowed, and then she put on that mask I'd seen so often when she was younger, the same one I'd seen when she'd arrived on my doorstep today. No emotion whatsoever. She said, "I'm tired. Think I'll take a nap."

"Don't leave," Tom said. "Come and talk to us."

"Like I said, I'm tired." She walked around the counter and started toward the hallway.

"You're not interested in a job prospect?" he asked.

Uh-oh. What are you doing, Tom Stewart?

She turned, that expressionless demeanor not giving anything away. "What kind of job?"

"You were a reporter, right? What did you cover?" he asked.

A flush raced up her neck and settled on her pale cheeks. "Most recently? Or do you want the whole resume?"

"Sorry if I'm upsetting you," Tom said. "I'll get straight to it. We have a sorry-ass newspaper in this town. One editor and one reporter. But unlike the big city, where everyone gets their news from the Internet, people here still read their paper every day."

Why did I feel like an interloper in my own home? How had this happened, and why couldn't I find my voice? But if I spoke now, I was certain I would anger Kara even more. A stranger she could handle, but me? Just as I'd done while

John was alive, I avoided any kind of unpleasant confrontation with her and kept my mouth shut. I decided I could slug Tom later for succeeding where I'd failed. Yes, with a Louisville Slugger. Maybe Rufus Bowen could lend me one.

Kara laughed. "You want me to take a job at some Podunk newspaper? And make what? A couple hundred dollars a month?"

"You could bring your big-city knowledge to this small town. And what you write will be read. If it's money you're worried about, I can offer you part-time work, too."

"*What?*" I blurted, unable to hold back on that one.

"She came to Mercy for your help, Jillian." Tom looked at Kara. "That's why you came, right?"

Tom the listener had turned into Tom the Mr. Fix-it. How I wished I could be a Ms. Fix-it for Kara.

She said, "I only came to crash for a few days and then . . ." Her words trailed off, and she averted her gaze.

"See, that's what I'm talking about. You haven't called Jillian since, when? Since your father died? And then all of a sudden—"

"You told him that?" she said. Clearly she was surprised by the idea that I might talk about her in her absence.

"She didn't tell me. I'm guessing, and it looks like I've touched a nerve," Tom said.

"The only thing I told Tom was that you lost your job," I said.

"But you *were* talking about me. Do you even want me here?" she said.

"Huh?" I shook my head. "Kara, of course I do. I can't tell you how glad I am that you came here. Listen, let's have some sweet tea and clear up these misunderstandings. Are you two good with that?" I glanced at my untouched coffee on the end table. Sweet tea would be better than coffee for this conversation. Tom's direct approach didn't work for me . . . and the thought of Kara staying longer than a few days—well, I'd never imagined or expected such a thing. I might have wanted that kind of relationship with her once, but she'd rejected me for so long, I'd gotten used to it. I wasn't quite sure how to start over.

Tom raised his hand to indicate that he wanted tea—tea he didn't really care for—so I guessed he was attempting to help me get through this little rough spot. Kara, to my astonishment, walked over and sat in her father's old leather recliner. I guess she'd changed her mind about needing a nap.

She smiled thinly and said, "Sure. Let's all have something sweet."

But of course, I'd drunk all the tea I'd made earlier. I walked into the kitchen, put the kettle on to boil and grabbed tea bags and liquid cane sugar from the pantry. Kara and Tom were chatting away, probably about this part-time job he'd conjured from out of nowhere. A nice, quiet conversation that I couldn't hear. Fine with me, because I wasn't sure I wanted to listen to how nice she could be to him while all I got was poorly disguised hostility.

I filled a heavy pitcher with tea bags and waited for the water to boil. That's when I heard the beginning of a cat-fight downstairs. *I should have told Kara to close the door when she left the kittens*, I told myself as I raced down the stairs.

At first, I was bewildered by what I found. Merlot and Syrah were in the middle of the game room, both their coats puffed out so they looked like blowfish. The "you better stay away if you know what's good for you" half hiss, half growl I was hearing came from my sweet Chablis. She was playing guardian angel to Dame Wiggins and her litter. The big-boy cats wouldn't be getting near them if Chablis had her way.

"Boys, I'm sorry." I bent to stroke their ruffled fur. "It's a girl thing."

Syrah, my dominant cat, slowly sat, never taking his eyes off his onetime best friend, Chablis. Merlot, the sensitive guy, turned and raced up the stairs. His feelings were hurt, but it wouldn't last. Chablis was playing—what?

Grandma?—and that made me smile. I felt the tension in my gut ease, and then I heard the whistling kettle call me.

By the time we all had glasses of tea, Kara seemed more relaxed than I had ever seen her.

Tom said, "She's a columnist, not a reporter, Jillian. I guess we both stand corrected." He gave me this raised-eyebrows look, one I understood to mean, "Go along with me."

"Sorry, I should have known there's a difference," I said. "Has Tom convinced you to save the *Mercy Messenger* from mediocrity?"

She laughed, but this time without a hint of derision. "No way. But something big has happened in this town—that's what you were talking about downstairs earlier, right? Both Tom and I think I could freelance on this. Animal mistreatment? A murder? That might be an interesting story."

"Who said the professor was murdered?" I glanced at Tom, who just shrugged as if to say, "Not me."

"No one said he *wasn't* murdered," she answered. "With Tom's private-eye skills and you being right there at the scene yesterday, I could get plenty of facts about the case and end up selling this story to the wire services." She turned to Tom, her eyes bright. "Or . . . what about this, Tom? A true-crime book. And that might just be the beginning of a big career. Bigger than anything stupid Houston had to offer."

Okay, she wants to stay, I thought. I liked that. Maybe I could work on breaking down that wall between us. Finally.

Twelve

When Kara did leave to take that nap she'd talked about, Tom came over and sat down at the other end of the sofa, spreading his right arm along the back of the couch until his hand was inches from my shoulder.

"I did good, huh?" he said.

I stared at him in exaggerated shock. I said, "You think so?"

He looked at me, but I could tell the confusion I saw was completely fake. "Okay, Jillian, I may have overstepped, but the girl's lost."

I sighed. "You're right about that, but the way you just took over, it really made me feel as if I should be the one to—" My cell rang, and I pulled it from my pocket. It was Candace.

"Can you meet me for dinner? I need to vent," she said.

"Sure. But can we both vent in front of Tom? Because he needs to be vented upon," I said.

"Meet me at the new diner. This sounds like fun." She disconnected.

I stared at the phone for a second, then closed it. "That was Candace. She's upset, needs to talk. Are you brave enough to join us?"

Tom rose. "Sure. Maybe I can help you understand where I'm coming from in offering to help Kara. Speaking of Kara, should you invite her, too?"

"She looked so tired, I think she needs to rest, so

I'll leave her a note and make sure she gets her dinner later."

Before we left, I peeked in on Kara. Yup, sound asleep after her drive. Merlot must have decided beds were a good thing after all. He was stretched out at the foot, his lovely, long coat spread out so that he looked even larger than he is. He gave me a look that seemed to say, "I've got this problem under control."

We took Tom's Prius since my van was blocked in by Kara's car. During the drive to the diner, Tom spoke first. "I'm sorry if I upset you. But you've lived here for over a year and no one's come to visit. After you came for Christmas dinner at my mom's house, she started asking me questions about your past. And I realized I didn't have much to say."

"You know everything you need to know about me," I said.

"See, that's the problem. You're as guarded as Kara in your own way," he said.

I smiled. "I already came to the same conclusion."

"When I opened my big mouth with Kara, I was trying to help you. She may not be a blood relative, but—"

"But she is a part of John," I said. "Like I said, I realize that."

"She's down and out, though she's trying to cover it up," Tom said.

"Her father left her plenty of money. Enough to relocate, enough to live on while she looks for a job, and yet she shows up on my doorstep. She never accepted me when he was alive, so can you understand why I might be a little confused? And okay, I'll admit it, I am hopeful she wants to connect with me, but it's hard. Even after all this time, we're still practically strangers."

"Maybe she needs a family and didn't know any other way to approach you except by dropping in unexpectedly," he said. "Even if she doesn't need a family, you do. I mean, who do you lean on?"

Good question, I thought. My parents died a long time

ago, way before I met John. So I guess he was the one who— I blinked. I couldn't think about this now, much less talk about it with Tom yet.

Tom pulled into an angled parking place in front of the Main Street Diner. "You didn't answer my question. Can we talk more later? I want you to let me in, Jillian."

"Sure," I said. But was I sure? I didn't know.

"Are we okay, then?" he asked.

"Certainly." I gently tapped the corner of his turned-up mouth. "Your smile fixed everything."

"That's a nonanswer if I ever heard one," he said as we both got out of the car.

The Main Street Diner had opened last month, and from what I'd seen from the outside, the restaurant suited Mercy's small-town ambience right down to the green awning, which matched all the other ones on the street. There must be some kind of town ordinance about those awnings, I decided. I mean, people couldn't all choose the same color by accident, could they?

I'd heard from Belle, who owned Belle's Beans, that this new diner was already cutting into her revenue. She once had a monopoly on coffee, breakfast muffins, pastries and ready-made sandwiches. I loved Belle, who was kind of wacky but made great coffee, and I almost felt like a traitor visiting this establishment.

Tom held the door for me, and when I walked in I felt like I'd stepped onto the set of an old movie. The twin aisles of booths to my right were high-backed wood. To my left was a long, curving counter accented by chrome. The red leather swivel stools had chrome pedestals to match. A sign told us to seat ourselves—it was early for supper—and then I saw Candace waving at us from the back booth.

I slid in beside her to give Tom plenty of room across from us. Even though the booth seats had no padding, they were comfortable. A small jukebox was attached to the wall behind the sugar, salt and pepper.

Tom immediately took a quarter from his pocket and began to flip the laminated pages for a song. He chose

"Jailhouse Rock" and settled back with a smile as the song started to play. I didn't move my knee away when I felt his rest lightly against mine. Maybe he had no idea, and my moving away would give him the wrong idea. Or maybe it was a kind of apology for stepping in with Kara without talking it over with me first. In any case, I had to admit that it felt nice.

A waitress in a pink and white uniform appeared, handed us menus and took our drink orders—iced tea all around.

I turned and looked at Candace. "Why the need to vent?"

She said, "Between Morris and Lydia, I might be checking into the Hotel California before this case is over. Or maybe I already have, seeing as how you can *never leave*."

"I'd love to help, but I don't think I have much influence with those two." I opened the menu, and the first thing that caught my eye was what was touted as the diner's specialty, a Texas chili dog. *In South Carolina?* That was kind of like serving a Whopper at McDonald's.

"Lydia can drive anyone nuts," Tom said. "She's nearly driven me to the edge more than once. What's going on?"

"You know Morris is acting chief?" she said.

"Jillian told me," Tom said.

"He won't listen," she said. "Not like he ever listened to me before, but we're losing time while he waits on Lydia to find a pathologist to do the autopsy. Tough to accomplish on the weekend, I know, but still, she seems to be in no hurry."

"Losing time?" I said.

"The first forty-eight hours are crucial in any investigation, and I spent the entire night and this morning collecting evidence." She began whispering then. "See, I *know* the professor was murdered."

"Not suicide and not an accident? You're sure?" I said.

"Yes, because—"

But Candace was interrupted by the waitress, who'd reappeared with our drinks and was ready to take our orders.

We all chose Texas chili dogs—which, from their description, sounded like nothing unusual, but since they were touted as "the special" we all decided we had to try them. Tom ordered fries and Candace added onion rings, but my mind wasn't on food any longer. My instincts had told me that man was murdered, so I was eager to hear what Candace had to say.

"Won't you get in trouble for talking about this with us?" I said.

"She knows we won't say anything," Tom said.

"But that means not saying anything to Kara, Tom. You understand that?" I said.

"Who's Kara?" Candace looked back and forth between us.

I hesitated.

"Okay, if there's a person who you might talk to about this case, then I've said enough." Candace looked ready to vent on me now. Her arms were crossed across her chest, and her lips were a tight pucker.

"I'm sorry," I said. "Kara is John's daughter. She arrived this morning, right after the bug man left."

"He had a daughter? And you never told me?" Candace said. She sounded hurt.

"Never told me, either," Tom added, who obviously sympathized with her hurt.

The whole thing made me pretty uncomfortable. It was hard for me to talk about Kara and explain to others why we weren't very close. It was one of those things that was easier left unsaid. "Can I explain when we're both not so . . . so tired and cranky?" I said.

"I'm not tired," Tom said.

"But you want to help Kara with her writing career, and—"

"Hold on, Jillian," Tom said. "I thought you understood." His knee moved away from mine. "Helping Kara does not involve telling her anything Candace says about the case. If the professor was murdered—and I have no doubt that's true if Candace says so, then—"

"Kara's a writer? What kind of writer?" Candace asked.

I sighed. And then I explained. "She lost her job and needs your support. I get it." Candace seemed to relax, and so did I. No secrets between the three of us now.

When our food arrived, Tom said, "Let's take a break from talking about Kara and the professor, eat these chili dogs and then get coffee over at Belle's. I, for one, will feel better about the three of us conversing as trusting friends once my belly is full."

"You're right," I said. "Stressful day. Nothing like a chili dog and fries to cure what ails you."

Turns out the "Texas chili dog" was like nothing I'd tasted back home in Texas. Instead, this dog had a chili sauce touched with cinnamon and came loaded with grated sweet onions. It had to be the best bad-for-you food I'd ever eaten. No one talked. We'd all gone to heart-attack-on-a-bun heaven.

When we were done, we walked one block to Belle's Beans in silence, but in a far better mood. Food is the quicker fixer-upper. As we made our way down the block, I could almost smell the impending rain, but the aroma of coffee was stronger.

As we entered the coffee shop, I wondered whether Belle had been exaggerating about losing revenue. The place was packed. After we gave our coffee orders to Tom, he stood in line while Candace and I went back outside. Belle set up wrought-iron tables on the sidewalk when the weather was nice, and we grabbed the only one that was unoccupied.

"Tell me why you think it's murder," I said. I glanced through the window to my right and saw that Tom still had three people in front of him. "Or should we wait with the questions until he comes with the coffee?"

But the questions would have to wait, thanks to the arrival of Lydia Monk. She stopped at our table and smiled. "If it isn't Cagney and Lacey."

I snuck a peek through the window. *Please stay in there, Tom. Please. The last thing I need is a crazy Lydia moment.*

"What are you doing in town?" Candace asked.

"Talking to Morris. He's not taking this case as seriously as he should." She glared at Candace. "Because strychnine is serious business. Surely you can find the poison source if you're as smart as you think you are."

I thought about mentioning Rufus Bowen and how I'd questioned him about strychnine this morning, but that might have been disastrous. Lydia had no idea whom she was messing with on this particular evening, but I did. From Candace's expression, I could tell it wouldn't take much for her to engage Lydia in an argument.

Candace stood, her coral Henley T-shirt and blue jeans a tad ordinary in comparison to Lydia's bejeweled and beaded black shirt with the plunging neckline.

"Are you trying to start something, Lydia?" Candace said.

"Hold on, you two," I said, hoping to avoid a public cat-fight. "You're both competent women who know how to do your jobs. Can we leave it at that?" Okay, lying to Lydia about Lydia tweaked my conscience a tad, but I was more interested in getting the woman to move along before Tom walked outside. And that would happen soon, I noted, since he was giving our order to the young woman behind the counter this very minute.

"Start something?" Lydia said, ignoring me. "I'm not that unprofessional."

Except for the hoop earrings, the tattooed eyeliner and the teased hair, I thought. Not unprofessional in the least.

I caught Candace checking inside the coffee shop, and she obviously realized what might happen if she kept up this disagreement. "Sorry, Lydia. You're right. Nice seeing you without a corpse nearby." Candace sat back down and folded her arms on the table.

Lydia narrowed her eyes and stared at Candace for a few tense seconds. Then she cracked a smile. "You know how to apologize. That's progress, Candy."

She looked at me. "Good night, Jillian. And stay away from crime scenes and certain security experts, would you?"

I mustered what I hoped came off as a sincere smile. "I'll try."

Lydia turned, and the rhinestoned spike heels she wore glittered in the light from a nearby streetlight. I watched as she walked away and released the breath I'd been holding.

Then Tom arrived with our coffee, and before he could speak, I raised a finger to my lips and nodded in the retreating Lydia's direction.

Tom set down the cardboard tray with two cups of coffee marked DECAF on the side and his own small espresso in a china cup. "That was close," he whispered.

"Okay," I said to Candace. "I'm anxious to know why you think the professor was murdered."

"Sometimes, when you find little or no evidence, that tells you a lot," she said. "Although I do prefer a nice fingerprint or DNA."

"And what *didn't* you find?" I asked.

"Strychnine. At least I don't think there was any strychnine in that house or outside. We found rat poison in the shed. But it was your usual grocery-store variety made with warfarin. And it was pellets, not powder." She sat back with a satisfied smile.

"Could strychnine have been substituted for the warfer-whatever? Sheesh. I can never say that word."

"Sure. But why? Do you think he was snacking on warfarin pellets and the murderer somehow knew that and made a substitution?" she said.

"You're right. Dumb question. I'm not thinking too clearly today."

Tom said, "I take it you didn't find any suicide note?"

"Nope," Candace said. "I'd say you'd have to be pretty damn sorry about something to strychnine yourself to death. I've been reading up on it, and you won't find me within a country mile of that poison."

I sipped my coffee, and it was just right. Tom had added milk to mine and none to Candace's. We hung out at Belle's at least a couple of times a week, and he knew how we liked our coffee.

Tom poured three packets of sugar into his high-test and stirred the pitch-black espresso with a tiny spoon. He said, "I worked a murder case involving strychnine once. Multiple deaths from bad cocaine. Dealers sometimes cut the coke with strychnine powder. But Candace probably already knows that."

"One of your private investigations?" I asked.

"Nope." His gaze was fixed on his cup. "This was back when I was on the force. Do you know why Morris doesn't think this is a murder case?"

"Morris wants the easiest solution," Candace said. "Thing is, no one knows much about this professor."

"Or why he was feeding cats that red goop and raw cow's milk," I said. "Research, maybe?"

"Yes. We've already tossed around the idea he was doing some kind of experiment with the cats' diet. But you know me," Candace said. "I hate guessing. No one seems interested in what I have to say, though."

"I'm interested," I said. "Maybe some animal welfare group found out what he was doing and didn't like it. But that doesn't explain the cats that were left behind. True animal lovers wouldn't have left them." I sipped on my coffee. "That still bothers me."

Half to himself, Tom said, "Interrupted."

"What?" I said.

"Maybe they were interrupted and couldn't take all the cats." He sipped at his espresso.

"Yes," I said, nodding as I realized that what he said could well be true. "Interrupted by someone else. By the killer. Maybe the people who went to get the cats weren't the same people who killed him."

Candace groaned. "Don't start making stuff up. I need evidence, and so far, all I have is a footprint. And from the size, it looks like it will come back to the professor. Oh, and a few fibers off the fence."

"The barbed-wire one? You might find all kinds of me on that particular fence." Like my skin. But the scratch on my backside was nothing, not even worthy of a tetanus shot. Now that the tension had finally seemed to dissipate, I felt more relaxed with my friends.

"I got a few strands of fabric off the chain-link enclosure, where someone probably reached through to grab a cat. Cat hairs, too, but those were all over the place and pretty much useless."

Tom said, "Wouldn't he be keeping notes about this possible experiment? Like on a computer or even talking into a recorder?"

Candace said, "Oh, he was. Jillian saw him writing things down. But that's actually an 'absence of evidence' and pretty darn suspicious. All I found in the house were lots of textbooks on animal nutrition, but no notebook and no computer. I think the computer must have been taken, because the professor did have a DSL line, and we found an instruction manual for a laptop."

"He had a PhD in animal nutrition," I said. "Do you consider his education evidence that he could have been researching cat food?"

"Who told you about his schooling?" Candace said. "I was with you the entire fifteen minutes we spent with the man, and I never heard him say anything about that."

"I Googled him. He had a wife. Has she been notified?" I said.

"Ex-wife. And two sons. The ex is on the way from Denman, but I don't know about the kids," Candace said. "All's I can say is, I sure hope the pathologist can get that grimace off the professor's face before the woman is asked to give an official identification."

"Did she sound upset?" I asked.

"Not so much, I have to say," she said. "But she said she had no idea he was living here and that she needed directions. She mentioned she'd need several copies of the death certificate and asked about insurance. No, the ex–Mrs. Professor wasn't too upset about anything but those nonhuman details."

Tom said, "I'm stuck on this notebook. Where did it go? Jillian saw it and, what, an hour later the guy's dead and the notebook's gone?"

"That's what I was talking about. Circumstantial evidence that makes me think this was a murder," Candace said.

"Most whodunit cases *are* built on circumstantial evidence," Tom said.

More cop talk, I thought. I sure wanted to hear about his cop days, as he'd told me very little before, but I needed to wrap my mind around the case at hand.

"Wait a minute," I said. "Here's something I know that might be useful. There's a difference between activists. The welfare types like Shawn and so many like him, and the fringe types that are more radical. More political. Maybe the notes will surface on the Internet if some group wanted to expose the professor's actions. But if people interested primarily in animal welfare took those cats, my bet is, you won't hear another thing. And those kinds wouldn't hurt anyone. Period."

Candace said, "Yes. Different kinds of activists. I've never met up with any of these folks, but if they carry strychnine around, I don't want to get anywhere near them."

"Welfare activists usually want to save animals from mistreatment, but the more militant types want humans to have no access to animals. Even as pets," I said.

"That's . . . almost impossible, I'd say," Tom said. He looked at Candace. "I'm still hung up on my interruption thing. What if *you* were the one who interrupted what was going on at that farm?"

"You mean the folks who took the cats were on the property when I showed up?" she said. "How would they—" Her hand flew to her mouth, and between her fingers she whispered, "I sorta screamed when I saw the meat on that counter. They could have heard me."

"But I was right outside, and I didn't hear—" My stomach clenched as I remembered the man in the van, the one who had waved to me.

"I can tell by your face that you remember something," Candace said.

"Before you came out of the house, a van drove by. It came from the opposite direction from the way we'd arrived." I closed my eyes, trying to picture what I'd seen. "The driver even waved at me."

"This is big," Candace said. "Can you describe this van?"

"White panel," I said. "Is there ever a crime committed without a white panel van involved?"

"Did you see the driver?" Tom said.

"A man. Maybe. Gosh, I was so worried about the cats, I didn't pay much attention," I said.

"Don't think too hard," Tom said. "You've had a demanding day, and when you're more relaxed, details might come flooding back."

"And if they do, you call me right away," Candace said. "I don't care if it's three in the morning. See, this fits, Jillian. When I was out at the farm this morning, I confirmed what I thought I saw last night. The grass was pretty trampled around the outside of that chain-link fence, probably by whoever took those cats. It looked to me like they'd cut a path to the empty property next door."

"Did you find anything over there?" I asked.

"Nope. And county records show the place has been empty a long time. I looked in the windows. No sign of anything amiss except that trampled grass," she said. "Not even a stick of furniture inside that I could tell."

"Not much cause for a search warrant if there's no homicide ruling," Tom said.

"You see why I'm a cranky-pants today?" she said. "Frustrating as hell that Lydia's dragging her feet about getting a pathologist." Candace lowered her head.

But her head snapped back up when a man came up behind her. "Let me help you out, then," he said. "You need relaxing, I'm your guy."

Tom stood and put out his hand. "Why, Darryl Tillson. Didn't I just see you, fella?"

The two exchanged happy greetings while Candace gave me an eye roll. Darryl owned the local feed store and had been trying to date Candace for the last six months.

I had to agree with her decision not to jump at the chance, though. The man often smelled of manure, which would not top *my* list of characteristics for potential suitors. But in truth, I didn't know him well enough to judge.

Tom said, "I put security cameras at Tillson Cattle and Feed last week."

"Going high-tech on us, Darryl?" I said.

"Gotta keep up with the times, but I think my daddy might be rolling over in his grave at the thought that I even need them," he said.

Candace kept her face down, her head supported by fists at her temples. "When you're being robbed blind, you do what you gotta do," she said.

"Candace, here, investigated the feed thefts. She's a smart cop for a girl. She's the one recommended you, Tom." Then Darryl caught sight of me for probably the first time. Candace *was* his priority, after all. "And, Miss Hart. How's the cat family? They like that new kibble I persuaded you to buy?"

"They love it," I lied. I knew Darryl's intentions were good, but in truth, Chablis refused to eat even one piece and moped the entire day. Syrah almost hissed at the dish, and Merlot walked off after one sniff. The next day I'd tossed out the bag and went back to their old standby. "But you do have to rotate with cats. Picky eaters. Next time I'm in, I might try something different."

"Y'all was talking it up, and I interrupted," Darryl said. "But I had to stop and say hey. See you all at the store." He walked around our table and into Belle's Beans.

As soon as he was gone, Candace stood. "I do not want to be here when he comes back out. Besides, I have to call Morris about that van." She pointed at me. "You will phone me if you remember anything else?"

"Of course." I came around the table and hugged her good-bye before she took off.

Tom and I talked for a few more minutes, and then I said, "I'm pretty tired myself. Mind taking me home?"

We walked back to the Main Street Diner, where we'd parked, and during the five-minute ride back to my place, we didn't speak.

I was thinking hard, though.

When he pulled up behind Kara's car, he turned off the ignition and said, "Don't beat yourself up."

"What are you talking about?" I said.

"You're kicking yourself for not remembering that van right away, for not paying attention."

I looked sideways at him. "Am I that transparent?"

He smiled. "You're getting to be. As hard as you're trying to stop me, I am actually getting to know you." And with that he leaned over and kissed me. A soft, gentle kiss on the mouth.

Thirteen

The following morning, I awoke to the smell of coffee and the memory of a kiss. And last night's guilt was fresh in my mind, too. I felt as if I'd betrayed John. Especially when I'd walked into the house last night and the first thing I saw was his daughter. Kara had been talking on her cell phone and waved at me in a friendly enough manner to warm my heart. Maybe there was hope for us after all.

I hadn't wanted to interrupt her, so I'd gone straight to my bedroom. Sure, John would want me to find another partner. But that darn guilt still kept me tossing and turning for a good hour before I'd finally fallen asleep.

Now I sat up, stretched and checked the clock on my nightstand. Eight a.m. Kara must have made coffee, and I almost felt pampered. Then I realized my cats weren't in the room. That bothered me. Routine is soothing, and this was a break from routine. I realized Chablis might be downstairs guarding her friends. But I wondered where my boys were.

Thinking about my visiting cats downstairs gave me a terrible thought. *Dame Wiggins and her litter.* Darn. *I didn't fill her dish last night*, I thought, getting out of bed. I nearly tripped as I rushed out of my bedroom and headed down the hall.

Kara was in the kitchen, and I said, "Good morning. Coffee smells great," as I hurried past her toward the basement door.

Kara seemed to know just what I was up to because before I made it to the basement door, she said, "Don't worry, Jillian. I fed her and gave her fresh water. But perhaps you could do the litter box?" she said.

I stopped and looked at her. "Oh. Thanks." I don't know why I was so surprised by her thoughtfulness. I guess it had just been a long time since I had been living with someone else.

"Don't you ever eat?" she asked. "I mean, you've got next to nothing but yogurt and tea. Tuna salad was good for lunch yesterday, but it's not really my favorite breakfast food."

"We can go to the Piggly Wiggly later. Or you can make a list and I can go," I said.

"I'll do the shopping." She wore shorts and a tank top and was leaning against the counter holding her coffee cup. "I'm meeting with Tom today, and I'll stop at the store after we're done. That way I can pay for the week's food."

Okay. Lots of info. She has enough money to pay for food, she's staying for at least a week and she's meeting with Tom. I smiled and said, "Sounds perfect. And thanks for feeding Dame Wiggins."

"Believe me, she came up here and told me to do it," Kara said.

"She left her litter?" She must have been as hungry as when she'd showed up at Ruth Schultz's farm to do that.

Kara smiled. She was so lovely with her flawless skin and gentle curves, and a decent night's sleep and a better attitude only accentuated her assets. "Go down and check out what's happening," she said. "It's great."

So I did. Merlot and Syrah were lying in the middle of the game room again. *Waiting for Chablis to grant them admittance to the bedroom?* Probably. When I went to the door, I had to cover my mouth to keep from laughing out loud—which would have surely hurt Chablis's feelings. Chablis lay on Dame Wiggins's quilt with those four babies cuddled close to her. Dame Wiggins sat at the food dish and stopped eating long enough to offer a sweet little meow.

I knelt next to Chablis, and I swore her purrs could have

been heard in the next county. Apparently this was a dream come true for her. I stroked her head, and she closed her eyes. Yup, a litter of kittens was the best thing that had happened to her since John and I rescued her from that shelter.

I guess she'd been wanting a family all this time.

After I came back upstairs, I told Kara I was off to shower and then had quilting orders to attend to. When I came out into the kitchen an hour later, she was gone. Off to meet with Tom, I guessed. I consumed the last two yogurts and then took my coffee down the hall. Syrah and Merlot bounded into my sewing room ahead of me.

I still had to bind quilts for promised orders. I make continuous bias bindings for all my quilts and hand sew them on during the last binding step for a nice, neat finish. I had yards of completed bindings and took a green and red tiny print from my binding drawer. A woman in Georgia had ordered a quilt for her cat Saint Nick and wanted, of course, green and red. I'd made a simple nine-patch with beautiful small-print fabrics and added a flying-geese border to this one. Custom orders like this are my favorite.

Long strips of fabric like bindings are a cat's dream, and I always keep several that my three can play with. I pulled out one of those, and Syrah was on that fabric like a bear on a fish. He grabbed it in his mouth and started to run toward the windowsill, but Merlot immediately snagged the other end. Too bad Chablis was missing out on this game, but she was probably having more fun downstairs.

I sat at my sewing machine by the window. No lake view on this side of the house, but there were the big hickories and oaks with lots of birds and squirrels to distract me. The binding was all ironed, and once I had machine sewed it all the way around the quilt, making sure to miter the corners, I would then flip the binding over the raw edges of the quilt and hand sew it on. This was my absolute favorite part of making a quilt—the part that relaxed me the most.

But I'd managed to get only the machine-sewing part of

the binding done when my cell phone rang. The small voice I heard at the other end took me by surprise.

"Is this Miss Jillian Hart?" whispered the boy.

"Jack? Is that you?" I said.

"Yes. I can't talk loud. I don't want Mom to hear. Can you come over and help her?"

My heart fluttered. "Is she hurt?"

"Nothing like that. She's called Candace like a hundred times, but Candace must be so busy with the professor's death investigation, she doesn't have time for my mom right now. Totally understandable to me, of course."

"Totally," I echoed, astonished again at this child. I wondered what it must be like to be so different from other kids. Difficult, was my guess. "How can I help, Jack?"

"Would you come over? Just for a little while. She's . . . well, you saw how she is. And it's worse because the professor died."

"I'll be there as quickly as I can. And I won't let her know you called me, okay?"

"That would be especially considerate. Bye."

I made a quick check downstairs and saw Chablis, Dame Wiggins and the kittens sharing the quilt. The kittens were suckling, and Chablis was curled close to Dame Wiggins's head this time. Syrah had carried the quilt binding downstairs and lay on his back on the game-room floor with the fabric between his paws. Maybe he thought he could tempt Chablis out of the bedroom with the binding and things could get back to normal for him. *Not anytime soon, buddy*, I thought.

After I turned the TV to Animal Planet for Merlot's entertainment, I was off. Fifteen or twenty minutes later, I drove down Robin West's long dirt driveway. I noted a new padlock on the barn and saw that the blinds on the house were all closed. If I didn't know better, I might have thought no one was home. I slid from behind the wheel of my minivan and felt a few splats of rain hit my shoulders. I hurried to the porch before the dark clouds released the storm that was about to hit.

I knocked on the door and at the same time shouted, "Robin? It's Jillian."

Nothing at first, and then I saw the blinds crack on the window to my right. I heard Jack yell, "Mom it really is Miss Jillian." His voice sounded muffled for some reason.

Seconds later, the door opened. Robin wore heavy-duty rubber gloves and had a surgical-type mask hanging around her neck. "Hi, Jillian. What brings you here?" Her smile was tight, her voice strained.

"In the neighborhood," I said.

"Let her in, Mom. It's about to storm."

I realized why his voice was muffled when I peeked around Robin. He was wearing *his* surgical mask.

"Sorry to be rude," she said. "Come in. Nice to see you again." She opened the door, and I stepped into her ultra-tidy living room. No dust lived here, that was for sure.

"Is someone sick?" I asked, as Robin led me through her living room to the kitchen.

Jack walked beside me, and he rolled his eyes and shook his head.

Robin removed her gloves and pulled out a kitchen chair for me. She said, "Sick? Why would you—"

Jack pointed at his mask.

Her eyes widened in understanding. "Oh. No. I'm doing a little extra cleaning today. Those chemicals can be very harsh on the immune system."

Jack removed his mask. "You're finished cleaning for now, right, Mom?"

Robin glanced behind her. A bottle of Clorox Clean-Up sat by the sink. "Yes. I suppose."

She looked like she hadn't slept in days, which was probably true, what with the cow and the professor and the stake-out. "You look tired, Robin. Having trouble sleeping?"

Robin looked at her son. "Um, Jack? Would you mind leaving us alone for some girl talk? You can use your computer for one hour, okay?"

His eyes lit up. "Cool. Bye, Miss Jillian."

He took off, and I felt like I'd already accomplished something. He could have a little fun.

"What can I get you to drink?" Robin asked.

"Water would be fine," I answered.

She opened the refrigerator, took out a glass bottle and poured water into a spotless glass. "It's filtered," she assured me. "And I don't like to keep the water in that plastic pitcher. Plastic is very bad for your health."

"You're not having anything?" I said.

"My stomach's a little queasy," she said.

I sipped my water. "You're upset, right? Because you heard about the professor's death?"

"Yes. I can't help but think that if I hadn't called Candace, if I'd left him alone and let him just take the milk—"

"Let him come on your property without permission and continue to steal from you? No. You did the right thing, Robin."

"But he's dead, and see, there's more. He called me. And I wasn't very nice to him. And I am so sorry for that." Her eyes brimmed with tears.

I reached across the table and placed my hand over hers. They were clenched together in front of her and icy cold. "I can tell you're the kind of person who takes on a lot of responsibility. But you don't have anything to be sorry for. The man stole from you."

"And I forgave him, but then on the phone, I just didn't like what he had to say, and—" She pulled her hands from beneath mine and stood. "I forgot the coaster."

Indeed, my glass was weeping and had left a wet spot on the table. I was the one who felt sorry now—for her and for Jack. Had she ever been treated for her over-the-top anxiety? Did she realize how much her behavior must be affecting her child?

She took her time wiping the wet spot, making sure the table was completely dry. She then placed a stone coaster decorated with a picture of the White House beneath my glass.

Thinking she might need to calm down before we continued talking about the professor, I said, "Have you been to the White House?"

"Jack met the vice president. My ex-husband even made the trip. My wonderful, brilliant son wrote an essay on saving the environment, and he got to read it to the vice president." She shook her head, and the tears returned. "He is so special, and I am such a failure as a mother. I drove his father away because I do this crazy stuff, and—"

"Jack is amazing. Do you think a crazy mom could raise a boy like him? You're doing a fantastic job." She certainly admired her boy, that's for sure.

Robin took a tissue from her pocket and blew her nose. "You think so?"

I smiled. "I know so." *In some ways*, I added to myself. "Now, tell me about this phone call—and pretend you don't feel guilty, even though you do."

She pulled a small bottle of gel hand cleaner from her pocket and started cleaning her hands. "He called late Friday afternoon. At first I thought he wanted to apologize again. But he never said he was sorry. And you know how he was stuttering when you and Candace caught him?"

"Right," I said.

"None of that," she said. "He sounded like a different person. Like a not-so-nice person."

"What did he say?" I asked.

"He wanted more milk. Said I'd promised him milk and I should come through." Robin's cheeks reddened. "Did I promise him that? Because I don't think that's what I said, and I told him as much."

"You didn't promise him anything. You said you would have given him milk if he'd asked, but that's not the same thing. And after what he did, I wouldn't have given him the time of day. He scared you silly."

She sighed. "Whew. That's what I thought, but then he died and maybe I should have told him we could barter like he wanted to. But I never got the chance, really."

I narrowed my eyes. "Huh? He wanted to barter?"

"He said he would give me cat food for Lucy—high-quality cat food, he called it—if I would give him raw milk."

"But you didn't take him up on this, I assume?" I said.

"I don't think I would have, but see, I heard his doorbell ring then, and he said he had to go, that he'd get back to me. And today I find out that he's dead. I feel so awful because I could have been more generous and understanding."

"You and I should write a book—*The Guilt-Lover's Manual*. I go overboard in the guilt department myself. I don't believe I would have handled that call with generosity and understanding if I'd been in your shoes, though."

She smiled for the first time. "*The Guilt-Lover's Manual*. I like that."

"Do you recall what time he phoned? This could be important information for the police." I was wondering whether Professor VanKleet's killer had actually come to his front door that day. Whoever freed the cats didn't ring any doorbells; otherwise, they wouldn't have had to cut the fence.

Robin said, "He called late in the afternoon, because Jack was home from school. Of course Jack started asking me questions when I hung up. I could tell he was upset."

"Because *you* were upset, right?" I said.

"Yes, but I didn't tell him anything. And now I still have to keep quiet. Jack shouldn't hear about people being murdered in our town. He'll have nightmares."

But Jack already knows, I thought. Via the Internet? Probably.

"So VanKleet called in the late afternoon?" I said, but didn't add that he was dead not long after. "The police will probably be looking at the professor's phone records. Your number will come up, and they might want to talk to you. For now, I can tell Candace about this call when I see her. Would that be okay?"

Robin's face relaxed, and I swear she looked ten years younger. "Would you do that? I hate bothering Candace all the time, and the rest of the police force is sick to death of me." She covered her mouth with her fingers. "Oh. Not sick to *death*. That's a horrible thing to say right now."

"Remember our *Guilt-Lover's Manual*? Are you writing another chapter this minute?" I said.

She smiled again. "You're right. Thank you, Jillian. Amazing you came by at the right time to reassure someone who needed reassurance."

Not as amazing as you might think, I thought. "I noticed a little guy with sad eyes when I got here. Can I offer a suggestion?" Jack had reached out to me, and I wanted to help him.

"Certainly," she said.

I saw a wariness in her eyes that almost made me rethink what I was about to say. And then I realized that this had been Tom's intent with Kara—to help, not to overstep. And that insight made me understand that I had to speak up for Jack. "This is just my opinion, but a child might not feel comfortable coming to the door wearing a surgical mask unless you've had a tuberculosis outbreak in the house."

"But the chemicals could—"

I held up my hand. "Maybe you could send him outside when you have to clean—and I understand you need to do that right now. I'll bet Lucy would love it if Jack came out and petted her. And there's ball and Frisbee and, oh, I don't know, *rock collecting*. Anything, Robin."

She didn't speak for a few seconds, and I thought I'd really pissed her off, but then she let out a big sigh and said, "I know you're right. I should do that. No, I *have* to do that. It makes me uncomfortable, but I know if I don't, he's going to end up hating me."

I put my hand on her upper arm. "I don't think anyone could ever hate you." Thunder rumbled and I added, "Maybe now's not a good time for him to play outside, but later. When there are puddles to splash in."

"Puddles. Oh boy." She wrinkled her nose, but she offered the third smile of the day. Might be a record for her.

I said, "And now I'm off to hunt down Candace and

tell her about that phone call you received from the professor."

I left, but after I dashed to my van to avoid as many
raindrops as I could and was putting my key in the ignition,
I saw the blinds part in the front window. Then Jack stuck
his hand through the slats and gave me a thumbs-up.

Fourteen

Once I was on the road, I tried Candace's cell phone, hoping we could meet at Belle's Beans. I wanted to tell her about Robin's contact with the professor, but my call went straight to voice mail. I checked my watch. Almost noon. She'd worked yesterday at the professor's farm gathering evidence, so maybe she was at her apartment, sound asleep.

Home sleeping with what she considered a murder investigation in progress? *Think again, Jillian,* I thought. Candace believed Morris Ebeling didn't value her input, and if I knew her, she'd be hard at work hoping to prove him wrong. "Bet I know where to find you, my friend," I said as I made a U-turn. I'd just passed the turnoff to Van-Kleet's place and decided I'd drive by the old farm. My hunch was that the evidence hunter might have gone back for yet another look around that property.

But what I saw far down the road made me clench the steering wheel. Even though it was pouring now, I saw flashing patrol car lights, a fire engine and, as I got closer, Candace, wearing a dark green hooded slicker. She was placing orange cones in the road so no cars could go any farther than right in front of the professor's farm.

Had they finally listened to her and decided this was a murder scene after all? But that wouldn't have caused the Mercy brigade to show up here again. No. Something else had happened. Not anything good, either.

Just then a van passed me at mach speed, spraying rain and mud in its wake. I recognized Lydia Monk's county coroner vehicle.

Uh-oh. Coroners show up for only one thing.

My chest felt tight as I pulled over near the ditch right before the professor's driveway. I caught a warning look from Candace as she took up a few cones so Lydia could pass. I stayed put until Lydia had driven on down the road to where the rest of the emergency vehicles were parked. Candace hurried toward me, but I grabbed an umbrella and was out of the minivan before she reached me.

"What's going on?" My gaze was focused down the road.

"No doubt about this one. Definitely murder," she said. "But you better get out of here before Lydia and Morris see you."

"Okay, but tell me the quick version first. We can talk later," I said.

"Finally got hold of an executive of the bank that holds the lien on that property next to the professor's place. That's where I think the cats were taken first and where that white van you saw came from. The house is in fore-closure, and the banker told me I didn't need a warrant—a warrant that would have been hard to come by, though the banker didn't know that. He said I could search the place all I wanted. But when I got here, Jesus, Mary and Joseph, there he was, dead as he could be."

"Who?"

"You might not know him. His name is Rufus Bowen. He's an—"

"Exterminator," I finished. I suddenly felt light-headed and placed my free hand on the van.

A gust of wind nearly knocked me over, and my pathetic umbrella blew away down the road. But though rain began to soak me, I didn't care.

Candace gripped my elbow for further support. "What's wrong, Jillian?"

"W-was he poisoned, too?" My voice sounded so far away.

"Whacked on the head. But what do you know about Rufus that I don't? 'Cause you sure as heck know something."

"I'm so sorry for him." I shook my head, barely noticing how soaked my hair was getting.

"Talk to me, Jillian."

I swallowed hard. "Rufus Bowen came to my house yesterday."

"Oh my gosh. You did say something about the bug man, didn't you?"

I nodded, unable to speak around the lump in my throat.

"You poor thing," Candace said. "Two men you've met this past week are dead. That would stagger anyone." She reached around me and started to open my van door. "You're gonna catch a chill. Climb back in your van, and—"

"No." I pointed in the direction of the property where the crime had taken place. "I need to go down there. You'll want to talk to me. Take a statement or something."

She cocked her head, rain sliding down her fair cheeks. "Why?"

"Because I called Rufus Bowen to my house yesterday to talk about poison. Strychnine, to be exact."

I'd never sat in a fire truck before, but that's where I ended up. Since no cats needed rescuing, I was spared the distress of walking by a dead man for the second time in three days and seeing firsthand the damage one human can do to another. Candace had turned me over to Billy Cranor's care while she went to inform whoever would listen that I might want to offer some insight into Rufus Bowen's final days on earth.

Billy had produced a yellow raincoat and helped me into it. He even found a towel for my soaking-wet hair.

I dried off as best I could but felt chilled to the bone.

Meanwhile, Billy climbed into the driver's seat. He pulled off the hood of his slicker and said, "What in heck are you doing here, Ms. Hart?"

This was how the grapevine began its work. Billy knew I'd been here Friday night, and now I was back. Though I was certain his concern for me was sincere, I had no doubt he also wanted to be the first person aside from Candace to hear the answer to why I'd shown up.

But I was with-it enough to know that whatever my reply, it would be all over Mercy within the next few hours. So I said, "I was driving by—I'd stopped to visit with a friend, and—"

"What friend?" he asked.

I was still so cold, my teeth began to chatter. This offered me the opportunity to ask for a blanket and to avoid answering his questions.

"Sure." He offered a wry smile that indicated he knew what I was doing. He climbed out and walked up to the emergency-response truck parked ahead.

One of the paramedics gave him a cream-colored blanket, and he tucked it under his slicker and started back to my side of the truck.

But Candace appeared just as he reached the passenger side. They exchanged words, he handed her the blanket and a few seconds later she joined me in the cab.

I was shivering from head to toe, and she had me take off the raincoat and then wrapped the blanket around my shoulders.

"Is that better?" she asked.

I nodded, but my teeth were still knocking together. "I should have asked Rufus more questions. Should have found out why he got so weird when I asked him about strychnine."

"Wait. I need to write this down. I'll be taking your statement." Candace reached inside her slicker and pulled her small leather-covered notebook and attached pen from her pocket. "Tell me about your talk with him."

"I'd looked up a few things about strychnine on the Internet, but I wondered exactly how accessible that stuff is. I tried to ask Rufus a few questions on the phone, but does he—I mean *did* he—have a family?"

"Divorced, no kids," she said. "But his mama is still alive. He took over the business when his father died about five years ago. But tell me why I need to be writing anything down, because it sounds like all you did was ask him a few questions."

I pulled the blanket tighter around me. "He reinforced what we saw, said that strychnine would contort the professor's body, but he also told me that I wouldn't need anything that strong to kill a mouse or a rat."

"You managed to get him to come to your house just to talk about strychnine?" Candace said.

"Not exactly. I told him my cats killed a mouse the night before—and that was true. So I guess he came over to the house thinking I needed his services."

Her pen was poised, but so far she'd scribbled only a few words. "Tell me the part where he started acting weird."

"See, when he first arrived he was all friendly. He stayed friendly even after I told him I didn't want any exterminating done and just wanted to ask him a few questions. But then, when I brought up strychnine, he got this look on his face, and a few minutes later he practically ran out the front door."

As she wrote this down, Candace said, "What kind of look?"

"Thinking back, I'd say he was scared. Now it seems he was scared to death."

Neither of us spoke for several seconds as the weight of my words sunk in.

Finally I said, "You don't have much to write about, I know. But you do trust me when I say something came over that man?"

"Certainly I believe you. And this could be important," she said. "I'm trying to decide what to say to the chief—and not about the strychnine, but about you calling Rufus up and having that chat."

"I shouldn't have done that, should I? You know me; I just got curious." And then my stomach tightened. "Did I get him killed, Candace? Is that what you're thinking?"

She took my hand and squeezed. "No. Of course not. Listen, Chief Baca's back from vacation, and—"

"When did that happen?" I understood Candace's concern now. Dealing with Morris was one thing, but the chief was her real boss.

"Lydia called him about Professor VanKleet's death. Guess she didn't think Morris was the man to handle a big investigation. Anyway, the chief decided to cut his trip short. Lydia knew where Baca was, seeing as how she likes to keep track of the objects of her affection, even the former ones." She looked straight ahead and didn't say anything for several seconds. "I guess I woulda eventually figured out that a bug man could get hold of strychnine—if that's what happened."

"Given more time, I'm certain you would have come to that conclusion," I said.

"Maybe," she said.

"And last night when we were out together, I should have explained why I called him. But I was distracted by Kara's sudden appearance. And besides, Rufus told me next to nothing. I guess I didn't consider that very important at the time."

"Don't worry; it's absence of evidence again," Candace said. "It's not what he said; it's how he reacted. Unfortunately, Rufus running off scared isn't enough evidence."

"Maybe not, but the man's dead, isn't he?" I said.

"Oh, he is that. Yes indeed."

Once I was feeling calmer, Candace and I made a run for my minivan with her holding the yellow coat over my head to protect me. That was an exercise in futility. This downpour bordered on torrential, and every square inch of me was now sopping wet again. Before Candace closed my van door, I heard her mumble that the rain was screwing up her crime scene.

I drove home thankful I didn't have to hang around and talk to Chief Baca or, even worse, to Lydia. I'd already been worried about how I'd react to seeing her after sharing that kiss with Tom. And we'd definitely *shared*. I feared Lydia would know the minute she looked into my eyes that Tom and I had crossed that line between friendship and ... well, whatever came next.

As I pulled into my driveway, I didn't see Kara's car, and then I realized I hadn't left her a key or the alarm code. Maybe she'd come back and left again when she couldn't get inside. Or maybe her meeting with Tom was a long one. He could have already put her to work installing security cameras at some fancy house on the lake or had her doing some mundane task like answering the phone at his home office.

Merlot and Syrah greeted me when I came in the back door. Their little noses twitched with interest as I bent to pet them. They were immediately intrigued by my being very, very wet. Since I figured Kara would be home any time, I left the back door unlocked and the alarm disengaged.

I hurried into the living room after abandoning my leather sandals. My favorite sandals. The rain had just cost me about seventy-five bucks. I grabbed the remote and turned off the TV before heading down the hallway. Merlot and Syrah darted ahead as I pulled my soaked T-shirt over my head. I stripped off the rest of my clothes in the bathroom.

Merlot and Syrah tentatively approached the sodden pile on the floor while I stepped into the shower, ready for a good steam cleaning. I stayed under the friendly water—so much kinder than rain—until my fingers shriveled. By the time I got out, the cats had disappeared.

After I pulled on jeans and a T-shirt and blow-dried my hair, I gathered my wet clothes and a few other pieces of dirty laundry. Time to visit the washer and then see what was going on with Chablis, Dame Wiggins and the kittens.

But I never made it past the living room.

I gasped and dropped the clothes the second I walked into the room.

A black-clad person, ski mask and all, sat on my couch holding my precious Merlot.

Fifteen

"W-what are you doing in my house?" Dumb thing to say. But there are no adequate words for a situation that made fear and dread do flip-flops in my stomach.

I focused on my cat and saw that the man was holding Merlot's scruff with a gloved hand. Merlot would have scratched his eyes out, would have been yowling, if not for that near-death grip.

My heart pounded against my ribs. Someone was sitting in my living room dressed in a Halloween disguise. And he did not likely have my best interests in mind. But all I cared about at this moment was Merlot.

"Dried off now, Jillian?" the man said in a harsh whisper.

Merlot squirmed, and he tightened his hold. He was now pulling so hard, my cat's eyes were drawn into near slits.

That got my Irish up.

Four quick strides and I reached the couch. The man started to rise, but I snatched Merlot before he could fully react, and then I gently tossed my cat in the direction of the hall. "Go, baby. *Run*."

But I had to turn to send him on his way, and the man took this opportunity to grab my right arm and bend it behind my back. Then he put a forearm around my upper chest. "You're the one I wanted anyway," he said into my ear. He twisted me around and practically threw me down on the sofa.

I raised my chin and stared into the only feature I could see—his pale blue eyes. I would remember those eyes, maybe for the rest of my life. But the remainder of my life might only be a few minutes.

I quelled my fear enough to sound brave when I said, "My stepdaughter will be here any minute, and she'll call 911. I suggest you get out of my house while you have the chance."

"You're telling me what to do? I don't think so." He reached into his pocket and took out several zip ties. "Where's your cell phone?"

"Gee, I must have misplaced it." Anger was trumping fear right now, and sometimes that's not a good thing.

He dropped the zip ties, grabbed me by both arms and lifted me up so roughly that my bare feet actually left the floor.

I bent my knee, ready to plant it where he'd hurt for a long time. But he set me down and held me back with long, strong arms. I never had a chance to make contact.

He switched one hand to my throat and said, "Try that again, and I will *really* hurt you. Understand?"

He was choking off my air, and within seconds my lungs began to burn. I nodded, and he released the pressure but kept his hand around my neck.

"Your phone?" he said.

I glanced down and nodded right, toward my jeans pocket.

He used his free hand to reach in and take it. Then he dropped it on the floor and stomped on it with the heel of his boot.

Black leather boots. Remember that, Jillian.

"I'm lowering you to the floor. Sit down and don't fight me." He knelt as I slowly went down and said, "Put your wrists together in front of you."

The hand encircling my throat tightened again, so I quickly complied. After picking up a zip tie, he used one hand to slip it around both wrists and tighten it—almost like he'd done this a hundred times.

Well practiced. Done this before. Remember that, Jillian.

Once my hands were bound, he let go of my neck. I felt tears stinging behind my eyes and wanted to gulp in air, but I wasn't about to let him see weakness. I willed back those tears and steadied my breathing. Then I glanced left and caught Syrah peeking around the corner of the sofa.

No. I wanted to scream. *Get away from here.*

My attacker was zip tying my ankles and finished just as Syrah started to slink toward the man.

Hoping to distract my captor, I said, "Tell me what this is about."

Unfortunately this guy hadn't missed Syrah's approach. He lunged toward my cat, but my nimble friend was too quick. He raced across the room and then slowly sat. He offered one giant open-mouthed hiss at the bad guy.

I could have lifted both legs and kicked the intruder, but I was sure it wouldn't do any good. He'd proven he was powerful enough to control me with one hand, and if I pissed him off, he might take revenge on one or more of the cats. I stayed still.

The man stared at me. "What do I want? I want you to stay out of this business."

This business? What exactly is this business? The murders?

He leaned close until our faces were only inches apart. His breath was clean, but the scent on his skin—from his shaving cream, maybe?—was distinctive. Citrus? Lime?

Remember that, Jillian.

"Your cats are mine if I want them," he said. "All of them. Even that brood downstairs. I'll let you keep them today. But only if you go back to making your little quilts and quit showing up where you don't belong. You shouldn't be keeping domesticated animals in the first place."

Uh-oh, I thought. Was he a radical activist? That's what he sounded like.

He stood and made a quick sidestep toward Syrah, but again my cat was too quick and avoided capture. But Syrah didn't leave the room. He slowly sat again near the foyer entrance, the tip of his tail twitching, ears flat against his skull. He never took his golden eyes off this invader.

The man laughed. "You're a little soldier. You'd do fine in the wild—and that's where you belong."

He sounds almost robotic at times. Like this is all scripted and he's a bad actor. Remember that, Jillian.

He was looking down at me. "Thanks for leaving the door open, but don't get comfortable thinking your security system will stop me. I'm prepared for anything."

He walked past me, and seconds later I heard the back door slam.

The adrenaline rush created by this . . . this *shock* wore off at once. My legs began to shake as if I'd been soaked in another rainstorm.

Syrah bounded from his spot on the other side of the living room and came to my side. He rubbed his head against my shoulder. Soon Merlot joined us, his coat so puffed out, he looked like a Pomeranian that had just been groomed. Even Chablis arrived to see what was going on, looking wary as she sniffed the air. But petting them with my hands bound wasn't very comfortable. The zip tie was brutally tight.

I leaned back against the sofa, every ounce of energy drained. But I held back the tears that threatened again, thinking how that man would pay for coming into my house and terrorizing me and my cats.

When I heard Kara call out, "Jillian, your back door isn't locked," I felt my shoulders slump with relief. I'd been sitting with my back against the bottom of the sofa for thirty minutes.

"Um, I need a little help in here, Kara," I called. I turned my head, and over the back of the couch I saw her put several grocery bags on the counter.

"Where are—*oh my God*." She hurried around the dining room table and knelt by my side, joining Merlot and Syrah. "Who did this?"

"Wish I knew. Can you grab some shears from my

sewing room? I am so very tired of these nasty plastic bracelets."

She left and a few seconds later returned and snipped off the restraints.

"Thank you," I said, rubbing my wrists.

She rested a gentle hand on my cheek and looked me in the eyes. "We need to call the police."

I pointed out the remnants of my cell phone. "Can I use yours?"

"I'll call 911. You're probably too shaken up to dial right now," Kara said.

"No, let me give you Candace's number. Everyone is busy in town with another crime."

"Another crime? What is going on in Mercy?" she said. Then she dialed the number I spieled off.

I was actually relieved she did the calling. Candace must have answered, because Kara explained how she'd found me. Then she disconnected and looked at me. "She's on her way."

I let out a long sigh of relief.

While we waited, we sat on the couch and I told Kara what had happened, spilling out words as if getting rid of them would also rid me of the memory of that horrible man. But I began to realize that her interested expression was . . . well . . . almost too keen. Was she making mental notes for whatever she planned to write about the current crime wave in Mercy, South Carolina?

When I finished telling my story, she stood, picked the zip ties up off the floor and said, "You'd better give me a key and the alarm code. Your door needs to stay locked at all times." She started toward the kitchen.

"Where are you going with those?" I started after her.

"To throw them out," she said.

"Candace will want them." I held out my hand.

She gave them to me. "That's true. Meanwhile, I better put the groceries away."

The doorbell rang, and I hurried to answer while Kara

continued on into the kitchen. Merlot and Syrah lingered just outside the foyer.

I opened the front door, and Candace immediately wrapped her arms around me. Rain was still falling, and her hug got me wet again, but I didn't care. And this time the tears could not be stopped.

Then over her shoulder I saw Chief Mike Baca standing on the stoop holding an umbrella.

I pulled away from Candace, swiping at my tears. "Sorry. Come on in."

"Glad to see you're okay," Chief Baca said.

"Thanks, but I'm fine." *Liar, liar.* For some reason, I felt embarrassed about him seeing me like this. But being manhandled and threatened had created a vulnerability I apparently didn't know how to deal with.

Candace removed her slicker. "What should I do with this?"

I handed her the zip ties. "We can trade. He used those on my feet and hands." I took her slicker and the chief's umbrella and hung them on the hall tree.

I was grateful for Candace's arm around my shoulders as Syrah and Merlot led us into the living room. My boys sat in front of the entertainment center as if waiting for the show to begin. A lot friendlier show than the last one.

Candace produced a plastic baggie from one of her uniform pockets and dropped in the zip ties. She then held the bag up for inspection. "You would have gotten out of these eventually. Cheap hardware-store variety."

Chief Baca said, "We don't use them. They break."

"Coulda fooled me," I said.

Kara wandered into the living room, and I introduced her to Baca and Candace.

"Where were you when all this happened?" Candace asked her.

"I had a meeting with Tom, and then I went to the supermarket," she said. "I felt so awful finding Jillian all tied up like that."

Baca said, "Your stepmother is a strong woman."

"Yeah, strong," Candace said. "But still upset. Can you get her some sweet tea, um . . . what's your name again? Kara?"

"Sure." Kara started back the way she came.

Candace added, "I could use some myself. How about you, Chief?"

"Nothing for me, thanks." Baca's gaze followed Kara's backside.

Oh brother. He's my age. Too old for her; that's for sure. And I could tell Candace didn't seem too thrilled to meet Kara. I needed to keep us all on track.

I said, "You two have more important things to do right now than listen to me. The guy came to warn me, and he did a good job." I sat on the couch and tucked my feet beneath me. Despite my protest to the contrary, I was still grateful for their presence.

"Warn you about what?" Baca said.

"Jillian's apparently messing in someone's business, or that's what the guy told her," Kara said. She gave Candace and me our glasses and then sat in her father's chair.

"She also looked scared to death when she answered the door," Candace said.

"Oh, she's better now. You should have seen her earlier," Kara said.

The heat of a blush warmed my cheeks. "It's in the past and I'm fine."

"Let me just say, the information you provided earlier concerning Rufus Bowen might help connect the two murders," Baca said. "Thank you for that."

"You're welcome, but of course I had to tell you about my talk with him. Should have done it the night before." Maybe Candace was right about the chief changing his tune concerning me. He did seem friendly and was perhaps trying to set things right between us after last fall's murder investigation.

"Did you say *two* murders?" Kara asked Baca.

"We can't discuss an ongoing investigation, right, Chief?"

Candace said quickly. She'd cocked her head, and she was glaring at Baca. I expected her to add another "Right?" but the look she gave him was enough.

His turn to go red in the face. "That would be correct. I thought Candace would be the best officer to come and take your statement about this intruder. If we need to call the paramedics or take you to an emergency room, then—"

"No. I don't need medical attention. I'm just kind of angry about this guy getting in here, terrorizing my cats and just . . . I don't know."

"That's a normal reaction." Candace pulled out her notebook so I could give my second statement of the day. "Tell us everything you can remember."

With one cat in my lap and one beside me, I related how I came out of the bedroom and saw the man sitting in my living room. I told them everything I'd told Kara: about the leather boots, his pale eyes, the citrus smell and how he slipped into robot speech every once in a while. As I finished my story, I said, "Whoever he is, he's had practice with those zip ties. I hardly had a chance to blink, and they were on."

Candace looked at Baca, eyebrows raised. "Law enforcement, maybe?"

"Could be." He looked at me. "He threatened you by mentioning your cats. He indicated they'd disappear if you didn't 'stay out of this business'?"

I nodded. "He's got to be the man in the white van, the one I saw the day of the professor's murder. That's the only explanation I can think of for him to use that phrase. Who else besides people we trust knew I was at the professor's place that day?"

"This town talks. You know that, so we can't make any assumptions yet. The guy was vague, and probably on purpose," Candace said.

"I know you like corroboration, but I haven't been involved in any other *business* that might lead to a man walking into my house, tying me up and tossing me around like a stuffed animal."

"She's right, Candy," Baca said.

Candace took a deep breath. "Okay. Let's say he's been following you since the professor's murder and sees you show up at the second murder scene. But why would he think you're a threat? You didn't see anything except a white van."

"He doesn't know I couldn't see the driver." But then a chill raced up my back. "Wait a minute. There could be another explanation. Maybe it's not about the murders. Maybe it's about the *cats*. Whoever took those cats was interrupted and probably didn't like it one bit. When he drove off, he saw me by the side of the road." Half to myself I said, "He said Syrah would do fine in the wild." I must have gripped Merlot because he meowed. "Sorry, baby." I returned to more gentle petting.

"What are you saying?" Baca said.

"He's probably one of those militant animal activists, the kind that thinks people shouldn't own pets. And he believes that's where I might focus my energy—on the cats that disappeared from the professor's backyard."

Candace's eyes were wide. "And he'd be right."

"Hmm. I see what you mean," Baca said. "Those kinds of activists are considered domestic terrorists. Many are violent offenders. But he'd only suspect you would focus on the cats if he knew about you. This person is aware of what you do for a living, and he may know more about you than you think. Like how you rescued those other cats last fall."

"Could be he knows Shawn and he heard that I made sure all those cats found loving homes," I said.

"But unless he followed you, how does he know you were at both murder scenes?" Candace said.

Baca nodded. "You didn't turn back any white vans at the scene, Candy?"

"No. But there were several other vehicles that came down the road before and after Jillian's arrival. That's why I put up the traffic cones."

I'd noticed Kara taking this all in, and she finally piped

up. "Let me get this straight," Kara said. "The two murders and this attack on Jillian are unrelated? Loosely related? What? And who's Shawn?"

"Never mind," Candace said, her tone none too friendly. "Guess we should have asked you to leave the room."

Baca said, "But she freed Jillian, so she's one of our witnesses. And this will be all over town tomorrow anyway. Not that anything we're saying is such a big secret. This is just a lot of conjecture." He turned then and looked at Kara. "You don't know anyone in town to talk to besides Jillian anyway, right?"

Kara said, "I know Tom Stewart. And to be honest, I do plan to write about this."

"For what publication?" Baca said. But he didn't sound alarmed. He sounded interested . . . No, that wasn't it. He sounded *captivated*.

Kara said, "I'm not connected to any newspapers, if that's your concern, though I am a journalist. This sounds like a big story. Bigger than Mercy."

I could read Candace's expression, and her tight jaw and narrowed blue eyes told me she was steaming. "Bigger than Mercy? Really?" she said.

Kara laughed. "You are intense, aren't you? Let me put it this way: If I write this story, Mercy will be bigger for it. How's that?"

"Really?" Candace pointed at Kara. "Let me tell you something. You won't be writing anything if you're any good. Not right now. If you're a decent *journalist*, you'll wait for the facts. We don't have enough, and that means you sure as hell don't."

Baca said, "Candy, please. You're overreacting. And publicity might be just what we need."

"My name is *Candace*. And if you think we need publicity, then good luck. Now, if y'all will excuse me, I haven't used the ladies room all day." She got up and stomped out of the living room and down the hall.

"She needs to regroup, Kara," I said. "She's a very dedicated cop and can get fired up easily."

"She doesn't bother me," Kara said. "She should be that way in her profession."

I felt a tiny bit of relief at her response. I don't do well with conflict. "Anyway, I could use some regrouping myself. And I'm hungry. What about you, Mike?"

Kara said, "There's actually food in the fridge. How about a turkey and avocado sandwich? Hummus and pita bread?" She smiled a smile that had all of John's charm and more.

I almost lost it seeing John's smile so unexpectedly, but I took a deep breath, lifted Syrah from my lap and set him on the floor. I stood. "Turkey sounds great. You, Mike?"

"We have two big cases, and I have to get up to speed. But thanks for the offer. I'll leave Candy here, though. For protection. I'll find out who did this to you, Jillian. I promise." He held out his hand to me.

I took it, and he drew me close, gave me a half hug. Awkward, yes, but much appreciated.

Candace reappeared a minute later, and when Baca told her she was staying with me, she didn't protest.

She asked him to send over her laptop, case notes and the one thing she could not be without—her evidence-collection kit.

But her reaction to his instruction to watch over me was puzzling. Instead of bristling over being left here while two murder investigations continued, rather than fuming about being stuck in my house with Kara, whom she seemed to dislike, she'd calmly requested her necessities.

That didn't make sense.

Sixteen

After changing out of her damp uniform and into a pair of my jeans and a T-shirt, Candace joined Kara and me at the kitchen table. I really wanted to know why she didn't put up a stink when Baca told her to stay with me. But now was not the time.

We were all hungry, and Kara and Candace acted as if their tense interaction earlier had never happened. We finished off the deli turkey that Kara had bought—with a little help from Merlot. I chose to forego the avocado, but Candace piled her sandwich with not only avocado but cheese and spicy mayo. If I'd had a tub of lard, she probably would have spread that on the whole-grain bread. She'd had a busy week and obviously needed all those calories.

After Candace had a decent meal in her tummy, she played nice with Kara, asking her about her former job.

Kara said, "I'm a journalist and just left my position as a columnist in Houston."

"What kind of column?" Candace asked.

"Pop culture," she said. "My current interest is social networking—Twitter, Facebook, the online dating trends, issues like that."

"You don't write about celebrities, then?"

"Only if it involves social commentary," Kara said. "I have written some pieces that touched on the music scene. The Tejano influence, for example, and rap music."

"No Britney? No *American Idol*?" Candace said.

Where was she going with this? I wondered.

"*Idol* is of interest, of course. There are cultural implications. But I stay away from anything too . . . well . . . *tabloid*." Kara examined her fingernails and seemed downright bored.

Uh-oh. Maybe attitude hadn't left the building after all. It had just taken a different form.

"Isn't that a sorry shame?" Candace said. "Those supermarket rags are my favorite. I love celebrity stuff. If you wrote for the *Enquirer* or one of those types of newspapers, then *you'd* be the celebrity."

I knew that it was Candace's mother who loved the *Enquirer*. Candace thought tabloids were trash and always made fun of the stories her mother believed to be one hundred percent true. So where was she going with this?

"Those tabloids aren't *newspapers*," Kara said.

"Coulda fooled me."

I noted the smile playing at Candace's lips as she stood and began to clear the remnants of our late lunch. She'd gotten under Kara's skin and now seemed satisfied. I resisted the urge to say something. I wasn't sure why Candace didn't like Kara, but I also wasn't sure how Kara would react if I got in the middle of their verbal sparring.

Candace said, "Rain's let up. After we clean up, time for me to see if our bad guy left any evidence on your back porch that hasn't washed away. Darn it all if I don't hate rain."

She put the condiments away while I started filling the dishwasher. Kara retreated, saying she wanted to record notes on what she'd learned about the murders. After she was gone, Candace whispered, "Did your husband raise that spoiled brat?"

"What makes you think she's spoiled?" I said.

"Intuition," Candace said.

"John did let her have everything she wanted—and I warned him that wasn't the greatest idea," I said. "He was trying to make up for Kara losing her mother and for him working long hours. I guess, most of all, for not giving his daughter the attention she needed when she needed it the most. But he had no clue how to raise a teenage girl."

"She was in college when you two married?" Candace said.

"A freshman at the University of Texas. A little late to set limits, and besides, it wasn't my place. I hope you'll cut her some slack, because I don't think she's over losing John or her mother."

"But *you're* getting there," Candace said. "You actually criticized John, and you've never done that before."

I picked up the sponge and wiped down the table's mosaic-tile top. "He was no saint, and neither am I."

"I took a grief-counseling course. To teach me how to say the right things to folks who'd lost loved ones. I recall that teacher telling us that once you stop idealizing the person who died, you're on your way to accepting the loss."

"Oh, I believe I'm accepting the loss, all right." I walked over to the sink and dropped the crumbs I'd cleared from the table into the disposal. I told her about the kiss Tom and I shared last night.

Candace shoved my shoulder and said, "No way."

I winced. I was beginning to feel sore all over after what had happened earlier. And I still had scratches and cuts from crawling over barbed wire.

She realized what she'd done and immediately apologized, then glanced toward the door. "Wish my stuff would arrive. I need to take pictures of your injuries. Did you know you've got bruises on your neck?"

My hand went to my throat. "No. And I don't think I own a turtleneck."

"You don't need to hide what happened to you, Jillian. It's not your fault."

"I guess you're right, but before another minute passes," I said, "I have to know why you're willing to stay here with me. There's something else going on."

"I thought you understood, especially after what we just talked about," she said. "I have to keep an eye on Kara. I can smell trouble a mile away, and she's trouble. So while

I'm protecting you, I'm watching her like a hawk. I don't want her all up in my business, and that's exactly where she wants to be."

"She's not dangerous. She's looking for answers, just like we are," I said.

"Answers that I need to find, not her," Candace said.

She seemed upset that I was defending Kara, but before I could reassure her, the doorbell rang.

When I answered, with Candace right beside me, Billy Cranor stood bearing gifts: the evidence kit with the camera, the laptop and a file folder. He stepped inside and brought Candace's prized possessions into the living room.

"Heard some butthead came around threatening you, Ms. Hart," Billy said. "Wish I'd been here."

I smiled. "I wish you'd been here, too."

Billy set Candace's things on the end table, and of course his appearance brought cats out from under the dining room table to investigate. They knew Billy and found him far less fascinating than Candace's belongings. But though Merlot and Syrah were all over that evidence bag, Chablis didn't come up from the basement to visit. She sure must have loved cuddling with her adopted kittens.

"Long time no see, Candy." Billy laughed. "What's it been? Two hours?"

She smiled and fixed a few wayward strands of blond hair over her ear. This was her fireman-calendar fantasy man, but he always treated her like a sister. And that bothered her. "Kind of you to drag my stuff around town. I appreciate it."

"No problem. We've got more trouble in Mercy than we know what to do with. Any way I can help, I will," he said.

"Hi," came Kara's voice from the foyer. "We have more visitors?"

"Kara, meet Billy Cranor," I said. "He's a volunteer fireman and also knows how to fix just about anything. Works at the hardware store."

She entered the room, and I couldn't look at Candace after I saw Billy nearly start panting at the site of Kara in her tiny shorts and tank top. I'd never seen Candace jealous before, but that might be about to change.

"Pleased to meet you, Kara. You got a last name?" he said.

"Hart," she answered.

"Are you Ms. Hart's sister, then?" He looked at me. "You never said anything about a sister."

Kara laughed. "She married my father, that's all. We're not blood relatives."

"How long you visiting for?" Billy said.

Candace was moving her evidence kit away from further cat inspection, but Billy's question made her head snap up. She and I were both interested in the answer.

"Don't know. Very cute town. And it's growing on me," Kara said.

"Mercy is the finest place you'll ever want to visit," Billy said.

"Except for the murders, you mean?" Kara said.

Billy's face reddened, and his interest in Kara seemed to go from "Gee, I'd like to get to know you better" to something more like "What's your problem, lady?" Did Kara have a clue how condescending she sometimes sounded?

"Still the best place in the world," Billy said. "Listen, I got to get back to work. Have an engine to clean after all this rain. Fire trucks gotta sparkle." He nodded at Candace and me. "Take care, ladies." To Kara he said, "Nice to make your acquaintance."

"One favor, Billy?" Candace said.

"Sure."

"That professor's family is due in town," Candace said, "but we don't know when. You've always got your ear to the ground, so will you call me when they get here?"

"You betcha," Billy said.

After he left, Kara said, "Nice body, but such a hick. Did my father really like Mercy and these types?"

"I thought you said the town was growing on you. Your father loved Mercy," I said softly.

Kara said. "He must have had his reasons, and that tells

me I need to understand the town better if I'm going to write the book that's starting to come to life in my head."

Candace, her cheeks rosy with what I assumed was anger, had her camera out. "Jillian? How's about we go to the bedroom and I'll photograph those bruises."

"Sure." We started down the hall together, but Kara was on our heels.

"Mind if I watch?" Kara said as we entered my bedroom.

Merlot and Syrah had the same idea and were already sitting on the bed.

"It's up to you whether you want an audience, Jillian," Candace said.

"I guess I don't mind," I said, though I really did. But saying no to Kara seemed to be as difficult for me as it had been for John. "Guess you want me to take off my shirt, Candace?"

"That's right." Candace surveyed my room. She walked over and closed the door that led to the master bath. "Stand in front of the door. The lighting will be right."

Candace proceeded to photograph my bruised neck, the blue marks on my biceps where the man had lifted me off my feet and the red abrasions on both wrists. My ankles hadn't been bound as tightly as my wrists, and there were no marks there. All the scrapes and bruises on my legs had come from my trek to the professor's house through the fields.

As I was putting my T-shirt back on, Kara said, "When I write my book about these murders and if it turns out Jillian's attacker was involved, can I get copies of those photos?"

"Not my call," Candace said brusquely. "As of now, these pictures are part of an ongoing investigation."

"I see," Kara said.

"This guy wore gloves the entire time?" Candace asked me.

"Yes," I said. I motioned to the cats. "Come on, boys. Time for wet food."

We all walked back toward the kitchen, but Candace stopped. "Wait a minute. He wore a black ski mask, right?"

"Right," I said.

"And he was holding the very red-haired Merlot when you came in the room?" she said.

"You think he left fiber evidence on Merlot?" I said.

"I better check him out." Candace had put her case on the sofa and now took out a pair of latex gloves, a large magnifying glass and a pair of long tweezers.

So while Syrah ate his salmon dinner and Merlot chomped down on his grilled beef, Candace sat next to him on the floor with her magnifying glass. She examined his long red coat one section at a time.

Kara stood above Candace, watching with interest.

I opened the fridge for some sweet tea and was surprised to discover that my refrigerator had become a foreign country. Candace had made lunch, so I hadn't looked in here since Kara went to the store. I saw a half dozen prepackaged containers of sushi rolls and enough Red Bull to energize a pro football team. It reminded me of when Kara had come to spend Christmas with John and me and always filled the fridge with some kind of new and trendy food. Thank goodness for the whole deli chicken and containers of potato salad and olives. I wasn't a sushi fan.

I asked if anyone wanted a drink but got no reply, so I shrugged and poured myself a glass of tea.

Candace's "Aha" came seconds later. She leaned back and held up her tweezers. From where I stood across the kitchen I couldn't see anything, but I assumed she'd found a teensy thread in all that fur.

She said, "Ski masks may be good at concealing faces, but they shed almost as much as Merlot here."

"Really?" Kara said.

"It's near impossible to come into someone's house and not leave evidence of your presence behind. Take you, for instance: long dark hair, obviously colored. Hard not to leave any of those hairs around. Some of them could even contain your DNA." Candace looked at me. "Would you mind getting an envelope out of my case? You know the ones I use."

When I brought her the small paper envelope, I also brought her a pen. I knew the routine.

Candace placed her tiny, fuzzy black fiber in the envelope and wrote the date, time and where she'd found the fiber on the front. Then she stood. "I'll check the sofa to see if there are any more of these."

She came up empty there and said, "I doubt the rain left us any nice tire tracks, especially since other vehicles have driven in and out of your driveway since the event. But did you hear anything after the door slammed? The sound of an engine, maybe?"

"The *event*? It wasn't exactly a rock concert." Then I felt awful for being sarcastic. "Sorry. Guess I'm still a little on edge. To be honest, I wasn't paying attention." I finished off my tea and said, "I was just glad he left. But something has me wondering—guess it was the food in the fridge that sparked something in my head. How did he know he'd find me alone?"

"The food? What are you talking about?" Kara said.

"You were at the store," I said. "How did someone know you wouldn't be coming home anytime soon?"

Candace shook her head. "The bad guy might not have even known she was staying here. He got lucky is all."

"But what if he *did* know?" I said. "If this was an activist, he's probably not working alone. Someone could have been following Kara, too."

"No way," Kara said. "I would have noticed."

"Not if they were good," Candace said.

"That settles it." Kara made a beeline for the back door and went outside.

Candace said, "What's with her?"

"Don't know," I answered, "but I'm guessing she's not fleeing in terror."

And she wasn't. Kara came back inside a minute later, making sure to wipe her feet on the mat by the door. She held something wrapped in navy felt and lifted the fabric for Candace's inspection.

Candace stepped back when she looked inside. "Is that loaded?"

"Yes. I was traveling alone. I have the right to protect myself," Kara said.

I was shocked but spoke as calmly as I could. "I have rights, too, and this is my home. I want you to unload that gun," I said. "You might accidentally shoot one of my cats. Or me."

Kara looked at me like I had a screw loose. "Are you crazy, Jillian? Someone came into your house and threatened you. Someone might be following me, so—"

"And that's why I'm here. For protection," Candace said evenly. "Jillian has asked you to unload your .38 snubnose or put it back where you got it."

"From what Tom told me," Kara said, "South Carolina has the same law that Texas does—the right to carry a loaded handgun in a concealed place like the glove box."

"Without a permit. I know," Candace said. "But it's not in the glove box now. So please do as Jillian asked."

"Is the safety on?" I said, still horrified at her bringing a gun into my house. Handguns can hurt their owners, too, and I was worried about Kara carrying that thing around.

"Revolvers don't have safeties," they both said in unison.

"Even more reason to get that thing out of here," I said.

"Fine, but I wanted both of you to know I have this. No one is about to intimidate me. *No one.*" She rewrapped the gun, whirled and went back outside.

Candace shook her head, her expression troubled. "John's daughter has issues, Jillian."

"But John's daughter happens to be my family. Can you be nice to her? For me?" I asked.

"I'll try, but you be careful, 'cause I can guarantee you I won't be turning my back on her."

Seventeen

The next day, I made pancakes for all three of us. When given the choice of sleeping on the couch, downstairs with a bunch of cats and their litter box or in my king-size bed with me, Candace had chosen my room. I'd told her she shouldn't feel the need to stay that close to me, but she'd laughed and said her choice was all about comfort.

Though Kara complained that the "overloaded with carbs" breakfast would make her bleary for the rest of the day, she ate twice as many pancakes as Candace did. And that's a lot of pancakes. Would she have to double up on her Red Bull today? And would I need extra coffee?

When we were finished, I decided to be proactive, take more of a motherly role, and suggested that Kara do the dishes. She agreed without so much as a pout. *Progress, maybe?* I thought.

As Candace and I left the kitchen, I said, "I have a couple new quilts I want to show you." I grabbed her elbow and squeezed before she could say anything. Candace had no interest whatsoever in anything that had to do with quilting, but I wanted to talk to her alone.

Chablis had joined us this morning—she does enjoy a few nibbles of pancakes—and she and the two boys led the way to my sewing room. Maybe she was getting over her love affair with Dame Wiggins and the kittens. Once the cats took their usual places—Syrah on the windowsill, Merlot on the cutting table and Chablis next to the sewing machine—I closed the door.

"I saw you were stuck to your laptop last night. Were you working on the case?" I said.

She nodded. "Chief Baca sent me information on the family. Plus he has ties with someone from the college and forwarded an e-mail from this person. A former associate of the professor indicated—and it's all in university-type lingo and thus kinda fuzzy—that VanKleet was terminated. I mean before he was *really* terminated. But I don't know why."

"Can you find out more today?" I glanced at the pile of unbound quilts I had to finish—and soon.

"Spring break, so it might be hard," she said. "Maybe a trip to that little college town to find anyone willing to sit down and talk about this guy is in order—that is, if anyone is around and not on vacation."

"Can't you have one of their local officers help you?" I said.

"I wish. You think Mercy's small? In Denman, they depend more on the campus police than their four officers. Baca e-mailed me a couple names of the campus cops. But they could be on spring break, too."

"I heard you get a phone call last night, too," I said. "From the look on your face before you left the living room with your phone, I'm guessing it was Billy."

Candace blushed. "You are way too observant. It was him. The professor's relatives had arrived in town even before I found Rufus's body. The sons are staying at the Tall Pines Motel, but guess where the ex and her boyfriend are shacked up?"

"How would I—oh no. The Pink House?" I said, referring to the grand old Victorian painted an outrageous pink where last year's murder had taken place.

Candace pointed at me. "You got it. Did you know the new owners advertise their bed-and-breakfast as haunted? What a crock."

"Will you talk to the professor's family today?" I said.

"You want to invite them all here for lunch? I don't think so," she said.

"We don't have to stay here like we're prisoners. I mean, don't you need clothes and your toothbrush?" I said. "We could pick them up at your place and then stop at the police station—try to time it so we end up there with the family."

"You want me to find out from the chief when and where he plans to talk to them and just show up?" From her half smile, I could tell she liked this idea.

"Sounds easy enough," I said.

"What about Kara? I don't want her within a country mile of our investigation," Candace said. "But if we leave her here and Mr. Ski Mask shows up, I'll be in deep doo-doo. Especially if she brings her weapon inside while we're gone and then feels justified in using it."

"We'll drop her off at Belle's Beans. From all that Red Bull in my fridge, I'd say she's a genuine caffeine addict. Plus, she said she wanted to learn more about the town. We'll just share with her the fact that Belle's is the best place to do that."

Candace grinned. "Perfect."

"There's one more thing you should know." Something that had kept me awake half the night.

"What's that?"

"I was so shaken yesterday, I wasn't thinking. We probably have the whole attack on video," I said.

Candace's eyes widened. "Your *cat cam*." She thunked her forehead with the heel of her hand. "I should have thought of that." She started toward the door. "Come on. Show me."

The cats and I followed as she hurried down the hall to my office. "I'll bring up the feeds, show you how to look at stored video, but if you don't mind, I'd rather not watch."

"I get it. No problem," she said.

A minute later, I left Candace in my office to view the man scaring the bejesus out of me. The cats didn't seem interested, either, and followed me out, but then took off in the opposite direction for my bedroom. It was nap time already. Oh, to be a cat.

Kara was sitting in the living room talking into a small recorder when I returned. She quit speaking and shut it off, but before I could tell her the plan that would get her started on her study of Mercy's proverbial flora and fauna, her cell phone rang.

She smiled after she said, "Hello," and listened for a second and then held out the phone. "It's Tom. He wants to talk to you."

"Thanks." I walked over to where she sat in John's chair and took the phone. It was more modern than I was used to and felt awkward in my hand, and even more awkward up against my ear. "Hi."

"Why didn't you call me yesterday?" he said.

"Um, my phone sorta went bye-bye," I said.

"I know," he said. "But why was Kara the one to call this morning and tell me what happened? You could have borrowed hers or Candace's and let me in on this. I thought after the other night . . . Hell, I don't know what to think now."

I turned away from Kara's probing stare and walked into the kitchen. "I was upset and didn't want to talk about it. I just wanted to go to sleep. I'm sorry."

"But you're all right? That jerk didn't hurt you?" he said.

I was touched, and I had to admit surprised, that he was so concerned. I realized I wasn't used to someone worrying about me like that. I softened my voice. "I'm fine. And Candace is here for—oh, but you already know." I lowered my voice. "Kara told you. I'm beginning to think she'll fit right into this town. It only took her a couple days to join the grapevine."

"That's what reporters do. I spent several hours with her, and she's bright and funny."

"She is, but she's hardly ever shared that side with me," I said quickly and with instant regret. "I'm sorry. That's my problem, not yours. Let's change the subject, shall we?"

"Okay, on to a safer topic. You'll need a new phone."

"I did plan to call you about that. Do they still make the model I had so I can get my live cat-cam feeds?" I said.

"They stop making the same model of anything techlike the day after it's on the shelf. I'll look at a few phones on the Internet that will support your videos, and then we can order one or maybe see if your local wireless provider has what we need."

I liked the way he said what *we* need.

Then he said, "Pass me back to Kara, would you?"

"Are you putting her to work?" I said.

"I'm thinking about it," he answered with a laugh.

I went back into the living room and handed Kara the phone. "He wants to talk to you."

I then went down the hall and met Candace coming out of my office.

Her face was tight with anger. "What that guy did to you was downright vicious. But the audio wasn't any good, and I didn't see anything that you haven't already described in excellent detail. Wait, I did learn one thing."

"What's that?" I said.

"I'm taking that man down, and when I do, he's gonna get some of what he likes to dish out."

At first Kara didn't seem thrilled with the idea of heading into town, saying she wasn't afraid of anyone sneaking in the back door. But when I said we'd be dropping her off at a coffee place where she could literally drink in Mercy's atmosphere, she abandoned her reluctance.

We piled into my minivan, and once we arrived, we decided we all could use a fix of the best coffee in the Southeast. We gave our orders to Candace and, no surprise, Kara ordered a large black coffee with a double shot of espresso. I pulled enough money from my purse to cover the tab. The white-haired and oh-so-sweet owner, Belle, sat at a corner table, and I led Kara over for introductions. Since I wasn't sure whether Kara liked my calling her my stepdaughter, I simply told Belle that Kara was John's daughter.

"Aren't you the cutest thing?" Belle said. Her coral lip-stick, as usual, was misapplied. The top lip had a straight line today, but the color on the bottom went well below her lip. Sometimes the top lip was as messy as her lower lip, but two things never changed: It was always wrong, and it always made me want to take out a tissue and fix it.

Kara's cheeks colored, and I guessed she'd decided that *cute* was not her favorite word. But to her credit, she kept quiet about this and said, "Thanks. This place of yours is cute, too."

Belle leaned close to me and whispered, "We got a whole lot of visitors in town since the murders. I heard you was with Candace when she found that first body. Horrible thing, poison. Just a miserable way to die. Heard they found strychnine at Rufus's place of business, too."

"*What?*" I said.

"Morris was in for his coffee and a nice big Danish—all sniffly and out of work on a sick day. He's the one who told me."

I raised my eyebrows in surprise. "Morris is usually more careful about keeping the details of a case from the public," I said, glancing Candace's way. She wouldn't like this slip one bit.

"The man's sick. Blame it on a fever and forget you heard what I said." Belle held her thumb and forefinger—both fingernails painted coral like her lips—an inch apart. "He's this close to retirement. And we don't want to get him in trouble."

"Probably best if you don't tell anyone else, don't you think?" I said.

Belle examined those well-manicured nails to avoid my question.

"You already have?" I was again thinking how Candace would react to the leak in the case. And then I reminded myself that this was Mercy and I should quit worrying about who knew what.

"I mentioned it to a few people. Poor Rufus is dead, Jil-lian. What are we gonna do? Talk about the rain?"

"You're absolutely right." I glanced at Kara and could see by her wide eyes that she was surprised at how much Belle knew about the case.

"Have these visitors you mentioned earlier been in here?" I asked.

"They're here *now*." She nodded quickly at the other corner without looking at the four people seated at a table.

A woman and three men. I recognized the woman from the newspaper photo I'd found on the Internet the other day, despite the change in hair color from blond to brunette: Sarah VanKleet. I assumed the two young men with her were her sons, and the older man with his wavy head of steel gray hair and matching goatee was the boyfriend. But he was no boy; that's for sure. He looked like an actor in one of those Viagra ads.

Kara said, "That's the dead man's family?"

"Well, aren't you cute *and* smart. You must be proud of her, Jillian," Belle said.

"I am proud, but I can't take credit. She's an accomplished young woman," I said.

Candace arrived at the table with our coffee. Kara picked up the largest cup and sat down in the chair that offered her the best view of the town visitors.

Candace took her seat, and the strangers captured her attention, too. Out of the side of her mouth she said, "That's them, isn't it?"

Belle laughed, and her generous belly jiggled with the effort. "See what I was saying, Jillian? There are no secrets in this town."

"Hush," Candace whispered. "Don't want them noticing us as much as we notice them."

"Oh, Candy, you are such a naive young thing," Belle said. "That woman over there is no dummy. By the way, I'm taking up a collection for Rufus. Word is he was about broke. Might not be enough for a casket or a burial."

I reached in my bag and pulled out my checkbook. I

wrote a fifty-dollar check from my money-market emergency fund since I'd used up most of my routine monthly cash. I gave it to Belle. Candace pulled a crumpled twenty from her pocket and handed the cash to her, too.

"Thank you, ladies," Belle said.

Without glancing our way, Kara said. "You two can leave. I'll be happy here with my laptop and my excellent coffee." Kara had already set her computer case on the table.

Candace glanced at her watch. "The family should be leaving soon. They have a meeting with Chief Baca in about twenty minutes."

"Then we need to get to your place and fetch your overnight bag." I looked at Belle. "Kara is a writer, and she would love to hear some stories about Mercy."

"Does she have all day? 'Cause you know me, Jillian," Belle said with another laugh. "But what's this about an overnight bag?" She glanced back and forth between Candace and me.

"Um . . . they might be painting my apartment, so I'm staying with Jillian," Candace said.

"Now, don't go lying to Belle. I won't pass on that you're staying with Jillian to protect her," Belle said. "Even though it was passed on to me not an hour ago. I just wanted you to confirm my source."

"Let me guess. Billy told you," Candace said through her teeth.

"I swear that boy knows everything," Belle replied. "He came in on the heels of that bunch in the corner. Think he followed them over here?"

"It would *not* surprise me," Candace said.

I tugged on Candace's arm. "We need to go." I looked at Kara. "I don't mind you sitting close and listening in on the conversation over there, but you need to pass anything important on to Candace."

"I do?" Kara looked momentarily confused. "Oh . . . to help with the case. They're suspects, aren't they?" Belle put her hand on Kara's forearm and looked straight into her eyes. "You should act like you're busy, but keep both ears open. I'll sit here with you and show you how it's done." She winked at Kara and then made a shooing gesture with her free hand at Candace and me. "Go on about your business. We got this covered."

We hurried out, and once we were back in my minivan headed toward Candace's apartment, she burst out laughing.

"What a great idea dropping Kara with Belle. Kara will get the complete lowdown on Mercy, and we might end up with useful information."

"You know Belle believes every citizen of Mercy is her child," I said. "I feel so calm when I'm around her. And speaking of that, promise me you'll stay calm when I tell you what I just heard."

"Of course I'll stay calm. I'm always calm," she said.

"And I'm Michelle Obama. Let me just spit this out. Belle announced to Kara and me that they found strychnine at What's Bugging You."

A long silence followed, and I took my eyes off the road for a second to look over at Candace. Her jaw was set, and she didn't appear calm at all.

But after a deep breath, she said, "I am most surely glad I heard this before I walked into the station. A cop who's the last to know about a key piece of information looks *stupid*."

A long and very quiet five minutes later we pulled into the apartment complex parking lot.

We always visit at my place because Candace's apartment remains mostly barren. There's a mattress, a treadmill, a futon and a television, but that's about it. She spends little time at home and only rents the place to have space away from her overprotective, overinterested mother, who would have preferred that she still live at home.

I packed her underwear, a few T-shirts and jeans into a canvas tote she threw at me. Meanwhile, she grabbed her toiletries and a uniform that had just come from the dry

cleaners. We were almost out the door when Candace realized that the telephone-and-answering-machine combo
that sat on the living room floor was blinking with at least
one unchecked message.

"Wait," Candace said. "That's probably from my mom.
She might need something." She set her bag and uniform
down and went over to the telephone.

But when she knelt and pressed PLAY, a familiar raspy
whisper made my heart skip. The male voice said, "Don't
think you can protect her. You want your friend safe, you
tell her she's done playing investigator."

Candace stood and pointed at the phone. "You don't tell
me what to do, you turd. You don't tell Jillian what to do,
either." She looked at me. "He's not getting close to you. I
promise."

I nodded, but I couldn't speak.

Candace's expression was steely as she pulled the cord
from the wall and picked up the phone. "Now. We go to the
station and I let the chief listen to this. Gives me a decent
excuse to show up there." She walked over and put her free
arm around my shoulder and squeezed. "He's a brute and a
coward, Jillian. And I like nailing those types."

I nodded again, but now I was frightened for her as well
as for myself.

Since Candace lives practically around the block from
downtown, we reached the courthouse in less than five
minutes. That's where the police station is located.

I had to run to keep up with Candace when she raced up
the courthouse stairs with her answering machine. We entered the lobby, and the security guard manning the metal
detector opened a gate so we could bypass this part of en-
tering the building. We headed left down the long corridor
that led to police headquarters.

Wrong name. That sounds way too fancy. Benches and
molded plastic chairs lined the hall leading to the police
station in this, the older and unrenovated part of the his-

toric courthouse. A woman with a swollen jaw and black eye was holding a squirming toddler. She was the lone person outside the police station door.

Candace stopped dead. "Margie?"

The woman looked up at Candace with sad eyes. The little boy freed himself and waddled across the hall. He climbed onto one of the benches and stuck his thumb in his mouth. He wore a diaper and a T-shirt bearing a red truck.

"You're here to press charges, right?" Candace said.

Margie hung her head.

Candace put her hands on her hips. "No. You are *not* bailing that bastard out. Please tell me that's not why you're here."

No response came from Margie, and Candace's frown showed her frustration. "I can't stop you. But you're making a mistake." She looked at me. "Come on, Jillian."

As Candace opened the door that led into the police offices, I thought about Kara. She should be here to see this side of Mercy. It wasn't so different from Houston or from any other part of the country, for that matter. Crime, domestic violence, even prostitution met up with law enforcement here.

Inside was another very cramped waiting area that had one advantage—it wasn't as smelly as the corridor outside. B. J. Harrington sat at the cluttered desk to the left. I nodded at him in greeting, but Candace was already headed down the hall.

Over her shoulder she said, "Wait here while I talk to Chief Baca. I'm thinking this guy is too smart to have used a traceable phone to call me, but we have to go through the motions."

I took the seat in front of the desk and smiled. "Hey, B.J. How's it going?" B.J. was a new addition to the Mercy PD. He was taking criminal justice classes at the local community college and did dispatch and paperwork when not in class.

"I'm thinking about sandwiches," he said. "There's a lot of different sandwiches these days. There's your regular kind, but then there's quesadillas and flatbreads and Hot Pockets, not to mention anything wrapped in lettuce. And if you fold your slice of pizza, that's sort of a sandwich, and—"

"You hungry, B.J.?" I said with a laugh.

The phone rang, and B.J. listened for a few seconds and then said, "We'll take care of that, ma'am." He hung up and got on his radio. "Deputy Dufner. Over."

"What is it?" came the staticky reply.

"We have a 10-79 near the residence." B.J. rattled off an address and said, "Over," again.

"A bomb threat? And not at the high school where they always are?" said the officer.

B.J. blinked rapidly. "Th-that's wrong. Wait." B.J. picked up a sheet of paper and scanned it. "I mean a 10-91b. Sorry. Over."

"Would you quit with the codes and tell me what this is, B.J.?" Dufner said.

I stifled a laugh, but I didn't hear B.J.'s response because the professor's family walked in at that moment.

Sarah VanKleet began talking to B.J. even though he was still on the radio, saying, "We have an appointment with the chief of police."

B.J. held up his hand as the officer asked for a repeat on the address.

I stood. "Maybe I can tell the chief you're here."

The gray-haired man, who looked like he could have been related to the Kennedy clan, looked me up and down. "You're a plainclothes officer?"

"Uh, no. But I can help." I hurried down the hall before they could say anything else and rapped on the chief's office door.

I heard him say, "Enter," and cracked the door. I saw Candace sitting in the chair on the other side of Baca's desk.

"They're here," I whispered. Why I was whispering, I didn't know.

"Good. Candace, Sarah VanKleet is mine. You'll interview the boyfriend. The kids will have to wait since Morris decided he needed a day off. Says he sick." Baca rolled his eyes. "Thanks for letting us know they've arrived, Jillian. Seems like we need volunteers in this place."

Candace followed me out to the waiting area.

B.J. started to apologize for being occupied, but Candace waved him off. "Mrs. VanKleet, you'll be speaking with Chief Baca." Candace looked at the man. "Professor Lieber, is it?"

The distinguished-looking man nodded.

"You'll be talking to me. I may not look the part, but I'm Deputy Candace Carson." She pointed to the badge she'd pinned on her jeans waistband. "As for your sons, Mrs. Van-Kleet, we'll be interviewing them when we're done with you two."

I took notice of the young men, who both looked to be in their early twenties, having paid little attention to them over at Belle's. One had wavy brown hair and dark brown eyes; the other had shaggy dirty blond hair and green-gray eyes. The only trait they seemed to share was their height. Both were over six feet and lanky. The professor had been a small man, but Sarah VanKleet was at least five foot ten, so they must have gotten their height from her.

Sarah VanKleet scowled. "Why can't we all talk to the chief of police together?"

"That's not how we do things," Candace said. "B.J., please take Mrs. VanKleet to the chief's office. Professor? Follow me." She turned and started down the hall, leaving Sarah sputtering in protest.

B.J. stood and smiled at Sarah VanKleet, but her mood didn't improve. She ignored him and looked at her sons. "I'm sorry about this, but it seems you'll have to wait here." She glanced around. "In *this* place."

The blond one spoke. "What about the death certificates? Don't we need those to get Dad's affairs in order? He's probably left us a mess."

She raised her eyebrows and offered him a "You better shut up" look.

The other son said, "Later, Evan."

Mrs. VanKleet smiled and said, "Thank you, Brandt." Then she followed B.J. down the hall.

I smiled at Brandt. "Hi. I'm Jillian Hart. I sort of volunteer around here." *Baca said it, not me*, I thought. I looked at the other young man. "Hi, Evan."

"Hey, what's happening?" He offered a straight arm and a fist, and we bumped knuckles.

"You guys want a Coke or something?" I said.

"Yeah, sure," Evan said.

B.J. came back around his desk, and I said, "You got money for the machine?"

"Oh. Sure." He opened a drawer and gathered several coins. But it wasn't enough.

"For all three of us," I said. I'd dropped by here enough to know that unless you were being arrested, you got free Coke.

"Sorry. Right. Um, thanks, Jillian," he said.

"This way, guys," I said to the VanKleets.

I led them out of the office and down the hall to the vending machines. We passed Margie, the baby and the husband, who must just have been released from the basement jail. *He* didn't have a black eye or a swollen face. And he looked smug. I hated that.

Once Evan and I had our drinks—Brandt refused—we went back inside the office. There was more space to sit out in the corridor, but the smell of vomit was particularly strong today.

B.J. found two folding chairs for the sons, and I reclaimed the wood chair. I decided to play dumb. "You must be visiting Mercy on upsetting business," I said.

"I saw you looking at us in that coffee place," Brandt said. "And I'll venture you know exactly why we're here."

"I didn't say otherwise. I'm only trying to be friendly," I said.

"We're not feeling very friendly," Brandt said.

"Speak for yourself, brother," Evan said. He swigged his Coke. "I like friendly, and you seem nice enough. So here's the deal if you haven't heard. Our father got himself killed."

"Shut up, Evan. Remember what I told you," Brandt said through clenched teeth.

"Oh, the law student speaks. Mea culpa." Evan looked at me. "Please make me shut up, Ms. Hart. Or read me my rights. Brandt can help you with those words, since I'm sure he's memorized them."

"Evan." Brandt spoke that one small name with so much contempt, I felt sorry for his brother.

"You don't have to talk," I said. "I know this is a rough time."

Evan laughed. "Rough time? This is easy compared to everything that's happened before. Except the mother unit latched on to *another* professor. Must be some kind of fatal attraction."

Brandt looked ready to drag his brother out of here before he said anything else, but all this family drama came to a halt when Kara walked in the door.

Oh boy, can she stop traffic, I thought.

"Hi, Jillian," Kara said. "Thought I'd walk down here and see what's going on. Interesting old building."

B.J. stood, his cheeks as rosy as two ripe peaches. "Can I help you?"

She flashed her charming smile and rested a hand on my shoulder. "Jillian's my stepmother."

B.J.'s eyes widened. "Really?"

"Are we like a circus act that you all couldn't get enough of in the coffeehouse?" Brandt said.

But Kara turned that smile on him, and the tense atmosphere in the room seemed to float away. "Strangers in Mercy are probably treated that way all the time," she said. "I'm so sorry you feel like some sort of spectacle."

"It's not that," Brandt said, his attitude melting by the second. "This has been a difficult time for our family."

"You want to get coffee and talk about it when you're done here?" Kara said.

There are some things a forty-two-year-old woman cannot accomplish that a twenty-nine-year-old one can. Especially one who looked like Kara.

Brandt stood and offered Kara his seat.

She took it and then looked up at Brandt, her smile still shining.

He reached into his creased chinos pocket and produced what looked like a phone similar to Kara's. "Give me your number, and I'll text you when we're done here."

While this was going on, Evan leaned toward me and said, "The pretty boy gets all the action."

I smiled. "You said he's a law student. Are you in college, too?"

"Not right now. I'll be heading back in the fall. If Mommy can get the boyfriend to help her with the finances, that is. There's been a cash-flow problem ever since my now-deceased father got fired."

"Evan," Brandt said. "Keep quiet. Please?" Not as much disdain in his voice this time, but I was guessing that was so Brandt didn't seem like such an ass in Kara's presence.

"That would be no, Brandt. I'm not inclined to keep quiet just because you think I should." Evan turned his chair, holding the Coke can between his knees. "While they bond, why don't we? I like you, Ms. Hart. What are *you* doing here?"

"The officer who's interviewing Professor Lieber is a good friend. We were together when she got the call to come in and help out. There's an officer out sick." A small lie about being called in, but Evan had already spilled plenty and I had the feeling there was more. Candace would want me to take advantage.

"So you're friends with Deputy Candace Carson? She's pretty darn hot for a cop. Think you can make sure she's my interviewer rather than me having to endure some stuffy police chief?"

I laughed. "I don't think I'll have a say in that."

He brushed hair off his forehead and smiled. Beneath the facade, I got the sense this was a nice kid who didn't know quite how to respond to murder. Who would?

"Had to try and see if she'd be the one I could talk to."
He gulped down the rest of his Coke and tossed the can in
the wastebasket near B.J.'s desk.

B.J. was on the radio again, that piece of paper with the
police codes in his hand. He was determined to use those
codes no matter what.

The Sprite I'd bought wasn't sitting well after that latte
I'd consumed earlier. I stood and put my mostly full can in
the trash, too, and slid the change meant for Brandt's drink
onto B.J.'s desk.

Kara and Brandt were deep in conversation, but Candace's appearance with the boyfriend interrupted them.
The look on Candace's face when she saw Kara said it all,
but she immediately put her thoughts into words. "What
are you doing here?"

Brandt said, "This is a public building. That means she
has every right to be here."

Showing off his law-school learning for a pretty girl.
Guys like to impress, no matter how old they are.

"Brandt," the boyfriend, Lieber, said, "I know you're on
edge, but can you tone it down a notch? Deputy Carson has
a job to do."

"Thanks, Dr. Lieber, but I can handle this," Candace
said. "Brandt VanKleet, come with me, please."

Brandt looked at Kara and made a motion with both
thumbs. I'd seen Candace do that before and learned it was
the "Text me" signal.

As Brandt followed Candace to the interview room,
Evan said, "Man, he gets them all. Guess I should consider
law school."

Lieber stood by Evan and patted his shoulder. "You
have a creative mind. There are better things ahead for
you."

Evan looked embarrassed and changed the subject, saying, "This is Ms. Hart, Doug. She's a volunteer. I can see
why they need one. I mean, for a police station there's
hardly anyone here." He gestured at B.J. and said, "Except
for him."

Kara said, "I had no idea you'd gotten into volunteer work, Jillian. You are full of surprises."

Thank goodness she didn't blow my story. From the gleam in her eye, I could tell she was enjoying this. But that little hint of conspiracy between Kara and me didn't get past Evan.

"What are you so happy about, Kara? Guess you haven't lost a father lately like we have," he said in annoyance.

"Oh, but I have," she said quietly. The gleam was gone in an instant.

Lieber gripped Evan's shoulder so hard, his knuckles turned white. "Cool it, Evan. I know you're stressed, but let's not take it out on strangers." He turned to Kara. "Douglas Lieber," he said, holding out his hand to shake hers.

Kara's small step into grief was over. She introduced herself, again referring to me as her stepmother. "What are you a professor of?" Kara asked.

"I teach sociology and an occasional chemistry course. Dual PhDs," he said. "I try not to be too boring, but freshmen are a tough audience."

"I wouldn't be bored," Kara said. "I just left my job as a newspaper columnist. I wrote about social networking, pop culture and trends, so I'm a big fan of sociology."

Evan looked at me with a silly grin. "Aren't they the intellectuals? What do you do, Ms. Hart?"

"I'm a quilt maker," I said.

"The simple life. Good for you," Evan said.

Sarah VanKleet marched down the hall toward us, her high heels clicking on the tile. She motioned to Evan. "Go talk to Chief Baca. And remember what Brandt told you earlier."

Evan rose, hiking up his loose jeans. "Certainly, *Mommy*."

B.J. started to get up and lead Evan down the hall, but Evan said, "I read every one of those *Where's Waldo?* books and found him every time. Sit down, bro." He took off for the chief's office.

Sarah glanced back and forth between Kara and me, her smile tight. "Douglas, who have you been talking to?"

Lieber gestured at me and said, "This volunteer who helped us earlier is Jillian Hart." He waved a hand at Kara. "And this is her stepdaughter, Kara."

I glanced at B.J. He was looking at me, obviously puzzled at that volunteer reference. But to his credit, he didn't say anything about charity work he knew nothing about.

Sarah examined the metal folding chair Evan had vacated, obviously looking for grimy police station crud. Apparently satisfied it was safe, she sat down. Lieber picked up her hand and held it between his own. She looked up at him, appearing nervous.

"That interview wasn't so awful, was it?" he said.

"I had to provide an *alibi*, so yes, it was awful," Sarah said. "Even the suggestion that I would be involved in murder is absolutely ludicrous. These people have a lot of nerve."

"I wish I'd been home with you Friday," Lieber said. "That would have made things easier."

Kara waved her hand back and forth between the two of them. "So you can't help each other out. That's too bad."

Douglas Lieber, it would seem, wasn't under Kara's spell, because he said, "Yes, too bad," in a curt tone.

Sarah looked at Kara. "I know why your stepmother is here, but what's your reason?"

"Just like you, I'm a stranger in town. Here for a visit. Jillian thought I should see more of the town. And for a writer, what better place to start than the police station? This is the pulse of Mercy, South Carolina."

What a load of dirty kitty litter, I thought smiling inwardly. The girl was quick. Good for her.

"I see," Sarah said. She again looked up at Lieber. "I want this whole sordid mess over. But I have to identify his body. I'm not prepared to walk into a morgue, Douglas."

"Maybe they'll allow me to do that," he said.

"If it helps any, you won't have to get near the body,"

Kara said. "They'll show his face on a video feed or wheel the body into a room. You'll be in an adjacent room with a window for viewing."

"Is that so?" Lieber said. "That should make things easier, right, Sarah?"

"I suppose." She sighed heavily.

"You seem to know a lot about that procedure, Kara. How's that?" I said.

"I once covered a rapper who'd come to Houston for a concert," she said. "Rap music remains an evolving and interesting part of the social landscape. Anyway, this man was shot in a drive-by outside his hotel before the concert. Since I'd done the research on him, the crime reporter let me share a byline. Part of the story involved interviewing the medical examiner—or trying to. All I got was a tour of the morgue's outer offices."

As she told us the story, Kara dropped her guarded facade. She seemed like that eighteen-year-old girl I'd met so many years ago. I could tell she'd enjoyed covering that shooting, and for me, that partly explained her interest in the murders. Maybe she was meant to be a crime reporter.

"That's horrible," Sarah said. "Murders there, murders here. It's making me ill."

Lieber said, "She was trying to help you feel more comfortable with the process; that's all. Knowledge is power, Sarah."

"So is prayer." Sarah bent her head, her hands clasped in her lap.

That certainly shut us all up. Sarah VanKleet remained in that position until her sons both came down the hall almost simultaneously.

She stood. "Were the officers polite with you?"

"We can leave, Mother," Brandt said. "That's all that's important." He allowed Lieber, his mother and Evan to go first, and before he left, he made that double-thumb signal at Kara again.

Down the hall I saw Candace walk across the hall and enter the chief's office.

B.J. said, "No one told me about you volunteering. That is so nice of you, Ms. Hart."

"I'm here to help," I said.

The phone rang, and he picked up.

"Do you really volunteer here?" Kara whispered.

"I did today," I said with a smile. "You did a little volunteering yourself."

She said, "I did make a genuine connection with that family, didn't I? I'll have Brandt VanKleet eating out of my hand—"

"Eating out of your hand?" Candace had arrived in the waiting area without either of us noticing.

"Just a figure of speech," Kara said.

"You keep away from our witnesses, understand?" Candace said. She was carrying a folder and said, "Let's go back to your place, Jillian. I have to transfer these statements to my computer."

Kara rose, her expression revealing what I interpreted as restraint. She'd wanted to fire one back at Candace, but she didn't. Instead, she followed Candace out the door. I suddenly felt like a mother with feuding daughters. Which made me about as comfortable as a cat being subjected to a bath. I started to leave, too, but stopped to wave good-bye to B.J. before we left. He was on the radio trying to explain what a 10-58 was to poor Officer Dufner.

Eighteen

When we got to my house, Candace carried her laptop and case files to my office. Kara left *her* laptop on the kitchen table, opened the fridge and popped the top on her first Red Bull of the day. She'd also taken one of her sushi packages out and asked whether I wanted some. I declined and grabbed several cans of cat food and the bag of kibble from the pantry. Then I went downstairs thinking that the cats would probably enjoy sushi if there were any leftovers. Dame Wiggins was nursing her kittens. I swear those four were twice the size they'd been when they'd arrived three days ago, especially the orange and white one. Chablis, meanwhile, was giving Wiggins a thorough cleaning about the head and shoulders. She didn't even stop to acknowledge my presence.

But when Syrah and Merlot came up behind me at the door, that got her attention. Chablis bounded across the room, swiped at Syrah and missed, but planted a paw squarely on poor Merlot's nose. My boys retreated to the center of the game room. Syrah, who'd stood up to a threatening stranger only yesterday, was scared to death of Chablis. Go figure.

My bossy Himalayan went back to her task of making Dame Wiggins the prettiest mom in the cat neighborhood. Wiggins, who had to be the most mellow feline I'd ever known, closed her eyes as she was treated to this massage.

I cleaned the dishes in the utility sink near the washer

and dryer, and soon Dame Wiggins had fresh food and water. I could tell by Syrah's twitching nose that he would have liked a sample, but he didn't get near that door again. I sat down next to mom, kittens and Chablis for some kitty love. Cats have a nerve connected to each hair and are calmed by petting, but I think I was more comforted than any of the felines. My stress-relieving escape was cut short when I heard Kara call my name.

I went upstairs and found Tom talking to Kara in the kitchen. He was leaning against the counter, and they both seemed relaxed, a scene so casual and friendly, I wanted to be part of it. Maybe the stress-relieving moments weren't over after all.

Tom held up several computer printouts. "Hey. Got ideas on new phones from your wireless provider. Want to make a trip and get you fixed up?"

"I would love to. Let me check with Candace," I said.

Kara said, "You think she needs to go along? Tom can protect you better than she can."

"She just needs to know where I am," I said. "It's part of her job."

"Good idea," Tom said. "Go fill her in, wherever she's hiding."

I turned and went through the living room, thinking I'd comb my hair and put on some lipstick while I was at it. I sure hoped I didn't smell like that police station.

Candace was busy typing away on her computer at my desk.

I said, "Tom's here, and he's offered to take me to buy a new phone. Then I expect he'll come back here and set up the video so I'll have my cat cam back."

"Does that mean I have to stay here with you know who?" Candace said.

"I know you don't exactly like her. She can be hard to like, but I'm trying my best, and I hope you will, too. But if you want to leave and help out Baca at the station, Kara's got a gun and swears she can take care of herself."

"The chief doesn't need my help right now. Once he

listened again to that nasty phone call—untraceable, as I predicted—Chief Baca said Morris was coming in to work no matter how sick he was. You're stuck with me as your houseguest. Besides, I'd only be doing the same thing I'm doing now if I went to the station."

"As long as you're okay with this," I said. "And I love having you as a houseguest. I'm just sorry you have to share a bed with me rather than have your own room. Be honest. Do I snore?"

"I couldn't tell you. I was tired last night, asleep in an instant," she said. "I'll send the chief an e-mail that you're heading out with Tom on an errand. A former cop can protect you just as good as I can."

"I do need a phone. I swear no one knows I even have a landline. I sure never use it."

"No problem; just make it quick. And pick me up a cheeseburger," Candace said. "I'm craving red meat." She tapped her temple. "Helps my brain."

I laughed. "I understand. You need anything else?"

"Nope. The chief forwarded Rufus's phone records. I need to figure out who he was talking to before he died. The chief's waiting on the vendor records for What's Bugging You. Maybe we'll have evidence that the strychnine came from Rufus."

"Sounds like you'll be busy," I said.

"Plenty busy. Need to write up the interviews, too. Interesting family, huh?"

"That's for sure. I'd love to hear your take on them," I said. "And Kara seems to have connected with Brandt. Promised to text him. She could help you."

"I caught that connection. Maybe she *can* help," she said begrudgingly. "Oh, by the way, I found out that besides the stolen kibble I told you about Saturday night, the town butcher reported a break-in last week. I have to give Gabe a call, see if he remembers anything else besides the stolen hindquarter."

Gabe Newton ran a busy butcher shop and specialized in making smoked-deer sausage during hunting season, not to mention preparing deer for those who just liked to shoot the animals and eat them while skipping the messy stage in between.

"You're thinking that the meat found in the professor's kitchen was stolen from Gabe?" I asked.

"Seems possible. But we don't have anything from the state crime lab yet on what kind of meat we found at the scene. When it's raw, it all looks the same to me." She wrinkled her nose in disgust.

I leaned against the doorframe. "So Professor VanKleet stole a cow, cat food and probably that meat? I wonder what else."

"I thought maybe the strychnine," she said. "I figured the professor could have stolen or bought that from Rufus, but if that were so, Rufus woulda come straight to Morris or me when he found out how the professor died. But he didn't do that on Saturday . . . and Sunday, he's dead."

"Do you think someone purchased strychnine from Rufus and that's why he freaked out when I brought it up?" And then I had an idea that made my heart speed up. "Rufus could have been the one who told Mr. Ski Mask that I was asking questions about poison."

Candace leaned back in the chair. "Yup. I've been going down the same road. Rufus went straight to Mr. Ski Mask, probably the poison buyer, and next thing you know Rufus is dead and you've got an unwelcome visitor. Why kill Rufus, though? I don't get that."

"And why not kill me, too?" I asked. The thought made the hair on the back of my neck prickle. Had I been that close to ending up like the professor and Rufus? And how close was I now?

"Wait a minute," Candace said. "What if Rufus didn't know his sale would lead to a murder? After you told him about the professor's death, he goes to this guy—pretty dumb move, I'm sorry to say—asks the wrong questions and gets himself murdered."

"And Mr. Ski Mask didn't kill me because I didn't know who he was—only Rufus did. Why didn't Rufus tell me—or tell you? He'd be alive today if—"

"Hold on. Don't go blaming yourself. Rufus made a bad decision. If he kept records, we'll find out who bought that poison," Candace said.

"Maybe it was the person driving that white van." I paused for a second. "But there's something else. A missing piece. I don't know exactly what that is, though."

Buying the new phone turned out to be a confusing experience. I came away with one that looked like Kara's—a "smart phone" is what Tom called it. Smarter than me, probably. But I trusted Tom when he told me I would get much better videos and be happy with his choice once he showed me how to use it. And I *so* looked forward to that part, sitting shoulder to shoulder with him.

Kara's car wasn't in the driveway when we got back. When I asked Candace whether she knew where Kara was, she said she remembered Kara popping her head in to say she was leaving.

Tom had followed me into the roomy study so he could program the new tech device and then I could receive my cat-cam videos.

"Where did she go?" I handed Candace the bag containing the burger she'd asked for and the side of fries I knew she wouldn't refuse.

Candace stood and took the bag. "She didn't say, even though I asked."

"Maybe she's meeting with Brandt, which doesn't make me all that comfortable," I said.

"She's a big girl, Jillian," Tom said.

"I know, I know," I said.

"Jillian *should* worry. Kara's a little overconfident, if you ask me," Candace said.

Tom looked quizzically at Candace. "Why don't you like her?" he said.

Candace's face reddened. "I like her just fine. But she busts into town and shows up at the police station like she owns the place. That's what I don't like."

"Sounds like you've got the confidence problem—in the opposite direction," Tom said. "Come on, Candace. You know how good you are at what you do, right?"

"He's right. You're a great cop, Candace. The best Mercy's got," I said.

"That's the absolute truth," Tom said. "Don't think Kara—or any reporter, for that matter—can investigate better than you can."

"Okay," Candace said with a small smile. "I surrender to the superior judgment of Jillian and Tom. But, please, Tom, promise me you won't share any case information you hear with Kara."

"You want me to recite the Boy Scout laws?" he said. "Trustworthy is one of them." He looked at the ceiling and smiled. "But you know what? I can't remember honesty being on that list."

"Don't be a smart aleck," Candace said. "I'll tell you both what I just found out, and it goes no further than this room for now. Right?"

Tom said, "Right."

"You know I don't tell secrets to anyone besides my cats," I said.

Candace set down the bag of food, placed both hands on the desk and leaned toward us. "Guess who got arrested and then kicked out of college for chaining himself to a campus truck shouting that the ferrets in his father's college lab should be set free?"

"Evan VanKleet," I said.

Candace looked deflated. "How did you know?"

"I can't see Brandt, the law student, partaking in civil disobedience before he's had a chance to graduate."

"Why are you so excited about learning this?" Tom said.

"That means he's an activist—or maybe a wannabe

activist. There were others involved in that little campus temper tantrum. And this was at the school where Evan's father used to work. Maybe his activities took a different form when he found out that his father was researching pet food at the farm," Candace said.

"You think Evan took those cats?" I said. "Or maybe even killed his own father?"

She said, "Maybe. It's a jump in logic, I know, but—"

"You got that right," Tom said.

She smirked at Tom. "Thanks for the encouragement. Anyway, it's a place to start. By the time I finish, I'm gonna know what Evan eats for breakfast and when he goes to bed. The chief said he wasn't cooperative and seemed to care less about his father. And he claims he was alone the night VanKleet died. No one in that family has an alibi."

"One thing's for sure. Evan didn't come here, tie me up and scare my cats to death," I said. "Not the right build; not the right eyes. And even though the bad guy was whispering, I'd still recognize his voice. Nope. Not Evan."

"You told me activists usually don't work alone, Jillian," Candace said. "Evan could have had a partner. He never could have taken all the cats by himself."

"Ah, the partner angle makes sense," Tom said. "I worked on a case once where a group of young people decided to bomb a mosque right after 9/11. All bright, articulate kids. And after I'd interviewed each one, I was positive not one of them would have planned that bombing alone. I like to call it collective terrorism." He'd moved behind my desk so he could use the computer.

Candace picked up her food and laptop and moved aside. "You need to work here. Will the Wi-Fi be down?"

"Yup. Give me twenty minutes," Tom said. But when he turned on my computer's monitor, his eyes widened. Then his jaw tightened. "This is him. This is that gutless asshole who—"

"I meant to shut that down. Sorry," Candace said.

"Don't be sorry," he said. "I want to see this, want to

study every move, every nuance. Because if I ever see this guy—"

"Can you call me when you're done, then?" My mouth had gone dry. That attack was the last thing I wanted to see.

Tom looked at me, and whatever he saw on my face made him hurry around the desk. He wrapped me in his arms and kissed the top of my head. Then he said, "I'm sorry."

"And I'm outta here," Candace said with a smile. She carried her laptop out of the room, shutting the office door behind her.

Tom held me close for a few seconds, and then he took my face in his hands and kissed me tenderly.

Nineteen

By Monday evening, I'd absorbed about all the information I could handle concerning my new smart phone. I practiced over and over how to make and receive calls and could bring up my cat cam videos with ease. Tom wanted me to learn the texting thing, too, but my brain was tired. By then it was dinnertime and Kara still wasn't home. She hadn't called, either. Maybe she didn't realize I'd replaced my phone and still had my old number.

Tom asked for a rain check on the pizza I'd ordered. Since news of the murders had spread, he'd had at least a dozen calls to set up security systems and was meeting with a potential customer.

Candace, Merlot and I were finished with the pizza—Merlot adores pizza—and she was ready to get back to work, when the doorbell rang.

Candace and I both got up.

"Hang on. Don't answer that yet," she said. She went to the hall closet, where her uniform hung. And her gun belt. She tucked her very large weapon into the waistband at the back of her jeans as I watched from the edge of the foyer.

Of course she had her gun. She always had her gun. But it hadn't registered until now that she might need it.

The doorbell rang again, and Candace nodded in the direction of the door and whispered, "Go ahead. I'm right beside you."

I checked the peephole and saw Evan VanKleet standing on the porch. "It's okay," I whispered before I opened the door.

The evening air, rich with the promise of more rain, washed over me when I greeted Evan and invited him in.

The sarcastic attitude he'd worn like a flak jacket earlier today seemed to be gone. He looked troubled and then surprised when he saw that Candace was with me.

"Um, I didn't know you'd be here," he said to Candace.

"You never know where I might show up," she answered.

"Come on in." I started walking toward the living room, and Candace made sure to fall in behind Evan. "Can I get you something to drink? A Coke? Tea?"

"Nah, I'm good," he said. He looked around the room for a few seconds. His jeans weren't the baggy kind he'd worn earlier, and his pale green shirt brought out the color in his eyes. But I noticed that those eyes were wide and that he seemed almost scared.

I took John's chair, and Evan finally sat down on the couch. Candace chose the overstuffed chair right across from him.

"I—I didn't come here to talk to the cops—I mean police," Evan said. He looked at me. "I thought that since you volunteer at the station and you seemed so . . . I don't know . . . *nice* . . . that I could explain some things to you."

"Things you didn't want to tell us directly?" Candace said.

"Yeah. I guess I thought Jillian could pass it along," he said.

"I would have told you to tell Candace yourself, so now you get two for one." I tried to sound light and reassuring. I could tell this was definitely difficult for the kid.

"Okay. I get that. Anyway, Brandt's the law student. He kept saying over and over before we got to the police station that none of us should say anything, that the family members are always suspects. But I've got to talk about this. It's the right thing to do. My father was murdered, and I want to help you catch whoever did it." Evan ran his hands through his mop of hair. "I haven't always done the right thing, but ... but—"

"Go for it," Candace said.

Before he could say another word, Syrah jumped on the back of the sofa right behind Evan.

"Whoa," he said as he turned. "He's not a regular tiger cat, is he?" He reached out his hand to let Syrah have a sniff, and my boy rubbed his head against Evan's fingers.

"He's an Abyssinian," I said. "His name is Syrah."

"Abyssinian. That means he's descended from ancient Egypt, huh?" Evan said. "His big ears look like those cats in the Egyptian drawings in my old world history book."

"That's exactly right," I said with a smile.

Syrah does like to be admired, and he climbed in Evan's lap.

Merlot, who had been in the corner of the foyer when Evan arrived, had followed us into the living room and now came from behind Candace's chair to claim his share of appreciation.

Evan looked so much younger tonight. Maybe he was only eighteen or nineteen rather than in his twenties.

He said, "How much does that one weigh?"

"Merlot weighs twenty pounds," I said. "But getting back to why you came. You want the police to know certain things, right?"

"I was being a punk earlier. I came to apologize to you, Jillian. To explain. I'm not like Brandt or my mother or Doug. My family is a freak show. The biggest freak is dead, or at least that's what people will say. But though it didn't come across that way today, I loved my dad. He was just screwed up."

"Chief Baca said you acted pretty belligerent. That you didn't seem to care that your father's been murdered," Candace said.

"I was pretending not to care. But I do," Evan said. "I want the police to find out who killed him. I didn't do right by him while he was alive, so I can at least be on his side now."

"How did you 'not do right' by your dad?" I said gently.

Evan stroked Syrah and didn't answer for several seconds. "I ratted him out." He looked at Candace. "No one but Brandt knows what I did."

"And Brandt, not quite a lawyer, by the way, decided information should be withheld from the police?" Candace's tone was hard.

That tone worried me. I was sure that getting angry with Evan wouldn't help. Hoping to maintain the connection between Evan and me, I said, "Brandt seems to have a lot of power in your family. That must be difficult to deal with."

Evan took a deep breath and blew out through his lips like he was inflating a balloon. "No kidding. He kept hammering into all of us that the relatives are always suspects and that we didn't have to tell you anything."

"You 'ratted out' your father," Candace said. "What does that have to do with his murder?"

"I'm not sure, except that's what led to him moving to that farm. See, I went to visit Dad in his lab about a year ago. The door was locked, but he'd given me the code, so I went in to surprise him. First thing I saw were these animal carriers, about five of them . . . and there were cats inside. My father was supposed to be doing research with ferrets and their immune system. But he had all these cats."

"So you asked him what he was doing," Candace said.

"Right," he said. "But what I didn't tell you today is that my dad was bipolar. He took medicine for it most of his life. He'd go off his meds every now and then, and I could tell that day in the lab that he was definitely off. It was his eyes, you know?"

Like the look he had in his eyes the day I met him at Robin's farm? That's what was wrong with him, I thought. "What about those cats?" I said. "Do you think he was researching their immune systems rather than working on the ferrets?"

Evan said, "I didn't know what was up, but I got a bad feeling because the cats looked thin. Not really sick, just thin. Since my father was a cat lover, that seemed odd. And when I asked him about them, he told me to forget what I'd seen and keep my mouth shut. Said he had a plan that was better than winning the lottery."

"Did you ask him what he meant by that?" Candace asked.

"He kept rambling on about amino acids and millions of dollars. He was obviously using the lab for something he shouldn't, and he needed to get back on his medicine. That's all I could think about."

"What did you do, Evan?" Candace said.

"I told my brother. He said I had information about improper use of a research lab and that what my dad was doing was a crime. He said I had to tell the department head. God, I didn't want to do that."

Candace said, "Brandt tells you to 'rat out' your father and then tells you to *not* talk when the police ask about his murder. That's messed-up thinking, Evan."

"I *know*," he said, his anger finally flaring. "That's why I'm here."

"Did you tell the department head about the cats?" I asked.

He took a deep breath, seemed to be trying hard to keep his emotions in check. "Brandt said I could do it anonymously. And rather than the department head, I sent a letter straight to the college president, thinking he'd know about my dad's illness, help him get back on his meds and send him back to work." His eyes grew moist, and his lips trembled with emotion. Syrah leaned his head back and looked up at Evan. He knew the kid was upset. "But that's not what happened. They fired him. And all because of me."

Syrah wasn't the only one who could tell this was tearing Evan up inside. I saw it, too. Evan knew his father had been doing something wrong, but he still loved him.

"You felt guilty, huh?" I said.

"Oh yeah. So I decided to leave the dorm and move in with him, make sure he stayed on his meds. Mom always made sure he took them, but see, she'd left him, and Brandt had been away for years. He didn't care if Dad took his pills or got in trouble or got fired. He hated him."

"I'm trying to understand, but I'm not sure what this has to do with your father's murder," Candace said.

I made room for Merlot, who wanted to squeeze in next to me on the chair. "I think I get it. It explains why Professor VanKleet was in Mercy," I said.

"Okay. That's true." Candace looked at Evan. "Please keep connecting the dots for me."

Evan said, "My dad was still obsessed with his research idea, whatever it was. Said he could make it without the college lab."

"That scared you, didn't it?" I said. "You knew he wasn't well enough for real research without his medication."

"Definitely, and the next thing I know, he'd disappeared. A mentally ill man with an obsession fell off the face of the earth. And Mom and Brandt couldn't have cared less." He sighed. "That's why he came here. To continue his research without Big Brother watching."

"That much I get," Candace said. "But there's something else that you didn't talk about at the station. You've had your own problems, right?"

"Brandt said you'd know all about it," Evan said. He'd lifted his chin, and the hostility was back. "But what exactly do you know?"

Candace leaned toward him, her arms folded on her knees. She said, "I know you got arrested and kicked out of school, but I don't know the details. Your father gets in trouble, then you. That's what I'm seeing—a pattern."

Evan rested his head back against the sofa, eyes to the ceiling. "We're both criminals, huh? That's what you see?"

"She's got to explore the possibility, Evan," I said. "If you're telling us what you believe led up to your father's death, you should tell it all," I said.

"Like she said, I don't see how it's connected to his murder," Evan said tersely.

He was shutting down. I had to get him back. I wanted to see that vulnerable, caring young man again. "Maybe it's not connected, but you want the killer caught. That means you have to trust Candace to figure it out."

"She thinks the bad boy of the family did it. I can see it in her eyes," Evan said.

"Then you're not reading these eyes too good, Evan," Candace said. "I'm a police officer. A victim's advocate. Your dad was a victim, and it sounds to me like you are, too. But if you're not straight with me, I can't help."

He stared at her, his defiance slowly fading. "Okay. Here's the deal. When my dad disappeared, I went a little nuts. Even thought I might be bipolar, too. I started drinking to kill the fear, made friends with a bunch of kids. They probably thought I fit right in, but they were frickin' weird. And just so you know, they found me; I didn't find them."

"I don't understand," Candace said.

"Here's how it happened. I got caught by a campus cop one night passed out in front of my dorm. He woke me up, filled me with coffee. He seemed like a nice guy, said he wanted to help me out. He didn't arrest me, just told me I needed to get my act together. The next day he introduced me to this girl Rosemary—said she was a great girl who had this rep for helping people out. Helping kids like me who didn't have any social skills and couldn't make friends."

"And of course Rosemary had plenty of friends?" Candace said.

"Yeah. Lots," he said. "It was all their idea, the thing with the truck. But they ended up with a reprimand. I got arrested and thrown out of school."

"Tell me about the thing with the truck," Candace said.

"They were protesters—or thought they were," he said. "After my dad got canned, everyone started talking about the lab and the ferrets. They decided the ferrets needed to be freed. And I decided that since I'd been worried about those cats, why not the ferrets, too?"

"Tell me about the truck," Candace repeated.

Evan's eyes were downcast. "We chained ourselves to a big campus truck. We were carrying signs about freeing the ferrets. We planned to stay all night, but I got rowdy and the whole thing came to an end pretty fast."

"You got arrested that night," Candace said.

"Yeah. Just me; none of the others."

"That doesn't seem fair," I said.

His hands were clenched at his sides. "Yeah, it was. I was drunk and they weren't."

"So you went to the Denman city jail? And your mom had to bail you out?" Candace said.

Evan's throat had red blotches that were spreading up to his face. "Douglas bailed me out. I don't think Mom had the money, and since she'd taken a job at the college, I think she was super-embarrassed about what I'd done."

Candace said, "So your new friends were some kind of animal rights activists?"

"Not really. They wanted to stand out. Be heard. But they weren't hard-core, bomb-making idiots. They were just holier-than-thou idiots. They should've done a spot on *Sesame Street* about taking care of pets and it would have been more effective."

"But you were the only one who got hauled off to jail," I said.

"Yeah, a real bummer, and you know what the irony was? The guy who took me there was the same one who told me Rosemary could help me. Those campus cops are a bunch of doofuses."

"This campus officer who helped you find these so-called friends took you to jail?" I said, incredulous. Not such a nice guy after all. And pretty suspicious. I wondered whether Candace was thinking the same thing.

"This was a public incident," Evan said. "He didn't have much choice."

"Rosemary's last name?" Candace said.

"Why do you want to know?" Evan said, looking cautious.

"Because I'm going to talk to her and find out exactly how unradical this girl is," she said. "Did you ever get the sense she knew about your father, knew about the cats in the lab? That she set you up because of what your dad did?"

Evan sat straight up, and this made Syrah leap from his lap and scurry into the kitchen. "Rosemary? That's crazy."

"She could have been more of an activist than you realized. Maybe she discovered where your dad went after leaving Denman," Candace said.

"She got close to me to find out about him? No way. She never even asked me questions about Dad," Evan said.

"Maybe I'm wrong," Candace said. "Lots of leads turn out to be dead ends, but we have to go down those roads, following the evidence."

But though Rosemary might be a lead, I was still stuck thinking about that campus cop. He seemed way too involved, and this whole "Let me lead you to some friends" thing seemed pretty contrived to me, even though Evan obviously hadn't thought so.

"Please don't bother Rosemary. She's just a weird girl who has nothing to do with anything."

Candace stared at him. "Prove to me you want to help us."

He hung his head. "Bartlett," he said. "Rosemary Bartlett."

"Now," Candace said. "Besides Rosemary, were there any other new friends who—"

But the sound of the back door opening made her stop. I was hoping it was Kara, but Candace wasn't taking any chances.

She stood and put a finger to her lips and reached into her waistband for her gun.

Twenty

Evan's eyes grew wide when he saw Candace's weapon. Meanwhile, my stomach tightened as it does every time she pulls that thing out.

But I already knew who was at the back door. I was sure Candace did, too, which was why I was so bothered about seeing that gun appear. It had to be Kara.

And it was.

But she wasn't alone.

I was relieved to see that by the time she and Brandt VanKleet walked into the living room, Candace had already hidden the gun.

They were laughing, and then Kara turned to me and said, "Hi, Jillian. You know Brandt? He and I have—"

"What the hell are you doing here, Evan?" Brandt said. "Have you lost your mind just like Dad?"

"I could ask what you're doing here, too, bro," Evan said. "Hooking up with a new one?" He glanced back and forth between Kara and Brandt.

All of this afternoon's derision seemed to have returned full force. *No brotherly love lost here*, I thought.

Though I didn't want to disturb Merlot, who was alert but apparently wanting to stay close to me, I hoped to turn down the hate meter, reduce that tension that seemed to envelop the room. I stood and said, "I'm glad you're back, Kara. Can I get anyone something to drink?" I looked at Evan. "Bet you could use a Coke."

"Yeah, that would be good." He set his jaw and looked toward the picture windows.

"Nothing for me," Brandt said.

"Thanks but no thanks," Kara said, settling next to a purring Merlot.

"Tea for me," Candace said.

Unfortunately, the seating was limited, and with Kara now in her father's chair, Brandt could only sit on the sofa next to his brother. He took a seat as far from Evan as he could get.

I went to the kitchen thinking that I didn't want to be a family therapist, but maybe I should take a course or two.

I heard Candace say, "Where have you two spent the day?"

Good question, I thought. Wherever Kara could best pump Brandt for information was my guess.

"We drove all over," Kara said. "Stopped a couple times to eat. I wanted to get to know Mercy. We found the property Brandt's father bought. Of course that farm and the house next door still have all that crime-scene tape to keep people away."

"And did you?" Candace said.

"Did we *what*?" Brandt said.

He sounded hostile enough to upset even the unflappable Dame Wiggins, I thought, as I retrieved a Coke from the fridge door. No wonder his brother can't stand him.

"*Did you stay away from the crime scene?*" Candace said, enunciating each word.

"We took pictures of both houses. Brandt tells me that's not intrusive or against the law," Kara said.

Brandt said, "Those run-down farms are a sign of the times, and the crime-scene tape just made it all the more interesting."

I poured myself and Candace glasses of tea, wondering exactly how much information Kara had shared with Brandt. Had she told him she planned to write a book? Brandt didn't seem like the type who'd enjoy publicity, especially a story about his mentally ill father's murder. I brought the drinks into the living room and gave Evan and Candace theirs. I sat on the floor near Candace, and Syrah immediately climbed into my lap.

Brandt turned to me and said, "Kara tells me you alerted the police to go to my father's property. Seems he had accumulated a large number of cats."

I glanced up at Candace, not sure what to say. Kara must have told him that much. Did she also tell him I now needed protection?

Candace didn't look at Brandt. Kara had her entire attention. "You discussed parts of this case with one of the victim's relatives?"

"Everyone in Mercy is discussing these crimes," Kara said. "We've been doing our homework concerning Mercy. What about you?"

Oh boy. Catfight coming, and not between the four-legged variety who lived here. Kara had no idea what button she'd just pushed.

Candace's fair skin reddened. "My job is none of your business. And if I found out you disturbed even an inch of crime-scene tape, you're in for trouble."

Brandt pointed at me. "What about her, Deputy Carson? She's the animal lover. Did you consider the possibility that she took my father's treatment of those cats very seriously and decided to release them? And what about her contact with the exterminator who ended up dead?"

I think my jaw dropped six inches. But before I could sputter a response, Evan was on his feet.

He pulled Brandt up by his shirt front so they were eye to eye. "Do they teach Asshole 101 in law school?" He then shoved Brandt back down onto the sofa.

I realized I'd been holding my breath, but I took a gulp of air when I saw that Syrah had decided he'd had enough of humans acting wacko in his house. But he went after Brandt, not Evan, leaping onto the arm of the sofa and hissing his displeasure.

I thought Brandt might tuck his legs up under him and cower—he looked that scared of a little old cat.

"Get your damn cat away from me," he nearly screamed.

Candace hadn't moved, and I swore Kara was holding back a smile. Brandt was definitely showing his less-than-tough side. He was no alley cat, that's for sure.

"I have no control over Syrah, Brandt. Sorry," I said.

But Syrah didn't need coaxing to back off. Done with his intimidation, he jumped down and walked slowly away with one backward hiss for good measure.

Evan still hadn't sat back down, and the hands at his sides were balled into fists.

Candace said, "Evan, Jillian doesn't want her house used for WrestleMania. Could you sit down?"

"No. I'm out of here." He turned and marched toward the foyer. Thank goodness he didn't slam the door when he left.

"Did you block him in?" I asked Kara.

"I did," Kara said. "Come on, Brandt. Let's settle this outside, and then I'll take you back to the motel. I don't think riding with Evan is a great idea."

"I'll walk you out and make sure this problem is handled peacefully." Candace got up quickly and went ahead of them so they could see the gun in her waistband.

I was certain a gun wouldn't be necessary, but it sure did speak loud and clear tucked in a cop's jeans. I breathed a sigh of relief after they went outside. Two cats immediately arrived to comfort me. Only two. Gosh, I missed my cuddliest kitty of all, Chablis. But she apparently felt the need to care for the guests who didn't cause a ruckus, the ones downstairs.

Kara and Candace came back inside a minute later.

"I thought you were taking Brandt back to the motel," I said.

"Evan cooled down and they took off together," Candace said. "I'm betting this kind of thing happens all the time between them."

I'd gotten up off the floor and was sitting on the sofa. Merlot was settling next to me, and Syrah had taken his spot on the couch back near my head.

"Still, I hope they don't kill each other once they get back to the motel," Kara said, heading past me for the fridge.

Candace stared after her. "Not great word choices."

"Sorry," Kara called. "People are dead. I know. But I have got to tell you guys what I found out today." She came back into the living room, a Red Bull in hand.

I looked at the can.

"What?" she said. "You want one?"

"Not this late," I said. "I like my sleep."

Candace removed her gun, set it on the end table and sat down again.

Kara reclaimed her father's chair. "I have info on your case. Be nice and I'll share."

Candace closed her eyes, seemed to be gathering herself. If she had to play sweet to get information, I knew she'd find her inner candy cane.

"What did you find out?" I said, hoping to give Candace a little more time to begin liking Kara, if only for tonight.

"Evan's got a record, for one thing," she said.

"We know," Candace said, her tone even. "Despite how the police station looks, we do have computers and access to databases."

"I figured as much," Kara said. "But did you know that the professor hadn't paid his wife any of his court-ordered support since they got divorced?"

"Have to admit, I didn't know that," Candace said. "How's that relevant?"

Kara leaned back and swigged her Red Bull before answering. "No money for support, but money to buy property. That didn't sit well with Sarah VanKleet."

Candace leaned forward. Now Kara had her attention. "She was angry?"

"According to Brandt, *furious* is more like it," Kara said. "Apparently the professor had bipolar illness and she'd taken care of him for years. She finally left, he went off his meds and then turned that into an excuse for forgetting to pay support. Or at least that's what he told the judge."

"She took him to court?" I said.

"Yes," Kara answered. "And according to Brandt—the biggest mama's boy I've ever met—he had to be there with his mother. He said the judge bought the professor's pitiful act. Gave him time to get back on his medication and find a job before paying the back support."

"Even though the professor had this property as an asset?" Candace said.

Kara nodded. "Brandt said his father could act crazy anytime he wanted to. And what better time than when he was in front of a judge and about to lose his precious farm?"

"So Sarah VanKleet had more serious money problems than the chief and I realized," Candace said.

"Yes. Even before the professor was fired—for doing illegal research," Kara said. "Brandt was ashamed of that."

I was impressed. Kara really had learned her trade as a journalist, and she'd done a great job getting information from Brandt. "Good work, Kara," I said.

"I thought it would be tricky," Kara said. "I couldn't misrepresent myself to Brandt if I wanted to use what he said in my book, but he loves to talk, so I never said anything about my plans."

"Guess he talked up a storm because you're not the police. He didn't tell me anything when I interviewed him. However, we did know about his father getting fired," Candace said. "But you're helping me understand the victim better, and that's the key to solving most whodunits."

Kara smiled. Not a smug smile, either. She seemed genuinely pleased to be helping. "Sarah VanKleet had to get a job, so she went to work as a secretary in the registrar's office at the college. She's less stressed now, despite the court ruling, according to Brandt. Seems she and Lieber are living together."

"And from what we found out, Lieber was friends with the VanKleets long before the divorce," Candace said, half to herself. "Sarah and Lieber becoming a couple apparently upset the professor big time, so—" She stopped herself.

"Go on," Kara said. "I didn't know about this part."

Neither did I. Candace must have learned this from Lieber earlier today.

Candace's face remained impassive, but I was sure she was mentally kicking herself for saying too much. "That's all. The professor was upset with his situation."

"I get it," Kara said. "Ongoing investigation. But I've been a good girl and told you all about today."

"And I thank you," Candace said. "Did you learn anything else that might help us find the killer?"

"Only that Sarah VanKleet had lots of questions about who would inherit the property," Kara said. "Brandt said he couldn't be sure until they know if there's a will. You didn't happen to find a will in the house?"

Candace just smiled. She wasn't about to spill anything else. "Sounds like you spent time with Mrs. VanKleet today, too."

"We did stop by the bed-and-breakfast where she's staying. They do a nice lunch there." Kara stood. "As for that will, I'm sure somebody in town will know. One thing I've learned is that people sure like to talk in Mercy. Belle is a wealth of information, and she might know by tomorrow."

"That's so true, I'm actually ashamed to call myself a cop," Candace said with a laugh.

I wanted to say, "See how fun it is to share, girls?" as if these two were five-year-olds. But I kept my mouth shut, appreciating the ease in tension between them.

Kara said, "Think I'll go to my room and talk to my little recorder before I forget what I learned today." She walked past us, Red Bull in hand, and left us alone.

"Tonight's information settles it," Candace said. "We're going to that college tomorrow to get the truth about what went on there."

"I'm game," I said. "But what's your focus now?"

"I need answers about what really went on in Denman. Brandt claims the professor was faking. Evan thinks he was a sick man. What's the truth?"

"I'm betting the truth lies somewhere in between," I said. "What about Kara?"

"She can't come. I'm charged with protecting you, but I'd have a hard time explaining her need to go with us. She stays here," Candace said.

"But I'm worried Ski-Mask Guy will come back." I thought for a second, then said, "I might have a partial solution, though."

"Partial works for me. What's your plan?" Candace said.

"I get Tom to give her a job to do tomorrow. Any job," I said.

"Think he'll be a willing spirit?" she said.

"Definitely. I get the feeling the more time he spends with her," I said, "the better he'll understand her. And then maybe he can explain her to me. I need all the help I can get."

Twenty-one

Though rain fell throughout the night and thunder woke me several times, by morning the sun snuck through the slats of my wood shades and one beam of light fell right across my eyes. There was no sleeping through that. Besides, we needed to get moving.

I shook Candace's shoulder, and she moaned in protest. "Five more minutes."

No five minutes for me. I needed coffee. When I swung my legs over the side of the bed, I was surprised to see Chablis sitting on the floor and staring at me. "Hey, sweetie," I whispered. "I've missed you."

In response, Chablis offered one of her more insistent meows and, fluffy chocolate-colored tail in the air, hurried out of the bedroom.

I knew that voice and that behavior. She wanted me to follow her. Cats do talk in their own way and have so many different sounds—more than a hundred by some estimates. I hurried after her.

Chablis led me to the basement, as expected. I filled one dish with dry food, even though it wasn't empty. I noticed that no one seemed interested in food—even the kittens were curled in the cutest little pile, fast asleep. But Chablis was licking away at Dame Wiggins back near the shoulder blades—and really going at it. She stopped for a second, looked at me and then started up again. This wasn't normal grooming.

I knelt by the cats and saw that Dame Wiggins's fur around this area was downright wet. "What are you doing, Chablis? Does she have an injury we don't know about?"

Wiggins could definitely have been bitten and developed an abscess after being around so many cats, so I lifted Chablis and set her next to me while I examined the area. Not an abscess at all. But definitely a small bump just below the skin.

Aloud, I said, "If they scanned her, no one told me. Bet they forgot." Indeed, Dame Wiggins had a pet-locator chip embedded under her skin. I'd have to get Shawn over here pronto. Dame Wiggins and her litter probably had a home to go to.

Candace's voice made me start when she said, "I've called the chief, and he wants us to go to Denman in a squad car. This is official police business. Let's get going."

This from the woman who wanted five more minutes of sleep? I told her about the implanted microchip and how I had to notify Shawn.

"It's been four days," Candace said. "Waiting another day to scan the cat won't be a problem. You're sure Tom can keep Kara occupied?"

"He was more than happy to help when I called him last night," I said.

"Let's go." Candace's eyes were bright with the promise of police work that was a little more challenging than babysitting a grown woman.

We took my van to the courthouse and drove around behind the building where the squad cars were parked. Kara had been awake when we left and questioned why Candace was wearing her uniform, and then asked where we were going. She'd noticed I had my purse and was fiddling with my new phone to make sure I knew how to bring up the cat cam. But Candace didn't get a chance to answer because Kara's phone started ringing. Candace pulled me out the back door, but not before I heard Kara say Tom's name. *Great timing, my friend*, I thought.

Soon we were on the road, and though Candace was driving, I felt fairly safe because she was always more careful when she drove a squad car. Once we were out of town and on the highway heading toward Denman, Candace shut off the police radio so we didn't have to endure hearing B.J. screwing up more police radio codes. But her phone rang a minute later.

She had her cell attached to the car somehow, and all she had to do was press a button and the call came out on the speaker feature. It was Mike Baca.

"Candace, I got the info you wanted on Rosemary Bartlett. She lives in town with her parents, and they said she's home."

"Good. What was your take when you spoke to her?" Candace said.

"I spoke to her parents. They didn't seem all that surprised that a police chief was calling. I got the feeling the father wanted to say, 'What's she done now?' but he just said she'd be waiting for you, that he'd make sure of it."

"Great. And the head of the college?" she asked.

"That's another story," Baca said. "I had to work him pretty hard, saying we didn't want to involve the college in our investigation beyond a few simple questions about the professor. Once he knew we were aware of why Professor VanKleet was fired, he said he'd cooperate."

"Sounds like we're all set. I downloaded a campus map, but give me the Bartletts' address." Candace pulled her notepad from her pocket and tossed it to me.

I wrote down the address Baca rattled off.

He said, "I've got to go. Lydia's decided to hand deliver the autopsy report, and I think she's just arrived if that shrieky voice I hear outside my office is an indication. What did I do to deserve this personal delivery? And what was I thinking—never mind."

He hung up, but I could have finished that question. What *had* he been thinking when he got involved with her several years ago? Miss Upstate Winnebago, as Lydia had once been titled, was a certifiable nutcase.

With all the rain, the South Carolina landscape was lush, and I was enjoying this ride. I'd brought several quilts to finish, but just when I was in a good stitching rhythm, it was my turn to receive a phone call—and thank goodness I'd practiced with the new contraption. The caller ID read ROBIN WEST, but it was Jack.

"Hi, Jack," I said when I answered.

Candace gave me a puzzled sideways glance.

"I wanted you to know that my mom took your excellent advice. I even got to play in the mud."

"That's great, Jack. Are you off from school?" I said.

"Yeah. Spring break, and it couldn't have come at a better time. My cat, Lucy, has new friends. Two of them. One is black-and-white and the other one is orange. Of course, Mom won't let them in the house."

"Two new cats? Did you go to Shawn and Allison's shelter to pick them out?" I asked.

Candace said, "Ah," while nodding.

"No," he said. "They just showed up. Very smart cats to find shelter during that awful storm we had the other night. They've been staying in the barn, and they don't seem to want to leave. And that's fine with me."

"How's Lucy handling two new friends?" I said.

"She wasn't thrilled at first. Lots of hissing and spitting the first day, since felines are very territorial. She's coming around."

"Yes, she'll be best buddies with them soon enough," I said. "I have three cats myself."

"Are they house cats, or do they stay outside?" he asked.

"They're indoor cats. But, Jack, glad as I am to hear from you, I sense a hidden agenda," I said.

"Yes. I am determined to have an indoor cat myself. And since you did so well with my mother before, well . . ." His voice trailed off.

"You want me to convince her to let you have a cat in your immaculate house? That's a tall order. Cats can destroy things, and your mom's vacuuming, which I'm guessing is already very time-consuming, might increase a whole lot more."

"Do your cats destroy things?" he said.

"No, because they have scratching posts and early on I trained them to behave."

"Here's my idea, though," he said. "My mom needs to quit obsessing. A cat might be a way for her to realize that she can enjoy something without having to constantly clean around it. She does love animals."

How did such a young kid get so smart? "Did you try to convince her with your logic?"

"I haven't brought it up. I thought I'd let you do that part because she doesn't listen to me."

He sounded so hopeful, how could I turn him down? But this would be a challenge. "I'm out of town on a little trip today. Can I meet your new cats another day?"

"Sure. I'm off school all week."

"I'll call you, Jack. Take care," I said.

"Bye, Miss Jillian. And thank you." He hung up.

I looked at Candace. "Did you get the gist of that?"

"You honestly believe that Robin West will allow a cat in her house? I don't think so," Candace said.

"At least I can try. Plus, those cats that showed up will need their shots and should be checked for parasites and feline AIDS, like we did the night the professor—oh my gosh."

"What?" Candace said.

"Ruth Schultz and Robin West don't live that far apart," I said. "Ruth had at least one stray that came from the professor's property that we know about and probably a couple more. What if these two that showed up at Robin and Jack's place came from the professor's farm, too?"

"Do you believe some of the cats escaped the evening of the murder and weren't carried off?" Candace said.

"It's very possible. And if there are more, Shawn will have his hands full," I said. "They'll come his way eventually."

"And he's so overloaded now that Allison's in school,

we had to work a night shift," Candace said. "Not that I minded. It was fun."

"That seems so long ago now, doesn't it? I have to volunteer more there," I said. "He needs the help. I hate to even tell him about the microchip I found on Dame Wiggins this morning because he'll have to make a trip to my place to scan her."

"Chief Baca told me that lazy Chester called the station to make sure Shawn scanned the cats left at the house," Candace said. "Chester's looking for any reason to bust Shawn. Scanning rescued animals *is* the law."

"Then we'll make sure Chester doesn't get Shawn in trouble," I said.

We settled into silence. I so loved the South Carolina countryside. Focusing on the budding trees and blooming flowers along the way relieved the stress I feared would return full force once Candace started asking questions at Denman College. Everything about the VanKleet family seemed to be connected to stress with a capital *S*.

Twenty-two

Denman is a tiny town, and according to what Candace told me, most everyone who lives there is connected to the college. We stopped at the police station first, or should I say the police *shack*. If I thought Mercy's police headquarters was ridiculously small, I never could have imagined that police officers in this country would be forced to work out of what was practically one of those backyard storage sheds you can buy at Home Depot. Only one officer was present, Officer Dooley, and he told Candace she was welcome to question anyone she could find who wasn't out of town.

"Courtesy call," Candace said as we got back in her squad car. "Don't want it to get around to any officers in town that I'm stirring up trouble on their turf. Let's talk to the college president now. Maybe we'll get new information about the professor from him. His name is Lawrence Johnson, by the way."

"How will you explain my presence?" I asked.

"Since I'm not about to let you out of my sight, we're back to Plan A, the one that started this whole thing. You're a ride-along—taking one of those citizen police-academy courses." She checked her small campus map and then put the car in gear.

"Me hanging around might make your job more difficult, though. I can wait in the car, or you can drop me at

McDonald's and I'll get coffee. Every college town has a McDonald's."

"Nope. That's not how this works. We are joined at the hip until this case is solved."

I sighed. "All I'm saying is that we're far from Mercy and any danger right now."

"Ski Mask could have followed us—though I was paying close attention and didn't pick up any tail. But who knows? Rosemary Bartlett might turn out to be more like Rosemary's Baby," she said.

"I give up. You're the one in uniform, and I must obey," I said with a laugh.

A few minutes later we drove onto campus, and Denman College turned out to be far different than I'd imagined. The buildings were a blend of very old and very new. We passed the infirmary, which obviously had been someone's home at one time, but there was also a residence hall that looked modern and was about six stories high.

The administration building turned out to be a beautiful large redbrick structure with white pillars. The landscaping was well tended, with shrubs surrounding steps on both sides that led to the main wide set of steps. We parked in a spot marked RESERVED right next to the president's parking place.

"Let them try and give a police car a ticket," Candace said as we got out and headed toward the administration building.

A cement plaque set into the brick next to the huge oak double doors said BUILT: 1910.

"Wow," I said as we went inside. "This place is a hundred years old, and everything looks like it's in perfect condition."

We learned from a posted building map that the administration offices were housed on the third floor. I saw a sign with an arrow pointing right that said MAIN DINING FACILITIES but heard no voices. The place was pretty much deserted.

We walked through what had once been the huge foyer of the building. Couches, chairs and coffee tables made for a nice relaxing place for students to visit. But not a soul was around.

The two elevators beyond this area seemed far more modern than the building. I'd expected old-fashioned cage-like protecting doors to close before the main doors shut, but that didn't happen.

President Johnson's office, as another sign told us, was at the far end of the hall to our right. There was no secretary in his reception area. Candace went up to another lacquered and gleaming tall door with a PRESIDENT LAWRENCE JOHNSON plaque prominent, and I hurried to keep up. I had been lagging behind admiring the high ceilings and beautiful arched windows.

She knocked, and a deep voice told us to come in.

President Johnson sat behind his massive desk, a slew of papers in front of him. Two dark wooden armchairs with padded blue silk striped seats and backs sat in front of the desk facing the president.

He stood and nodded. "Deputy Carson." Then he looked at me. I had left behind the jeans and T-shirt and had chosen a khaki linen skirt and blouse, but as nice as my outfit was, I in no way looked like a cop. His puzzled look was no surprise.

"Jillian Hart," I said to the man, who had to be Harry Belafonte's long-lost twin. The guy was gorgeous.

Candace quickly added, "She's in the Citizen's Police Academy. And she's signed confidentiality documents. Ms. Hart's learning how we do the people's business in South Carolina."

He'd been looking skeptical before she said "the people's business," but that phrase seemed to have worked, because he said, "Very well. Have a seat, ladies. This is an unpleasant business, something I certainly didn't think I would have to revisit."

"We know what happened with Professor VanKleet here at your college. All I'm looking for is corroboration. Let's get right to it. Why did you fire Professor Van-Kleet?"

Lawrence Johnson sat back in his leather swivel chair and rested his intertwined fingers on his abdomen. Bet he had a six-pack under that starched white shirt. The man seemed to be in awesome shape, so much so that it was impossible to tell how old he was. Since his dark head was shaved and shiny, there was no gray hair to give away his age.

"Why did I fire Hubert?" Johnson said. "Let me first say, I did not like doing it. At one time he was one of the most brilliant minds on the faculty."

"At one time?" Candace said.

"The man was ill." Johnson tapped his temple. "Everyone knew that, but in higher education, eccentrics are common. Oftentimes it accompanies genius—and that was the case with him."

"But he must have done a good job at some point," Candace said.

"While he was married to Sarah, he did more than good. He brought an enormous amount of research money to this college. But he began to cross the line from peculiar to almost frightening right about the time their marriage fell apart. I know Sarah. She works for me now, and she did try her best, but when Hubert stopped taking his medication, things got very, very bad."

"What's very, very bad?" Candace said.

Was he making jars of red goop here, too? I wondered.

"Bad, in that students started to complain not only to this office but to their parents. He was behaving oddly in class, not lecturing, not following curriculum. We cannot have that here," Johnson said, his dark eyes hardening for the first time.

And at what college could you have that? I thought.

"That's why you fired him?" Candace said.

"No. His research was too valuable," Johnson said.

Translation, I thought, *he brought too much money to the college to let him go.*

"I reprimanded him—in the kindest way I could, of course," Johnson went on. "I did not wish to condemn the man for something he could not control—his mental illness. But I did put him on probation and took away his course load. He was to focus on his research until I saw that he was fit to return to the classroom."

"Did he ever get back in the classroom?" Candace asked.

"Unfortunately, no," he said. "He continued to deteriorate. I even offered to take him to a colleague, an abnormal-psychology professor who was still a practicing psychiatrist. Hubert refused."

"So you did everything you could," Candace said.

This brought a smile to Johnson's lips. "I would do anything for the people at Denman—the students, the faculty, the families. It is what I *must* do to maintain our reputation."

"But then VanKleet really went off the deep end, right?" Candace said.

Johnson closed his eyes, shook his head. "I could not believe what I saw in that laboratory."

"Did you visit his lab often?" Candace asked.

She was trying to get information without giving away anything that she knew, and she was good at it. "No. That's not my practice. The bright men and women who work here do not need the president looking over their shoulders. I only went because I was informed there was a problem." His last sentence was terse.

"And who informed you?" Candace said.

"I don't know. It was anonymous, a computer-generated letter placed on my administrative assistant's desk."

"Do you get anonymous letters often?" Candace said.

"More often than you might think," he said. "One professor slipping information about a colleague he or she is still working with, students telling tales on their friends whom they've fallen out with; you name it, it's happened. For the most part, I ignore this kind of thing."

"But you didn't ignore this anonymous tip?" she said.

"Hubert was already on probation, and the details in this letter were too serious to ignore. I had to see for myself if this was true. Sadly, it was. We do not do research using cats, but there they were, and though they didn't seem to be in ill health, they shouldn't have been here."

"Did you save this letter?" she said.

"I did," he said. "But unless you have a legal document such as subpoena, I don't believe I'm obligated to share it with you. Just speaking with you is a favor to your chief of police. He is a friend of a friend."

"The professor's dead," Candace said.

This was the first time I detected any of her usual impatience.

"But his family is not dead," Johnson said. "His ex-wife still works here, and I have an obligation to keep unseemly information about her deceased husband away from those who might make life more difficult for her."

Or for Denman College, I thought.

"Could your decision not to share this letter—which you have every right to do—have anything to do with another VanKleet who was sent packing?" Candace said. Her tone was tougher now.

She obviously was on to the fact that this man wanted all the secrets to stay in the Denman College closet.

"I should have expected that you would know about Evan." Johnson smiled. "I underestimated you, Deputy Carson. My mistake. Forgive me if I was unprepared, but I wasn't informed I had to talk about him."

"You do," she said. "My biggest question is why he was kicked out of school and the others weren't."

He tented his hands. "I believe I will decline to answer that. As I said, I am unprepared and should consult with the legal counsel who advises me on such things before I say anything."

"You think he might sue you or something?" Candace said.

"It's been known to happen," Johnson said curtly.

"Was his being drunk that night the reason you kicked

him out, or was it because he owed the college a chunk of change?" Candace said.

I read the surprise in Johnson's eyes. "I will not get into that. Not today. Are there any other questions I can help you with?"

"Tell me about Sarah VanKleet. How did she handle all the trouble surrounding her family members?" Candace said.

He seemed to relax some at this change in direction and said, "Sarah is a hardworking woman who did the best she could with all she had to deal with. Her older son went to school here and has gone on to law school. She's quite proud of him, as is Denman College."

"She lives with Professor Lieber now?" Candace said.

He repositioned himself in his chair and blinked several times before answering. "I am not in the habit of inquiring about my employees' private lives. Professor Lieber is well respected here. And loved by the students, I might add. He is unmarried, and if he has a relationship with Sarah, that's certainly not my business."

Like heck you don't know about them, I thought. *I'll bet you know every detail of what goes on around here.*

"Were Professor Lieber and Professor VanKleet friends?" Candace asked.

I wasn't sure whether Candace had worn him down and he was tired of dancing around the truth, but he said, "Yes. They were friends. We have what I like to call a tight-knit family here at Denman."

"Were you surprised to learn Professor VanKleet died a horrible, painful death?" She'd leaned in and was probably looking for his nonverbal response to this very direct question.

"Why, of course. Why would you ask such a thing?" He was rattled now.

"Because he brought shame on this college, didn't he? Some people might be glad he died that way. At least one person did—the killer."

"I—I can't believe you're saying these things to me,"

Johnson said. "I tried my very best to do right by Hubert. Gave him every opportunity."

"But you gave up on him in the end, just like everyone else," she said softly. Then she stood.

I was so taken aback by her switch to this hard line that I felt like a robot and just followed her lead, standing as well.

Lawrence Johnson didn't stand. He sat in his big chair in his fancy office, and I read sadness on his face. Even his eyes had filled. Candace had been tough on him, but I now understood that though he loved his college, he had also cared about Hubert VanKleet.

Candace said, "Can you tell me where the Bartletts live?"

That brought Johnson out of his reverie. "You mean Rosemary Bartlett? You're talking to her, too?"

"I'm hunting for a killer. I might interview everyone in this whole damn town," she said.

He looked a little stunned now, nothing like the calm, cool and collected academic he'd been when we first walked in. "Um . . . where did you park?"

"Right next to you," Candace said.

"Then you can walk to their house. There's a path on the far side of the lot that leads to Hawthorne Street. They live in a small house about a block to the right. Number 405."

"Thanks," Candace said and started to turn to leave. But then she stopped. "Does Mr. Bartlett do a good job janitoring? Is that why Rosemary got to stay and Evan didn't after that little protest?"

Johnson opened his mouth to reply, but Candace said, "You don't have to answer. I think I already know."

I followed her out, and when we were in the elevator I said, "You didn't tell me Rosemary's father worked at the college, too."

"I mentioned that everyone in town works at the college, didn't I?" she said with a smile.

"You did. I have to say, I've never sat in on anything like that. You were awesome."

"He could have been a suspect, you know," she said.

"Because VanKleet tarnished Denman College?" I said.

"Maybe, but even though I didn't act like it, I believe he's a genuine guy doing a difficult job. VanKleet went rogue on him, and he had no choice but to fire him."

"I agree you didn't leave President Johnson with a warm, fuzzy feeling," I said. "He might be worried you'll come back."

"This is murder, Jillian. There's nothing warm or fuzzy about it. If I need to return with a subpoena for that letter Evan said he wrote, I will," she said.

"Maybe Evan kept a copy. I could ask him," I said.

"Good idea. Now I'm ready to hear what Rosemary Bartlett has to say."

Twenty-three

The Bartlett home was about a ten-minute walk from the college, and Mr. Bartlett answered the door of the small brick house. He was a burly man with muscled arms and a ruddy complexion.

Unlike Lawrence Johnson, he invited us both in without even questioning my presence. Maybe he was old-school. If a cop comes to your house, you don't ask any questions.

The living room was small and neat, with a big flat-screen TV the centerpiece on the far wall.

Bartlett said, "The wife's gone. Said she didn't want to be here when you questioned Rosemary. It's better that way. She'd probably cry the whole time. I mean the wife, not Rosemary. I wish I'd see that girl cry over something. Worries me sometimes how she can be."

Candace said, "This is Jillian Hart. She'll be sitting in on the interview, taking notes." She took her notebook from her pocket and handed it to me.

Okay, I thought. *I can take notes.*

"Where is your daughter, sir?" Candace said.

Funny how she'd never used the word *sir* with Johnson—a powerful man—but chose to do so now with a guy who obviously respected Candace without reservation.

"I'll get her. Go ahead and sit." He left the room and went left down a hallway.

"Do you really want me to take notes?" I said.

"Yes. And sit on the sofa next to me. That way the girl

can only choose one of the easy chairs and I'll be right across from her.

We sat on the beige sofa, and I noticed the vacuum lines on the carpet. A police visit required tidying up. Yup, this was far different from sitting in a college president's office.

Rosemary walked into the room after her father, her head down. The hair grabbed my attention first. Purple and magenta, cut in spiky layers. Her bangs covered one eye.

When she sat across from us, I noticed a piercing in her lower lip, but the ring had been removed. *Sullen* was a kind word to describe Rosemary Bartlett's expression.

Her father took the other easy chair, a plaid rocker, and said, "Go ahead. Talk to the officers."

She addressed him, not Candace. "What am I supposed to say? I'm sorry?"

He pointed a thick freckled finger at his daughter. "Quit with the attitude. These policewomen have come a long way to talk to you. I told you they want to know about Evan VanKleet. And I'd sure like to hear about him, too."

Rosemary raised her eyes and then faced Candace. "How can I assist you, *Officer*?" But she didn't sound in the least like she wanted to assist anyone.

"First of all," Candace said in her kindest voice, "let me tell you that I've spoken with Evan. He was cooperative and very much wants to find out who murdered his father."

Rosemary's heavily penciled brows knitted. "You're lying, right? He cooperated with the cops after they put him in jail for no reason?"

"I didn't put him in jail," Candace said. "And from what I could tell, he got a raw deal."

"No kidding. We do have the right to protest in this country," she said. "That's all we were doing."

"That's not why he went to jail, Rosemary." Bartlett looked at Candace. "I heard he was drunk. Is that true?"

"True," she said. "By his own admission."

"And he's sorry about that," I added. "I helped interview him, and he's trying to get back into school, straighten his life out. But he's so upset about his father's death. Can you help us help him?"

Rosemary said, "He's okay, then? My father wouldn't let me bail him out or even talk to him afterward. But Evan is such a cool guy."

"I get your father's concern," Candace said. "Because that's what it is—concern. To answer your question, Evan seemed fine when I talked to him—aside from being torn up about his father dying."

Candace knew exactly the right words at the right time, it would seem, because Rosemary said, "Man, I so wanted to call him after the story was in the paper. But I don't have his number anymore."

"We wanted her to have no contact with Evan and the other students involved in the incident afterward," Bartlett said. "Rosemary is on scholarship at Denman, and she could lose it all."

"Yeah, and instead I lost my friends." She began to chew on an already ravaged fingernail.

"How did you meet Evan?" Candace asked.

"Patrick. He told me that Evan needed friends, that he was bummed after his father got canned," Rosemary said.

"Patrick who?" her father said before Candace or I could ask the same question.

"Hoffman. He's pretty cool for a cop," she said.

"You call Officer Hoffman by his first name?" Rosemary's father said.

"We all do. You know he always walks me home when I stay late, right?" she said.

"No, I didn't know. How friendly are you with this man? And how old is he?" Bartlett said.

Rosemary sighed heavily. "Jeez. It's not like that."

Candace quickly said, "You can talk about all that later. So Officer Hoffman mentioned Evan?"

"Right," she said. "He knows my friends are all the weirdos on campus—I mean it's like frickin' high school all over again here. Patrick thought Evan would fit right in with us. And he did."

"Tell me about this protest," Candace said.

I realized I hadn't been writing anything down and decided to start looking official. I poised my pen over the blank notebook page.

"Did Evan tell you about that?" Rosemary said.

"Yeah," Candace replied. "This protest, the one where Evan got arrested, that was about the ferrets?"

"Yes," she said. "Most of us are science majors. Evan wasn't, but his dad was some big science freak, so he knows a lot more than he lets on. Saving even the small animals is important, even in Denman, which is a tiny place, I know."

"And is giving you a *free* education," her father added.

She turned to him again. "I could go somewhere else where you aren't watching me every second. I've got the grades and the smarts, you know."

"You do sound like a very intelligent young woman," I said, hoping to avoid a complete meltdown between Rosemary and her father. "So you decided to focus on the ferrets?"

"Yes," Rosemary said.

"Were the ferrets being hurt?" I said.

"Maybe. By the flu shots they were getting. Ferrets don't get the flu," she said.

"Actually, I think they do," I said. "Both cats and ferrets have immune systems similar to those of humans. Last year cats even got the H1N1 virus."

"Okay, maybe they do get the flu, but people have to stand up for them. That's all we were doing. Just a small protest we hoped might make more than just the Denman College newspaper. We tweeted about it, and lots of kids showed up from the surrounding towns for support."

"Tweeted?" I said. What the heck was that?

"She's talking about Twitter," Candace said.

"Oh. I know about that," I said. But I didn't know much.

"You had an audience, then?" Candace said. "Bet that didn't go over well."

"You got that right," she said. "I think Evan got arrested because President Johnson felt as if he had to do something about the protest. Make a statement. Evan was the scapegoat."

"Rosemary, you know that's not true. The president told me himself he knew nothing about what you and your friends were doing that night."

She said, "And you believe him, Dad? You are so frickin' gullible."

"The campus police took Evan to jail?" Candace said.

She nodded. "I have to admit, he was pretty stupid to drink before we chained up to the truck. Plus he had a flask in his back pocket. Our protest wasn't some prank. We were serious. We wanted to say something, but when someone's drunk, it makes it seem less . . . important."

"Why do you think Evan was so *stupid*, as you put it?" I asked gently.

"Because she picks stupid friends," Bartlett said.

"I do not," she practically shouted. Then she took a breath and seemed to calm down. "Evan was so upset about his family situation. His father was gone, his mother was screwing Professor Lieber and—"

"Rosemary," Bartlett said. "Watch what you say."

"Whatever. Lieber is very cool, by the way," she said.

"You're talking about Douglas Lieber?" I said.

"Right. Anyway, after we were chained up, ready to go all night, I realized Evan was wasted. He was rambling on about how his father hadn't paid his tuition. I felt so bad for him."

Maybe Lieber, who seemed to be friends with the students, was the reason Evan seemed to be clean and sober now. His mother apparently hadn't been much help; that was for sure.

Candace said, "Let me get this straight. The campus police arrived and used Evan's being drunk as an excuse to stop your little demonstration? Do I have that right?"

"They didn't stop the rest of us. Only him," she said. "But after that, our heart wasn't in it. We quit."

"And you've heard nothing from Evan since that night?" I asked.

"Not a text, not an e-mail," she said. "If you see him, will you tell him to call me? He has my number."

"Hold on, Rosemary. This young man is trouble." Bartlett looked at Candace. "Do you think he might have killed his father?"

Rosemary reached over and shoved her father's arm. "That is the most stupid thing you have ever said in your life."

He grabbed her wrist. "Do not disrespect me, Rosemary."

I could see why the mother didn't want to be here for this. Rosemary was one little spitfire.

"Rosemary," Candace said. "Listen to me. Your dad has a right to worry about you, okay?"

"But he doesn't even know Evan," Rosemary said.

"I know more than you think," Bartlett said. "When I was cleaning Professor Lieber's office, I heard him talking on the phone to Sarah VanKleet about the kid. They didn't know what to do with him."

Rosemary glared at her father. "You never told me that. What other crap have—"

Candace held up a hand. "Let me finish. We have no evidence that Evan harmed his father, Mr. Bartlett." Rosemary was leaning back in the chair, arms folded across her chest, head down.

Bartlett looked over at her and then at Candace. "You're being straight with me? He didn't kill him?"

"This is an ongoing investigation, but Evan is cooperating. He seems honest and obviously loved his father. That's all I can say at this time," Candace said.

"Then maybe I was wrong to judge him so harshly," Bartlett said.

"Oh," Rosemary said, "you believe them but not me. So typical."

"He's trying to understand, Rosemary," I said. "Give your dad some credit."

"Maybe you're right," she mumbled.

Candace stood, so I did, too. She reached across and shook Bartlett's hand. "You've been a big help. Appreciate you talking to us." She looked down at Rosemary. "Thanks for being straight with us. You've helped your friend."

She started for the door, but I stopped in front of Rosemary. "I'll have Evan call you." I looked at Bartlett. "If that's okay with you?"

He gave a short nod, and Rosemary almost smiled.

As Candace and I walked back to the college, I said, "If I had to deal with clown hair and pierced lips and that much attitude every day, I don't think I'd have as much patience as Mr. Bartlett has—even though he seemed almost at the end of his rope."

"Deep down she's probably a good, caring kid," Candace said. "You saw how she stood up for her friends. But now I want to talk to that campus cop, Patrick Hoffman. I still think it's hinky that he helped Evan and then arrested him not long after. I'm betting President Johnson had a hand in that, no matter what Bartlett thinks. Yup, I want to hear what Hoffman has to say."

But when we took the small path back into the parking lot, I saw we wouldn't have to hunt down the campus cops. A uniformed man was standing, arms folded, staring at the Mercy squad car.

"No way. He is *not* giving me a ticket." Candace started marching toward the man, and I had to jog to keep up.

But then the man turned and saw us.

Fear grabbed at my gut.

Those eyes. Oh my God, those eyes.

Twenty-four

"Candace, stop," I called, my voice cracking. "That's *him*."

She halted and looked at me, puzzled.

But my throat felt so tight, as tight as the day he put his hands around it, that I couldn't seem to get any words out.

The look on my face apparently told her what she needed to know. She resumed her pursuit, even faster than before.

I saw something glint in the guy's hand and shouted, "He's got a—"

But before I could finish the sentence, the man quickly stabbed the right front tire on the squad car.

"Hey," Candace shouted, her arms pumping as she picked up even more speed.

But he was on the run now, too.

She took out her gun but kept it pressed at her side.

I tried to follow but couldn't keep up. We hadn't run far before my chest felt so tight, I couldn't get enough air. The sight of that man had frightened me, and I felt breathless and paralyzed.

Candace stopped briefly when she reached the car. She pulled the keys from her pocket and tossed them back toward me. "Lock yourself in the car and stay there. I'm going after him."

I had no time to argue because she was gone in an instant, sprinting in the direction he'd gone, toward the administration building.

I did exactly what she said, but now my own fear was coupled with worry for Candace. I'd felt that man's hand around my neck. I knew what he was like, how strong he was.

So I began a little mantra to calm myself. *She'll be okay. She has a gun. She'll be okay. She has a gun.*

But maybe he has one, too, I thought as I sat in the passenger seat, my legs drawn up to my chest. And then I realized I could do something to help. I pulled out my brand-new phone that I hardly knew how to use and dialed 911. The dispatcher seemed unruffled by my near hysteria or my gasping explanation.

She told me the call had come in to a location not in Denman but close by and that she would contact the local police. An officer would come to the college parking lot.

"No," I said, hoping I didn't sound like a nutcase. "The officer has to go after *him*. Someone has to help the Mercy police officer who's chasing *him*. Her name is Deputy Candace Carson. She's wearing a green and brown uniform."

"And who is 'him,' ma'am?" she said.

"I don't know. He's wearing a gray uniform and has blond hair. She chased him behind the administration building, and where they went after that, I have no idea," I said.

"Stay on the line until the officer arrives to help you," she said.

"No, you need to help Candace—Deputy Carson," I pleaded. "I'm locked in her squad car. I'm safe."

"The caller ID says this phone is owned by Jillian Hart. Is this Jillian?"

"Yes. You have to help her. He might have a gun," I said.

"She's a police officer, you said?" the woman replied.

"Yes, but—"

"Then she's well trained. She'll know what to do. How

about you? You said you feel safe where you are?" she said.

"Y-yes. I think so. But I'm scared for—wait. I hear a siren," I said.

"Good. Stay on the line, Jillian, until the officer arrives."

I wasn't talking her out of sending the officer to me, so I did as she said and stayed on the line. When the squad car reached me, I saw it was the same guy we'd met earlier, Officer Dooley. He had his weapon drawn when he climbed out of his cruiser, but then he seemed to recognize me. He motioned for me to roll down the window. I did, and he took my phone and talked to the dispatcher. He seemed to be able to manage my phone better than I could because he disconnected without a problem.

"You okay aside from the flat tire?" he said.

"Deputy Carson is chasing down whoever slashed the tire. You should help her," I said.

"I'm the only guy on duty, and they could have gone a dozen different ways. I got the word out to a state constable, though, and he should be here soon."

"Please go after Deputy Carson. She went that way." I started to point in the direction of the administration building, and that's when the fist that seemed to be gripping my heart let go.

Candace was walking toward us. Strands of her hair hung loose, and her cheeks were red with exertion. When she reached the squad car, she stopped and bent, resting her hands on her thighs. Her breathing was rapid, and she nodded at her fellow officer. Between ragged breaths she said, "Thanks for showing up, man."

"Are you okay?" I reached out the window to her, and she grabbed my hand.

"I lost him, damn it. Or more like I got lost." She looked at the Denman officer. "Campus police wear gray?"

He nodded.

She squeezed my hand and let go. "You know one with blond hair and blue eyes? Strong guy?" she said.

"Yeah. That's got to be Patrick. The rest of the campus cops are graying or bald. But are you saying he did this to your tire?" The officer's expression said he didn't believe it for a minute.

"Oh, that's what I'm saying, all right," Candace said. "My friend and I both saw him do it. We need an APB on him now. Can we use your cruiser to head to his place?"

"Wait a minute. I know Patrick Hoffman. He's not into vandalism," Officer Dooley said.

"He is if it means that with a flat tire I can't follow him," Candace said, her anger controlled but very apparent. "As of right now, he's wanted for assault on this woman right here." She pointed at me. "He attacked her in her home several days ago."

Dooley shook his head. "I don't get it."

"You don't *have* to get it. You have to take me to his house now," Candace said.

"The constable is on the way. Why don't I call him to check out Patrick's place?"

"Just do something. He's getting away," Candace said.

Dooley returned to his squad car while Candace reclaimed the keys and opened the trunk. I got out, too, but she waved off any help from me as she pulled the spare tire out.

She was mumbling to herself as she used the tire iron to loosen the lug nuts.

After making his call, Dooley saw what she was doing and hurried over to the Mercy cop car. "Let me do that," he said.

She looked up at him with a venomous stare.

He held up both hands in mock surrender and said, "Okay. I understand. Let me check with the constable. See where he's at."

Candace didn't turn around but shouted, "Get Hoffman's plate number and put out an APB. If you don't, you'll be sorry. He is one bad wannabe cop."

Just then Lawrence Johnson appeared as if out of nowhere. But I had been a little preoccupied, as in *terrified*, so no surprise I wasn't paying attention to anyone but Candace.

"What's happening out here?" he said.

Candace had the car jacked up now and said, "Here's what's happening. Your campus cop is a bad guy. He could be a murderer. Can you pull the personnel files on Patrick Hoffman?"

Dooley said, "You never said anything about murder."

"I just did." Candace removed the slashed tire, and I swear she almost kicked it once she laid it on the pavement. "Does he drive a squad car?" she asked.

"They use bikes. It's a small campus." Johnson picked the spare up and positioned it for Candace so she could complete changing the tire.

She didn't give him the evil eye, just accepted his help. "Guess I won't find any evidence on his bike." She wiped her forehead and left a grimy streak on her skin.

Between the messy hair, the dirty face and her obvious anger, Candace seemed about as stressed out as I've ever seen her.

"I'll finish this," she said to Johnson. "Meanwhile, can you give me everything you've got on Hoffman?"

Johnson nodded and headed back toward the administration building. Seems he was wise enough to assess the situation and realize he needed to help any way he could.

Dooley's cell phone rang, and he answered. He turned away from Candace, probably hoping he wouldn't agitate her by anything he might say to the caller.

As Candace was easing the cruiser down with the jack, Dooley turned back around and said, "Hoffman's van is gone, and no one answered the door at his place. He's probably skipped. But the constable did get the plate number from the database. He's put out the APB."

"Van? What kind of van?" Candace said.

"White. He has a commercial license, but why, I don't know," Dooley said.

"White van. That fits," Candace said as she held her hand

out to Dooley. "Sorry if I've been a jerk. I'm just pissed that rat bastard got away from me."

They shook hands.

Lawrence Johnson came back to the parking lot and brought us all very welcome bottles of cold water as well as copies of Patrick Hoffman's personnel files. The constable, Hank Myers, showed up a few minutes later, wanting to get a more complete picture of the situation. South Carolina has a constable system made up of retired officers or volunteers with police experience.

Constable Myers said he'd be glad to lead us over to Hoffman's neighborhood so Candace could poke around there, check with the neighbors about what kind of person he was. Candace took him up on the offer.

Unfortunately, Hoffman lived in a section of small homes that turned out to be rentals mostly occupied by students. At least the one student who hadn't left town told Candace and Constable Myers as much. Candace decided she'd be wasting her time canvassing this neighborhood. Before we took off for Mercy, Myers said that if that guy was anywhere in his territory, he'd find him.

We drove home in silence for the first hour, but I kept checking my cat cam, fearing that Patrick Hoffman would show up at my house and make good on his threats to hurt my cats, or perhaps harm Kara. But the two cats who still liked to live above the basement were sound asleep. No Kara, and thank goodness no Hoffman to be seen.

"We're missing something, aren't we?" I finally said.

"Maybe, but we've found a huge piece of the puzzle: Patrick Hoffman. Now we have to figure out how he's connected to VanKleet's death."

I nodded. "Since he was on campus all the time, he could have seen what the professor was doing."

"Maybe he was upset about the cats and the ferrets, too," she said, "but was he working alone? Lawrence Johnson said he didn't know anything about Hoffman's private life, or who his friends were aside from the other campus cops."

"Could students have been helping him?" I asked.

"Perhaps. Though after interviewing Rosemary, I think Evan was right. This student group doesn't seem all that organized. Rosemary just wanted to be heard about something—about anything. Militant activism—and I don't see her as that kind—seems like a cause that you carry with you, and is pretty secretive, right?"

"True. But there is one person who might know more about Patrick Hoffman than we learned today," I said.

Candace smiled and pressed down on the gas so hard, we almost lurched. "You're absolutely right."

Twenty-five

We rolled back into Mercy around dinnertime. I'd made a call to the Tall Pines Motel, hoping to talk to Evan—the person who probably knew more about Patrick Hoffman than anyone else we could think of. Now that we knew Hoffman drove a white van, we were pretty certain he was the person I saw at the crime scene, which made me fear that Evan may not have told us the entire truth about his relationship with that campus cop. But Evan didn't answer his motel-room phone, and I'd never thought to get his cell number.

Since we were both famished, we stopped at the Main Street Diner. Candace and I were craving those Texas chili dogs. Old-fashioned French fries in a white cone were on our minds, too. Neither of us had eaten anything but the stale protein bars in the cruiser's glove box since this morning.

But before we even went inside the restaurant, I pointed down the street. "That's Kara's car," I said. "Wonder what she's been up to."

Candace kept walking, reached the door and held it open for me. "Come on."

We went inside and saw Kara sitting with Tom. He immediately waved for us to join them.

They were sitting across from each other in one of the larger booths, and both slid to the inside to make room for us. They had Cokes in front of them, so maybe they hadn't ordered and we'd all be having dinner together.

I sat next to Tom, but Candace told me to order her a large tea and went off to the restroom. She took my purse with her, I assumed so she could use a comb and some makeup.

"What happened to her?" Kara said. "She looks like a train ran over her."

"We got a lead on a suspect, and Candace got very busy doing things that police officers do," I said.

"A suspect? Who?" Tom said.

I rested my foot next to his. "If Candace wants to discuss her case, that's up to her. Right now, bring on those hot dogs smothered in chili and onions."

Candace joined us a minute later, her hair neatly pulled back in the elastic band it had escaped from earlier. The waitress arrived and took our orders.

Kara said, "I found out a few things today that you might want to follow up on."

I glanced at Tom and then at Kara. "You worked with Tom today, right?"

"You don't think for one minute I truly needed a baby-sitter?" Kara said.

"I thought you'd be safer with him while we were gone; that's all," I said.

"Sorry," Tom said. "She can take care of herself and told me so in no uncertain terms. But she did do a *little* work for me."

"Filing," Kara said. "Not exactly how I want to start my career as a crime writer. So I texted Brandt and we got together."

"Again?" Candace said. "Are you falling for the guy or what?"

"He's a jerk. But he knows things. Like how badly his mother wants to get her hands on that farm the professor left behind."

Candace's features softened. Kara was endearing herself to Candace lately—in spite of her opinion that Kara was as spoiled as my cats. Candace turned slightly in the booth so she could look at Kara. "And how badly does Sarah Van-Kleet want that farm?"

"She's found a lawyer in town already, one who knows about wills, estates and trusts. Brandt, who thinks he's the legal wonder kid, helped with that." Kara sipped her Coke through the straw, eyebrows raised. Then she said, "But your Chief Baca hasn't been very forthcoming about whether he knows of any will or life insurance policies found in the house. That has Mrs. VanKleet a little irritable."

We'd been thinking on the way back to Mercy about Evan's relationship with Patrick Hoffman, but what about Sarah? She worked on campus and probably knew Hoffman, too. Douglas Lieber probably knew him as well, for that matter. I didn't want to say anything about Hoffman without Candace's okay, though.

Candace said. "Well, Sarah VanKleet can stay irritated. She divorced the professor."

"But sons don't divorce their father," Kara said.

I said, "Did Brandt tell you that's how she hopes to get her hands on any assets? Through her sons?"

"He didn't come right out and tell me that," Kara said, "but that's the feeling I got."

"Feelings," Candace said. "Those aren't facts, and that's all I'm interested in right now. Who's the lawyer? Jim Stevens?"

Tom removed his straw from his Coke. "That's the only estate guy in town. Has to be him." He took a drink.

"Wait a minute. Tom said cops rely a lot on instinct. And instincts aren't facts, either," Kara said.

"You're nitpicking now. And I'm not really in the mood to talk about stuff you know nothing about," Candace said.

Kara said, "But I've just given you valuable information, and—"

Tom held up a hand. "Hold on. You had an obligation to do exactly that, Kara. You did the right thing. Now, can we relax a little? Maybe enjoy each other's company?"

"That's a good idea," I said. I'd had enough tension in the past few days to last a lifetime. Patrick Hoffman might have harmed Candace today, and I still couldn't get that thought out of my head.

"You're right, Tom," Candace said. "Sorry to be snippy, Kara, but it's been a long day."

At first I thought Kara might pout and give us the silent treatment like she used to do years ago. But she said, "I think we got off on the wrong foot, Candace. You're doing a great job, and I can see Jillian has found a true friend. I kind of envy that."

I smiled at Kara. "Candace is awesome. But so are you, the way you've tried so hard to help."

Kara answered with her eyes—with the same warmth her father had so often shared.

And the Texas chili dogs made everything that much better.

Kara had to take Tom home since she'd driven them both to the diner. Meanwhile, Candace and I went to the courthouse to drop off the cruiser and pick up my van. Though Candace had spoken with Mike Baca both while we were in Denman and again on the ride back to Mercy to fill him in on the day's events, she called him on the way to my house to tell him what Kara had said. She did more listening than talking, however. Then she said something that I hadn't expected but should have thought of myself.

"Concerning Kara Hart, you think I should warn her?" A short silence followed, and then she went on. "Inform her about Hoffman, give her a description. Since she's staying with Jillian and Hoffman's out there, we need to protect her, too."

More silence, and then she disconnected.

"You're right about Kara," I said. "She needs to know about Hoffman. Why didn't I think about that?"

"It's been a crazy day. Your mind is probably scrambled almost as much as mine. And you know what? If Kara is good with that gun in her glove box, I can't think of anyone more deserving of a bullet than Hoffman. I'll tell her just to wound him, of course," she said with a laugh.

"Let's hope it doesn't come to that." The thought of Kara or even Candace having to shoot anyone made those chili dogs in my stomach churn a little.

"Here's what else Chief Baca told me," Candace said. "He learned that Sarah VanKleet could be broke, since her credit cards are maxed out. But getting any bank info will take time. The question is, does she know something we don't about the professor—like if he had money stashed or had life insurance?"

"Good questions. She's probably living off Doug Lieber," I said. "Do we know if she started an affair with him before she separated from VanKleet?"

"Why would that matter?" she said.

"The stress of an affair could have made the professor act even more bizarre. And maybe he withheld money from his wife because of infidelity during the marriage," I said. "He decided she didn't deserve anything from him."

"You're reaching," Candace said. "We have no evidence of that. But then, I didn't get into personal details when I interviewed Douglas Lieber. I was trying to establish alibis, understand his attitude toward VanKleet. From what he told me, he and the professor were friends, and stayed friends even though he and Sarah were involved."

I said, "I understand you're the evidence queen, but I like to imagine what might have been going on, so humor me. Maybe Sarah VanKleet, in debt and with two kids in college, decided she'd be better off getting back with her ex, and Douglas Lieber didn't like that idea. The professor was doing experiments. He said whatever his plan was, it would be like winning the lottery. Was that kind of thinking the product of a confused mind or the truth—some scientific breakthrough concerning pet food?"

Candace laughed. "The pet food I get. He left evidence of that in the house. But you're saying Lieber was jealous because Sarah was reconsidering her divorce? That he killed VanKleet over Sarah? Come on. Really?"

"Okay, that's far-fetched," I said. "Here's another thought. What if VanKleet led Sarah to believe there was money coming, that he'd pay her everything she was owed and more, and she found out it wasn't true?"

"And then she kills him. In the most painful way possible," Candace said. "You might be on to something there. But I could see Brandt being that pissed off, too. The person who clobbered Rufus was strong. Brandt could definitely smash the man over the head and kill him. And even though I know you like him, we can't eliminate Evan. We saw his temper firsthand."

I did like Evan and didn't want to believe he could harm anyone, much less his father, but I had to put my feelings aside. Why did that seem so difficult? Maybe because Brandt seemed to be the decision maker. I said, "Did you check Brandt's finances? Law school is expensive."

"He told me when I interviewed him that he's on some kind of scholarship," she said. "Some wonderful ship that's taking him on that trip through law school for nothing."

I laughed. "You know what? We're both too tired to think anymore about this tonight. This could still be about militant activists. But Patrick Hoffman as that activist? My gut says no."

"I think it's more about people closer to VanKleet, but I *am* tired," she said. "I need to rethink everything when my mind is firing on all cylinders."

I pulled into the driveway a few minutes later and saw that Kara wasn't home yet. Maybe she could take care of herself, but I still worried. I mean, Patrick Hoffman was on the loose. Having a name to go with those eyes didn't relax my upset stomach. Or maybe the second chili dog was to blame.

I disengaged the alarm at the back door, and we went into the kitchen. Merlot and Syrah sat waiting by their empty food dish. Candace gave them each a little scratch on the head and said she was heading for a much-needed shower.

After filling their bowls, I went to check on the cats in the basement. Chablis didn't come to the steps to greet me;

that's how dedicated she was to her new family. When I entered the room, several cans of cat food in hand, she was again cleaning Dame Wiggins on that shoulder. She might lick the poor cat raw if she kept this up.

This behavior reminded me that I had to call Shawn right away. Maybe he could scan Dame Wiggins tomorrow.

After I spent time petting everyone, I finally relaxed a little. I went back upstairs and sat at the breakfast bar, ready to phone Shawn. Syrah took up residence on the counter within petting reach. Merlot was on the window seat and gave me a sleepy-eyed glance. But he was apparently too tired to move.

As I was dialing, I heard Kara's key in the back door, and she came in a second later. I gave her a small wave and a smile. She smiled back and walked past me. I turned and saw her go through the living room and down the hall.

Shawn answered on the third ring, and by his gruff "hello" I feared I'd called at a bad time.

"Hi. It's Jillian," I said.

"Oh, glad you called. We've got a problem," he said.

"We do?"

"A stray-cat explosion. Ruth Schultz had six more show up at her house this morning, and I've had people bringing me cats all day," he said.

"Uh-oh. I heard Robin West had two cats appear at her farm, too." I was stunned by my next thought, but mostly because I hadn't considered it before. "Could this mean the cats from the professor's farm were actually let go, not taken away?" I said.

"That's what I'm thinking, and if there are fifty strays running around, I'll need all the help I can get," he said.

"I'll do whatever I can. I know a few people who can foster cats," I said.

"Good. Doc Howard's coming back tomorrow to give more immunizations and do stool and blood tests. Thank goodness Allison is off school this week, or I'd really be going nuts," he said. "But I'm sure you didn't call to chat. Is Dame Wiggins okay?"

"She's fine. Sweet as can be, and her kittens are getting fat. But there is something. Did you or Doc Howard scan her for a chip?"

Silence followed before Shawn finally said, "I was trying to go back over that night in my head, and you know what? I don't think so. I've got to take care of that, and the sooner the better."

"She could have a home to go to, Shawn." I told him about the small lump on her shoulder blade.

"Tomorrow morning, okay?" he said.

"Sure," I said.

We settled on a time, and he hung up. I remembered Patrick Hoffman's words, how he said something about how the cats should be free. At the time, that seemed to me like a militant. If he really was—though his words had sounded scripted to me—he was the type who thought no cats or dogs should be owned by humans. But maybe he didn't care about the cats at all.

Candace walked into the kitchen a few minutes later dressed in a pair of my shorts and a T-shirt. "Forgot a few things when we swung by my apartment. Hope you don't mind I'm wearing your stuff."

"What's mine is yours," I said.

She poured herself a glass of water and pulled out a barstool.

I told her what I'd learned from Shawn, how lots of stray cats were showing up around town.

"Meaning they were let go, not taken?" she asked.

"That's what we're thinking," I said. "And for some reason, I don't think Patrick Hoffman was an activist with an agenda. I'm thinking he tracked VanKleet to Mercy."

Candace said, "That could be true and fits with something I realized while I was in the shower. Sarah VanKleet lied when she said she needed directions to get here the night she was notified her ex was dead. But from what Kara told us, she obviously knew the professor was here because she'd taken him to court about that farm. Maybe she told Hoffman where the professor was and didn't realize she was sealing her ex's death warrant. But why would Hoffman want to kill the professor?"

"I don't know, but Hoffman seemed to be reading off a script when he came here. Like someone told him what to say."

"You're saying Hoffman wanted it to *seem* like activists were to blame for the murder?" Candace considered this for a moment. "If that's true, someone else is behind all this and maybe for more mundane reasons. Like money. I definitely need to talk to Sarah VanKleet. But let's keep everything on the table, not completely discard this activist theory. Can Shawn help us identify exactly which group Hoffman might belong to if there really is a connection there?"

"I have no idea," I said.

"That could be a way to find Hoffman. If he's a domestic terrorist, he has to have friends exactly like him," she said.

Kara walked up to the breakfast bar on her own little cat feet. "Maybe I should have closed my ears," she said. "I heard the name Hoffman. Is that your suspect?"

Kara's dark hair was pulled back, and she had white night cream on her forehead, under her eyes and along the sides of her nose.

"Yes, that's our suspect," Candace said. "We all have to be careful because we don't know his whereabouts. He's the guy who attacked Jillian, and he got away from me today." She shook her head. "I was so close to taking him down."

"Why would he come back here?" Kara said. "He's busted now. If I were him, I'd run as far away as I could get."

"She has a point," I said to Candace.

"I get that," she said. "He probably murdered two people, he's on the run and he's desperate. But if he's connected to the VanKleet family in any way, he might expect them to help him. And they're in Mercy."

"Help him with money, I assume? But they don't have any," Kara said.

Candace looked frustrated for a second but then seemed to relax. "Brandt told you that?"

Kara nodded.

"You realize people lie," Candace said. "What evidence do you have that he told you the truth? I agree, there appear to be money issues, but we haven't had a chance to find out if there's money hidden somewhere that we don't know about."

Kara seemed to ponder this, and then said, "You didn't find any money in the farmhouse, right?"

"No, but let's focus on Patrick Hoffman. Something tells me this guy is coming back. For one thing, he's had contact with Evan VanKleet on at least two occasions, and I'm willing to bet he's had contact with the rest of family. After all, Denman is smaller than Mercy, so there are no strangers there. Bottom line, you need to be careful." Candace went on to describe Hoffman.

"He talks like he's reading off a bad script, too. And he smells like limes," I said.

"What?" Candace said.

"Remember? That's what I told you about him—and those are the good things," I said.

Candace leaned close and hugged me. "I am so sorry I didn't nail him today."

"It's okay," I said. "I was so amazed how you didn't hesitate. Just went after him."

"That's the job," Candace said.

Kara held out a small glass jar to Candace. "You look so tired. This stuff is great for those dark circles."

Candace cocked her head and didn't speak for several seconds. Then she took the jar and smiled. "Thanks, Kara."

Twenty-six

Shawn arrived at eight the next morning, before Kara and Candace were even awake. The coffee was on, and he smelled it the minute I let him in through the back door.

Merlot and Syrah were at his feet almost immediately, and he knelt down to greet them. They adored Shawn, seemed to love the way his strong hands massaged them. They probably missed John's masculine touch, and Shawn's kind of petting seemed to make up for their loss a tiny bit. "Where's Chablis?" he asked.

"She has become Dame Wiggins's protector and groomer, and a second mother to those kittens. That's how I found the microchip. Chablis thinks she can lick the thing out of Dame Wiggins."

Shawn laughed, and after he'd given both cats an equal share of attention, he stood and said, "Tell me there's enough coffee for me, 'cause it smells good enough for me to wade across a cold river to get some."

I filled a large mug and handed it to him.

"This might just get me through the day," he said.

I picked up a stack of cat quilts—I always have quilts squirreled away for emergencies. "These are for your new rescues. They'll need some comfort. I'll set them by the door so you don't forget them."

Shawn smiled. "Every cat goes home with a quilt since I met you. Thank you, lady." He held up his scanner. "Now lead me to Dame Wiggins."

I set the quilts by the small table at the back door, and we went downstairs with Merlot and Syrah leading the way. But cats learn quickly, and the boys stopped in the middle of the game room and sat down.

"What's with them?" Shawn said as we went to the bedroom.

"That's as far as they're allowed to go, according to their boss, Chablis," I said.

He smiled. "Your cats have the craziest personalities, Jillian," he said as he went into the bedroom. He had brought his coffee and took a hefty swig.

"They *are* the best cats on the planet," I said.

Chablis was curled up with the kittens, and Dame Wiggins was napping. Wiggins lifted her head and meowed when we came close. But Chablis wasn't sure she liked this invasion and was on her feet and between Shawn and Dame Wiggins in an instant.

We both knelt, and all it took was a few strokes from Shawn and Chablis started purring. She even plopped down and turned over on her back. Yup, all the cats loved Shawn.

Before scanning Dame Wiggins, he scratched her under her chin, and she, too, began to purr. I took this opportunity to gently pet the kittens Chablis wanted all to herself.

Shawn searched with his fingers and found the small lump. "Yup. She's got one all right. This might be good news for someone." He held the scanner over the area, pressed a button and then looked at the display.

And appeared totally confused.

"Something's wrong," he said.

"With your scanner?" I asked.

"Maybe. I should get a number, one we can match in a database. But there's no number. Just a bunch of computer gibberish." He felt around again. "This is bigger than any chip I've ever implanted, too."

"All the chips are the same?" I said.

"Not exactly the same, but never this big," he said.

"So what do we do now?" I said.

"Like I mentioned, Doc Howard is due in this afternoon

to help me immunize and test the new cats that have arrived. Mind if we come back? He's more up on this microchip system than I am," he said. "I just know how to put them in and do the paperwork."

"That would be great. I had another question, though," I said.

"About Dame Wiggins? She looks great, and those kittens seem healthy just by looking at them, if that's what you're worried about," he said.

"It's not that. It's about animal activist groups," I said.

"Oh." He held up his mug. "Then that information can only be bought with more coffee."

I laughed, and we went upstairs.

Once Shawn and I were settled at the kitchen table, both of us with fresh coffee, I said, "Tell me what you know about these groups."

"Um, that might take all day, and I've got to get back to the sanctuary." He held the mug between both his hands, looking distracted now.

"There are some who believe animals shouldn't be domesticated at all—shouldn't be kept by people, right?" I said.

"Very true. Those are the worst kind. You know why?" His tone was harsh now.

"Why?" I said.

"Because they just want to dump them. They don't really care about the animals. It's all political. They think they know how all of us should live our lives. Man, do not get me started on those types."

"Are there any of *those types* around here?" I said.

"Probably. But you know, when I saw that meat in the professor's house, I was thinking this was about the raw-food movement. That's what he was feeding them, right? Raw food?"

I shook my head, confused. "What?"

"You have to know about the raw-food people, Jillian. You're smart about everything that has to do with cats," he said.

"Well, I do know a little about that. I know some folks think animals should eat unprocessed and raw food, like they would in the wild. But that's not anything radical. I mean, some advocates of raw food go a little overboard, but it's become a commercially viable—" I put my hand to my mouth, felt my eyes widen. "*That's* what VanKleet was doing. That's why he thought he was going to hit the jackpot. Because he thought he was making a commercially viable raw pet food."

It was Shawn's turn to look confused. "What are you talking about?"

"I just figured something out, thanks to you. Anyway, back to these activists. Do they have names for their groups?" I said.

"Only the big umbrella organizations. But I can tell you one unique way they operate. Actually, Allison figured this out. She's the computer geek." He sipped his coffee.

"So tell me," I said.

"They use the Internet to communicate. Ever heard of Twitter?"

"Yes, but I don't know much about it," I said.

"Well, Twitter isn't the only game in town. There's another thing like it—can't remember the name right now. Anyway, Allison says they send each other these little coded messages about where animals are being held and if they don't think it's a good situation. Like in a lab, or even like what was going on at the professor's place."

"Coded messages? Like Morse code?" I said.

"Almost, really. I guess on these sites you can only use so many words. Allison's the expert on this, but she says she's followed some of these messages, and they give addresses. Send out the alarm. Like, 'Anyone in the area of such and such address. Ten chimps need help.' Stuff like that. Of course, sometimes the messages are good. There are people who inform about cats or dogs that are about to be euthanized and plead for people to go adopt."

"Oh, that is a good thing," I said. "I guess these people are networked and ready to act when called on. But you're saying the problem can be what they decide to act upon?"

"Exactly." Shawn drained his mug. "Wish I could tell you more, but I got to get back. Thanks for the jump start with the coffee. Doc and I will be here later today about that chip. And I'll ask Allison if she knows anything more about this activist stuff on the Internet."

I thanked him and gave him a big hug before he left.

Kara, I thought, as I locked the back door. *Kara could show Candace and me how this network thing works.*

I made a fresh pot of coffee, hoping a second round of that wonderful aroma would rouse the sleeping beauties. It worked, at least for one of them.

Candace stumbled into the kitchen, rubbing sleep out of her eyes. "You get up way too early, Jillian. I'm supposed to be watching you, so you need to stay in bed until I get up." She grabbed a mug from the cabinet and poured herself some coffee.

I grinned. "Shawn came to scan the chip. Someone had to be awake."

"Oh yeah. You're gonna miss Dame Wiggins when he takes her to her owner, huh?" she said.

"His scanner couldn't read the number," I said.

"Broken equipment?" It was Kara. Chablis was supposed to be the stealthiest one around here, but Kara had her beat.

Unlike Candace, Kara was dressed in cropped pants and a peasant shirt. Made her look younger than twenty-nine.

"Shawn thinks the chip's the problem, not the scanner." I went on to explain about the chip being too large. "But his visit was valuable in other ways."

"Can we sit and talk?" Candace said. "Chasing that stupid coward yesterday has taken a toll on my thighs. I haven't been on my treadmill since this case started. And that's not good for a cop who's supposed to be in shape."

We went into the living room and sat down, Kara in the chair that had become her favorite spot. "I am allowed to listen, right?" she said.

"Certainly. And I'm hoping you can help me understand something," I said. "But first, we forgot about one piece of evidence—not that there haven't been distractions. Remember the *meat*?"

"We're gonna talk about that meat before breakfast?" Candace said. "I'll try not to puke on your fine wood floors, Jillian."

"Shawn understood why that meat was there, but he probably assumed we knew, too. At least he assumed I did. But I didn't put two and two together until I talked to him today. I think the professor was experimenting with a raw-food diet for those cats."

"That makes sense," Candace said. "There was blender-ized meat in those jars; that's for sure. But we've learned the professor was two slices of bread short of a sandwich, right? That diet he was creating could have been completely bogus."

"Maybe not. He was a pretty respected scientist, despite his mental health problems. And raw-food diets have gotten lots of attention and are now commercially available. Expensive, but available," I said.

"They are?" Candace said. "In cans, like what you feed your cats?"

"No," I said. "Grocery stores are putting in refrigerators just for raw pet food."

"No way," Candace said.

I nodded. "Yup. So maybe VanKleet's missing notebook contains valuable information. He may have had issues, but President Johnson called him a genius. He could have been developing something innovative concerning the raw-food diet."

"He did tell Evan he was about to win the lottery," Candace said.

"This is about a formula for pet food? That's the motive?" Kara said.

"Not very glamorous, huh?" Candace said. "But what if this formula or whatever he'd cooked up—or maybe *didn't* cook up is what I should say. Anyway, what if this was all in his head?"

"Then why did someone take that notebook?" I said. "I saw it, and an hour later it was gone."

Candace said, "Good point. We should be looking at people who knew about this experiment and believed the professor could make millions."

"Who knew?" Kara said.

"Lots of possibilities. Evan, for one," Candace said. "Or anyone else in the family. Maybe even the guy who fired him. And let's not forget Hoffman. Maybe he and the professor were in cahoots." Candace stood. "I need to get on the phone with the chief about this. Thanks, Jillian."

"You should thank Shawn for reminding me what we all saw that night," I said.

Candace left the room, and Kara looked at me. "You said there was something I could contribute."

I explained what Shawn had mentioned about activists communicating on the Internet.

"He's right. I don't know about animal rights people, but remember the election rebellion in Iran? Twitter was invaluable at getting the word out of the country about the protests and the resulting brutality."

"Lots of people use this way to communicate?" I said.

"Millions. It's mostly innocent stuff, but I can see how a terrorist might use this form of social networking to talk to other terrorists. How can anyone possibly follow all the hundred-and-forty-character messages going out every second of every day?"

"One hundred forty characters, not words?" I said.

"Right. Tweeting is a new language full of abbreviations. It takes some studying to get the hang of it," she said.

"Shawn said there are other sites like Twitter. What do you know about those?" I said.

"There are. Twitter is big business and wouldn't want their network used for anything even bordering on illegal," she said. "They suspend suspicious accounts all the time. But some of the clones probably aren't as careful."

"Can you show me on my computer how this works?" I said.

"I can show you on your new phone," she said.

A few minutes later, Candace joined us as I learned how to join the Twitter world. She learned a few things, too, though she already did have a Twitter account herself. But the bad news was, Kara doubted we could ever backtrack to identify anyone who was sending messages this way. Social networking was her thing, and she said the technology wasn't there yet. How could anyone track the millions of messages going out every second?

But at least I felt more up on this now. And then while I was closing down the application, my phone rang.

I nearly dropped the thing. "Is Twitter calling?" I said before I pressed the TALK button.

Not Twitter—not even close. The female voice said, "This is Sarah VanKleet. I'd like to talk to you, if you have time."

"We're talking," I said.

"Not over the phone. Can you come here? To the bed-and-breakfast where we're staying? It's called the Pink House."

I kept myself from admitting I knew. "What's this about?"

"My sons. Please? Can you humor me?" she said.

"Sure. When?" I said, wondering why she was calling me instead of Chief Baca or Candace.

"They do a very nice lunch here. Say, eleven thirty?" she said.

"I'll be there," I replied.

After I disconnected, I told Candace we had a lunch date.

Twenty-seven

The Pink House is an old Victorian, one of the first houses built in Mercy. I knew the place well because it had also been the scene of the murder last fall. I had stayed away from the place since then, so I was amazed by what I saw today. Less than a year ago, the house had been about to fall down. Now it had a fresh coat of salmon pink paint, and all the gingerbread trim was once again white. Flowers and manicured shrubs lined the walkway up to the front stoop.

"This is amazing," I said to Candace as we reached the front door. "I never thought I'd come back here, but I'm glad I did."

Kara had promised she wouldn't wait alone at my house while we were gone and would instead take her computer to Belle's Beans, the place she called the "hotbed of Mercy gossip." I knew she was right about that, and I realized I actually looked forward to what she might learn while she was there. I had to admit, I'd come to admire how intelligent Kara was. And she'd loved her dad, loved cats, and maybe one day she'd care for me, too. I wanted her in my life. She was my family.

I rapped on the door using the gleaming brass knocker—definitely a new addition—and a petite woman with short brown hair answered. She seemed about my age but probably had plenty of those little jars of face cream like the one Kara offered Candace last night, because her skin was creamy and smooth.

"Anita Stone," she said, glancing back and forth between Candace and me. "Can I help you?"

"Jillian Hart. I'm having lunch with Mrs. VanKleet."

Anita Stone smiled. "Ah yes, but we only expected one guest."

I thumbed at Candace. "She goes where I go."

Candace held out her hand. "Deputy Candace Carson, Mercy PD."

I didn't think Anita Stone's skin could have gotten any paler, but she did lose color. She finally took Candace's hand in greeting and said, "Please come in. I'll tell Phillip we'll have one more for lunch. He's my husband and does all the meals."

We followed her through the large foyer, and though I knew the layout of this house well, the place had been transformed back to what it had once been probably fifty years ago. The wood banister and trim were shiny with polish, and fresh flowers sat on an antique table we passed. No dust mites or musty odors, either.

"You've done an amazing job renovating this house in such a short time," I said.

"That's for sure," Candace said.

"You know the history, then?" she said as we reached the dining room. Then she shook her head. "How stupid. Of course you do. You're the police." Anita looked at me. "Are you an officer, too?"

"No. And I'm not signing up anytime soon." I perused the dining room. The massive oak table that had once been here was gone, replaced by four round tables sporting white linens. A vase of fresh daisies and yellow mums sat on each one.

"I'll talk to Phillip about the menu and get another place setting. Mrs. VanKleet and her professor friend should be down shortly."

Shortly was right. They came into the dining room mere seconds after Anita left.

Sarah glared at Candace. "What are you doing here?"

Douglas Lieber rested a hand on Sarah's back. "It's okay. I've told you that you have nothing to hide. Perhaps it's better that Deputy Carson came along."

But Sarah still didn't look happy. "I can't throw you out, can I? First of all, this isn't my home, and second of all, you're the police."

"And you'd be right," Candace said with a smile. "You can't."

"Shall we sit down in the parlor while we wait for lunch?" Lieber said. "I assume you've met Anita?"

"We did. She's making sure I get to eat, too." Candace walked across the polished wood floor to the parlor.

We all followed. The huge pieces of furniture that had once filled this room had been replaced as well. Smaller antique dressers and tables were used only to display artwork or showcase beautiful candles and Lladró figurines. Slipcovered easy chairs and a love seat against the wall sandwiched a coffee table. We all sat down, with Sarah and Lieber taking the love seat. He immediately took her hand in both of his.

I ran my fingers along the arms of the chair, admiring the gorgeous floral fabric, but Candace was all about business.

"Why did you ask Jillian here today?" she said.

"The honest truth?" Sarah said.

"That's the best kind," Candace said.

"Um, we were hoping for a friendly conversation," Lieber said.

"I'm not real good at friendly when two people are dead," Candace said.

"But I'm glad you called me," I said quickly. Candace was being the touchy cop again, and I had a feeling that wasn't the best approach with these two.

Sarah smiled at me. "I called you here to apologize, for one thing."

"For what?" I said, totally confused. I didn't even know this woman.

"I understand my sons created a disruption at your

home the other night," Sarah said. "They argued in front of you and nearly came to blows. For that, I am very sorry."

"Brandt tell you about that?" Candace said.

"He did. Will you accept our apology?" Sarah said.

"I'm not sure I understand why you're apologizing for the actions of your grown kids," I said. "But it was really nothing. Tempers flared. I didn't think twice about it."

"Brandt told me how Evan was there at your house when he arrived with his new friend, Kara," Sarah said. "And apparently Evan was quite emotional. I am worried about him. What did he say?"

So that's what this is about, I thought. "Did you ask him?" I said.

"I don't want to set him off. Evan has been troubled ever since the divorce, and . . . and—"

"We think Evan blames Sarah for his father's death," Lieber said.

"He thinks she killed him?" Candace said.

"Nothing like that," Lieber said quickly. "But though Evan and I remain friends, he wasn't happy about my relationship with his mother, or about the divorce. He thinks her actions—really our actions—might have made Hubert go off the deep end."

"He did tell me his father's mental illness had worsened recently, but he didn't blame anyone," I said. "Evan was trying to make sense of the murder—something I can never make sense of, by the way."

Candace cleared her throat, and I took that as a cue to be careful about what I gave away concerning Evan. She said, "You have money issues, right, Mrs. VanKleet? And that's made you bitter about your husband's failure to pay support?"

Her cheeks flushed. "He took everything we had. And it's my fault I never knew how much that was. I still don't know. But he had enough money to purchase a silly farm."

Lieber squeezed her hand. "Remember what Brandt told you?"

"To keep your mouths shut?" Candace said. "Innocent people don't need to keep secrets."

Lieber sighed heavily. "I suppose what she's just told you does make Sarah seem vindictive, but it wasn't like that. She took care of Hubert for twenty-five years. She's a loving, caring person. Hubert may have pushed her too far, but she would never hurt anyone."

Sarah seemed to be fighting tears. "I loved that crazy man once. He could be so funny and brilliant and—"

"And he had a plan to make a lot of money," Candace said. "Have I got that right?"

Whoa, Candace wasn't falling for the tearful act; that was for sure. But I wasn't so sure it *was* an act.

Lieber laughed. "You mean his experiments? The man was mentally ill and getting worse by the day."

"Did you know about the experiments?" I said.

"Only what he told me," Lieber said. "None of it made sense. I'm no biologist like he was, but I do have a science background. I couldn't follow anything he said."

"Maybe it will make sense to me," Candace said. "Go ahead. What was his plan?"

"Something to do with animal nutrition. That's all I know," Lieber said.

Sarah seemed to have pulled herself together. "But Hubert's research isn't why I asked you here, Jillian. And I didn't count on you bringing the police along."

"She did, though," Candace said. "Back to the big question that you seem to be dancing around. What was the professor's big secret experiment, Mrs. VanKleet?"

"Oh, what's the difference if I tell you? You know all about him now. He was obsessed with a formula for pet food," Sarah said. "His dream was to be the scientist on board with a major pet food company. Then he would have more freedom to develop this new food."

"Why is that such a big secret? Or did he have something in the works already?" Candace said. "Something he could sell to, say, Purina, for a lot of money?"

"He might have thought so," Lieber said with a smile. "Hubert was a dreamer."

"Are you saying you knew nothing about him having stray cats all over the place and that he was controlling their diets?" Candace said.

"Evan did mention a few cats, but that's all we heard," Lieber said.

"If you're not being truthful, we'll find out," Candace said. "You already told one little lie, didn't you, Mrs. VanKleet?"

She looked confused. "I never—"

"About needing directions to Mercy. You knew exactly where Mercy is," Candace said.

"Oh. That," she said, raising a hand to her throat.

"What does Sarah seeking the income she was promised have to do with murder?" Lieber said.

"She lied because she knew we'd be curious about her money issues," Candace said.

"It was a mistake," Sarah said, her eyes downcast. "I'm sorry."

"But you asked me here," I said. "Why?"

She glanced nervously between Candace and me. "Well, I spoke with the coroner, Lydia Monk, and—"

"*Deputy* Coroner Monk," Candace corrected.

"Yes. Anyway," Sarah went on, "Deputy Coroner Monk is in charge of issuing the death certificates, correct?"

"That's right," Candace answered even though Sarah continued to look at me.

"She told me that you, Jillian, were her good friend," Sarah said.

Really? What is Lydia up to now? I thought. "We know each other, yes. What else did she say?"

She cast a quick look at Candace and then focused on me. "She told me you were quite friendly with the police and perhaps you could encourage them—" She paused and turned her gaze on Candace. "I suppose since you're here I should appeal to you directly. We need to know when the house will be released to us so we can get in there and see if

Hubert left anything of value. My sons have to go to school, and that means I need money."

"First of all, Chief Baca will decide when the crime scene will be released, not me," Candace said. "But I'm not sure the house will be released to you. You divorced the professor."

"Semantics," she said tersely. "I've consulted an attorney, and my sons will probably be awarded that property."

She seemed awfully impatient about that farm. Did she think it was worth a fortune? Because I sure didn't. "But the police have to follow their timeline concerning this crime scene," Lieber said. "Isn't that right, Deputy Carson?"

"True," she answered.

"Can you guess when the house might no longer be under your ... what's a good word? Your jurisdiction?" Lieber said.

"A couple days to a week," she said. "We'll want to get back in there for one more thorough search."

"That long?" Sarah said.

"That long," Candace replied.

We heard the knocker on the front door, and a few seconds later, Anita escorted Brandt into the parlor.

"What are you doing here?" he said when he spotted us.

"Your mother invited me," I said.

He narrowed his eyes at Sarah. "She's lying, right?"

Candace stood and walked up to him. "What is it with you, Brandt? Got something to hide?"

Lieber stood and put a hand on Brandt's shoulder. "Calm down, son. We were hoping to get a few answers about the house, that's all."

He craned his neck to look around Lieber and spoke to Sarah. "Didn't I tell you that the police always suspect the family first? You shouldn't be talking to them at all. And where the heck is Evan? Is he here?"

"No, I thought he was with you," Sarah said.

"You need help finding Evan?" Candace said, sounding worried.

"We don't need anything from you," Brandt said.

"Fine. This conversation is over." Candace looked down at Sarah. "If you want information about your ex-husband's belongings, property or whatever else might have to do with the crime scene, you go through Chief Baca." She gestured for me to follow her. "Come on, Jillian."

She marched past Brandt, brushing her shoulder against his arm. I went with her, even though I was a little disappointed I wouldn't get to taste what was for lunch at the Pink House.

Twenty-eight

Candace fumed in silence on the drive back to my house, and I was so glad I was driving. The angrier she gets, the faster she drives, so we would have made it home in record time. Or we would have found ourselves wrapped around one of the hickory or pecan trees that line my driveway.

"One of those VanKleets did those murders," Candace said as we came in through the back door.

"You said yourself that Sarah wasn't strong enough to kill Rufus." After I petted our greeters, Syrah and Merlot, I opened the fridge looking for something to eat.

"Yeah, but what about poison?" Candace said. "She could do that. They do say women are usually poisoners, not men."

"I don't want to talk about poison when I'm hungry." I'd skipped breakfast, anticipating a big lunch. Sadly, I was confronted with Red Bull and sushi rolls. The chicken had somehow disappeared, so I took out the container of Greek olives and the tea pitcher. I poured us both a glass. I needed to get to the grocery store soon. Heck, I was even out of bread. Kara's disdain for carbs was a definite problem. We'd have to work on that.

Candace picked up her tea and gulped down half the glass. "Sarah looked strong enough today to smash anyone's head in, so maybe I was wrong. She is such a manipulator. Fake tears, fake nice. She thought she could get you over there and sweet-talk you. Then you'd do her bidding and get the crime scene released so she could raid the house for buried treasure."

I popped an olive and ate it before I answered. "She does seem a little desperate. Maybe her new boyfriend is refusing to come up with the tuition for Evan. Did you notice how she attempted to play on our sympathies there?"

"Oh, I noticed. Little does she know, we're aware that Brandt doesn't have to pay a penny for his schooling." Candace opened the pantry door and stepped in.

Merlot joined her immediately. One door that always stayed closed was the pantry door, and he wasn't about to miss a chance to explore in there.

Candace emerged with potato chips. "I am starving, and olives aren't my favorite." She tore open the bag.

Meanwhile, Syrah had joined Merlot in the pantry, and before I could shoo them out, Syrah emerged carrying a bag of catnip. He took off before I could catch him, Merlot on his tail.

I laughed. "I guess they deserve a treat. It's been tense around here the last week, and I know they feel it," I said.

"Can I have some of that catnip, too?" Candace said. "Doesn't it make cats all happy and playful?"

"Some cats," I said, grabbing a handful of chips from the bag Candace held. "Some are completely unaffected. Scientists believe it's genetic whether a cat gets a tiny high off catnip."

"You had to say the word *scientist*," Candace said. "I've decided I don't like experiments or labs or even scientist's kids."

"Or their friends or their ex-wives," I added.

"Them, too," she said and popped a chip into her mouth.

"Do any of those people have an alibi for the evening of the murder?" I said.

"Brandt refused to answer, saying he didn't have to— are you surprised?" she answered. "Sarah said she couldn't remember."

"How convenient," I said.

"Lieber said he was at home, but he didn't supply an alibi for his live-in friend, Sarah," she said. "He said he *thought* she was playing bridge."

"Maybe he didn't want to get caught in a lie," I said.

"That's the feeling I got," she said. "He may act like he adores Sarah, but if she's involved in a crime, I'll bet he runs as fast as he can in the other direction. Anyway, Evan said he was driving around that night. I love the 'driving around' alibis. So helpful."

I was done with the potato-chip-and-olive lunch and grabbed a paper towel for my messy hands. Candace took one, too. Good timing, because my cell phone rang and I wouldn't have wanted to get oil all over the new phone.

It was Shawn, and he said he and Doc Howard would like to come over if it was convenient. I told him yes, and he said to expect them in about fifteen minutes.

"One mystery will be solved today. The mystery of the enormous microchip," I said.

"Enormous?" Candace said.

"I'm being silly. This has been a bad week, and if we can find Dame Wiggins's family through that microchip, that will be a sign things are turning around."

When Shawn and Doc Howard arrived as expected fifteen minutes later, Candace, Syrah and Merlot came with us down to the basement.

Doc Howard brought his medical kit as well as his scanner. After he made friends with Syrah and Merlot, who continued to stay behind the imaginary line in the sand drawn by Chablis, we all went in the bedroom.

Chablis was not happy about so many invaders at once and arched her back and hissed. I went over and picked her up, holding her close to settle her. A few seconds later she was purring as Doc Howard talked to her.

"Gorgeous cat," he said before he focused on Dame Wiggins and her litter. "Those kittens are twice as big as the last time I saw them. But that will be her last litter if I have anything to say about it."

After he gently made friends with Wiggins—not hard

to do—he located the spot on her shoulder and separated her fur.

I saw his brow furrow, and he bent to get a closer look. "Hmm. I brought a four-protocol scanner."

"Is that what you have?" I asked Shawn.

"Yeah," Shawn said. "There are four common types of animal microchips, and I never know who will have which kind when I do a rescue—that is, if I find one at all. But maybe my scanner was not reading whatever type Dame Wiggins has implanted."

Doc Howard raised his scanner over the cat's shoulder and pressed the button, just as Shawn had done earlier. He looked at the results on the readout screen and said, "This is not a pet chip. It is some kind of integrated circuit, though, because data is being transmitted. But not an ID number."

"Why would she have this thing in her, then?" Candace asked.

"I don't know, but whatever it's for, it may not be encased in the biocompatible material that's used for pet chips." He set the scanner aside and separated Dame Wiggins's fur even more. "Look here. She's getting irritation around the microchip."

"Chablis has been licking that shoulder like crazy," I said. "Could she have caused that?"

Doc Howard shook his head. "No. See this red delineation around the chip? If Dame Wiggins will cooperate, I think I'll take this object out. She's reacting to it."

"How will you do that?" I said. *And will Chablis allow this?* I thought.

"A little local anesthetic, a tiny cut, maybe one stitch," he said. "The skin in this area is not all that sensitive. Since she's nursing, I can't take her to my mobile clinic and put her under. Anesthesia in Dame Wiggins's system might harm the kittens through her milk."

"This won't hurt her?" I said, feeling as if I needed to ask for myself *and* for Chablis.

Shawn said, "He's the best. This will take five minutes max, right, Doc?"

"That's right," he answered. "But I prefer it if just Shawn stays in here to help. Chablis seems very nervous about me even touching her friend, so take her and wait upstairs, okay?"

Candace and I left for the kitchen, and sure enough, five minutes later Shawn and Doc Howard came back upstairs. Doc went to the sink and used a damp paper towel to wipe off what he held so carefully between his gloved thumb and index finger.

He then offered it to me. It looked like a tiny glass capsule. "This is a microchip, but not like anything I've seen used in animals."

"Then what the heck is it?" I said.

Doc Howard smiled. "I only know about radio frequency identification technology as it pertains to animals. I will leave this little thing for you to figure out."

Shawn shrugged as if to say he had no clue, either.

"And," the doc said, "I didn't have to use a stitch. I used some surgical glue to close the skin. But I'd keep Chablis away from Dame Wiggins for a day so the area can heal."

And then they left.

I placed the chip in a small jar and screwed a lid on, saying, "Get ready to be kept awake all night by one very nervous Chablis. She'll probably howl and screech when she finds out she can't get back to her adopted family."

"What about this chip?" Candace said. "Maybe forensic tech services will have a look, since the cat was found at a crime scene."

"How long will that take?" I said.

"Could be years," she said. "Okay, I'm exaggerating, but months, maybe."

"Then I'll call my own tech expert," I said with a smile.

Twenty-nine

I phoned Tom, and while I waited for him to arrive, Candace started working. First she called Baca to tell him about the conversation with the VanKleets, and then she pulled out her laptop to update the case file.

"The chief's planning to have another talk with those people." Candace sat on the sofa, waiting for her system to boot. "And guess what he told me? Evan does have an alibi. With Lawrence Johnson's help, Chief Baca put out a few feelers in Denman. A convenience store owner spotted Evan's car pass at least three times. Guess 'driving around' can be a real alibi after all."

"I knew Evan was being honest," I said with a smile. "He's probably the only person who cared about the professor at all."

I heard Tom's familiar knock on the back door and went to answer. But only Syrah and Merlot came with me. Chablis had planted herself at the door to the basement bedroom, and I decided that's where she would stay until she was again allowed to care for her precious family.

I was surprised when Tom cupped my face and kissed me when he came in. But what a nice surprise. Then he held up a leather satchel. "Where's this microchip your brilliant kitty wanted you to remove?"

I handed him the glass jar from the counter.

He held it up to examine the contents. "That's a microchip all right. Let's go to your office and see what the computer tells us."

"The computer? Are you going to put that inside my computer?"

He laughed. "No, but after I scan it and retrieve the data—"

"Wait. They already scanned it, and they didn't find any ID number, so—"

"You mentioned gibberish, though. Did you see this gibberish?" he said.

"Yes. It looked like a bunch of ones and zeros," I said.

Tom smiled. "That's good. We call that binary code. I can scan that, record the information and input it. That should lead me to something."

"You can do that?" I said.

"I'm in the security business. I know plenty about RFID technology. And spies know *too* much about it," he said.

"RFID? You're hurting my brain. Just do what you do," I said.

"And tell us all about it when you're done," Candace called from her spot. "We need to solve *something* today."

Tom walked into the living room, carrying his satchel. "Hey, Candace. How's it going?"

"Could be better. Is there ever such a thing as cooperating with the police? Because I haven't seen any cooperation lately," she said.

"I think that's always an uphill climb." Tom looked at me. "Come on, Jilly." Tom tucked the jar into his briefcase, took my hand and pulled me with him to my office.

I glanced back, and Candace mouthed, "Jilly?" with a questioning look. Then she gave me a thumbs-up.

The minute the office door was shut, he took me in his arms and gave me a more intense kiss than the one at the back door. Though I loved this, the jar in his satchel was pressing into my back. And pressing on my mind. I pulled away.

"Can we do this?" I said.

"Sure. You want to see how I work?" he said.

"That's why I'm here," I said. But though I am an extremely curious person, microchips seemed way over my head. And certainly not as fascinating as they seemed to Tom.

He took from his satchel what I now and forever more will recognize as a scanner along with the microchip.

"Why do you need one of those? Somehow I got the notion you'd have to take the chip apart," I said.

"The chip has an antenna. It's sending a signal. We just need to read what it's telling us," he said.

"It's not talking to me," I said. "Cats talk to me, but not little electronic devices."

The doorbell rang, and I left Tom alone with his tiny antennas and signals. I assumed Kara must have forgot her key when she went off to who knew where. Candace once again had her gun stuffed in the back of her jeans. She was looking through the peephole, and before I could ask who was there, she threw the dead bolt and opened the door.

Brandt VanKleet stood on the stoop. "Is my brother here?" he said, trying to look past Candace and me.

"We haven't heard from him," Candace said. "Is there a problem?"

"I don't believe you. He's here. I know it," Brandt said.

"He's *not* here," Candace said. "I tried to offer you a little help earlier, and—"

"Let him in, Candace," I said. "He may act and think like he's ready for the Supreme Court, but I can tell he's worried."

Candace sighed heavily. "Here's the deal, *Brandt*. First of all, I'm armed. Second of all, there's a very strong man, an ex-cop, working on something in the other room. You pull anything funny, and one or both of us will take you down. Understood?"

"All I care about is Evan. He's depressed about our father's death. I *need* to find him," Brandt said.

And that's where the worry was coming from. He really did care about his brother, even though he apparently didn't want anyone to know.

"My rules if you come in here?" Candace said.

He nodded, and I had to say, his arrogance was quickly fading. He looked frightened.

Candace opened the door wider so he could enter. Once again, she made sure he walked ahead of her into the living room.

He glanced around. "You're being straight? He's not here?"

"We're being straight," I said quietly. "But you haven't been, have you?"

Brandt exhaled and looked at the floor. "I never lied."

"You just decided we didn't need to know things. That's a mistake, Brandt," Candace said. "Sit down, and let's see if what you've withheld might help us find Evan. That is, if he's really missing. I'm sure you haven't checked everywhere in town. Maybe he wants his space."

"My brother and I may argue, but we do communicate. He said he was sleeping in—and that kid can sleep—but his room was empty." Brandt plopped onto the sofa looking defeated and troubled. "Lawyers are supposed to be tough. And I know the law; I know that we didn't have to say anything to the police. But that didn't help us any. And it sure didn't help you." He raised his head and looked into Candace's eyes.

She'd taken the seat opposite him. "He could have driven into town. It's not that far. But since you're concerned, you can help us."

I sat next to Brandt. "Why are you so worried? Something happened, didn't it? Another argument?"

Brandt looked at me with a troubled stare. "No. President Johnson called my mother. He told her that Officer Hoffman came here and attacked you for some reason. And that he took off and can't be found. Is that true?"

I nodded. "Very true. Caught-on-videotape true."

Candace's face was taut with anger. "Why in the heck did Johnson tell you anything?"

"He cares about my mother," Brandt said. "He's worried that since Evan and Patrick Hoffman were friendly once, that could mean Evan might be . . . involved in this bad business going on here. Can you see why I was afraid my mother might have told you that today?"

"But you're more worried about what Lawrence Johnson told your mother. You think Evan is with Patrick Hoffman?" I said.

"Not willingly. And, yes, that's why I'm . . . afraid." Brandt didn't look down, didn't stare out the window. He'd settled his gaze on Candace now, and he wanted help.

"Okay," she said, her tone no longer tinged with anger. "Tell us everything and start with why you think they might be together."

"It all started when my brother got drunk one night and passed out. Patrick Hoffman was there to pick him up, dust him off and steer him, so he said, in the right direction—to those wacko kids who adore Doug."

"Those *wacko* kids?" I said. "Your brother considered them his friends."

"Yeah, but Doug fed them all sorts of hype about global warming, saving the rain forest, treating animals ethically, things like that." Brandt's face reddened. "Don't get me wrong. Those issues are important, but—"

"Yeah, they're important," Candace said. "But you're saying Douglas Lieber might have had something to do with that protest the night Evan was arrested?"

"Something to do with it? He *planned* it. Evan told me so the other night—after we had that argument. We got our acts together and went to his room to talk. He was pretty upset because now Doug is saying he isn't about to pay Evan's tuition."

"And yet he'd gotten Evan in trouble in the first place," I said half to myself. "Was Lieber friends with Patrick Hoffman?"

"I don't know about friends, but they knew each other," Brandt said. "I've told you Doug was behind the protest, but how will it help you find Evan? Because I want to make sure he's okay."

"Because you think Hoffman came to town?" I said.

"Right. Or maybe he's disappeared for another reason. I mean, our father had awful highs and lows. Sometimes he wouldn't get out of bed when he was on summer break from the college. Maybe Evan is depressed enough to do something worse than stay in bed."

"You're talking about suicide, huh?" Candace said.

Brandt nodded solemnly.

"Suicidal people are sometimes drawn to water," Candace said. "We have one officer who runs rescues on the lake. We could send him out to check around the shores and the docks."

"No," I said. "My gut tells me Evan's not suicidal. He wants the police to find the killer, wants to see that happen. You said you tried to reach him?"

"Like a hundred times. Voice mail over and over." Brandt closed his eyes for a second, took a deep breath. "Something is wrong."

"Wait a minute," I said. "Kara might know where he is. She's been looking for information she can get from any source for her book."

"Her book?" Brandt said.

"Never mind," I said, unsure exactly what she'd told Brandt. "She programmed her number into my phone. Let me call her."

I grabbed my phone off the end table. But I got voice mail, too.

"Text her," Candace said.

"You think I know how to do that?" I said impatiently.

Candace took my phone, brought up a screen and used the tiny keyboard to type in the words *phone home*. When she was done, Candace said, "Now let's hope she calls and that she knows where Evan is."

"He likes to drive around," Brandt said. "His rental is one of those tiny cars, a white Ford. He's probably traveled the roads around here, and—"

"Your father's place. Could he have gone there?" Candace said, her eyes alive with excitement.

"We did go there the other day—but I made sure we didn't cross the crime-scene tape," Brandt said.

"How much you wanna bet that's where he is?" Candace said.

But before he could answer, my phone rang. Guess text messages work better than regular calls, because Kara's caller ID came up. I started to ask her about Evan, but she interrupted me.

The fact that she was whispering was my first clue that something wasn't right. I had to ask her to speak up.

"I was just texting you when I got yours. That guy is here at the professor's farm. We looked in the window and Evan recognized Hoffman. You need to send the police."

"So Evan's with you," I said, looking at Brandt and nodding.

His features relaxed, and he smiled.

"The police need to come without sirens, or Hoffman will run. That's why I was afraid to call 911," she said. "Hurry or he might leave."

"You and Evan need to get out of there. Now," I said.

"We're leaving," she said and disconnected.

My heart was beating a mile a minute as I explained everything to Candace and Brandt. Candace called Baca immediately and then went to the closet and came out with her holster. She strapped it on and put her gun in place.

"You two stay here with Tom." She held out her hand. "I'll need your keys—and Kara's phone number."

I showed her the number in my phone's address book, and she must have committed it to memory because she simply repeated it. We went to the kitchen, and I grabbed my keys off the hook. "Maybe you're blocked in," I said.

But when we looked in the driveway I saw that Tom had parked his Prius alongside my van, and I didn't see Brandt's car, so he must have parked in the road.

Candace left, and now the worrying began for me as well as for Brandt.

"She's good," I said. "And Chief Baca's good. They'll catch this man. Then maybe we can understand why he killed your father and Rufus, because I'm convinced now that he did."

"I might have an explanation." It was Tom. He'd come into the living room and held his hand out to Brandt in greeting. They shook hands.

"What are you talking about?" I said.

Tom held up several sheets of paper with printing on them. "This explains why Professor Lieber did what he did."

"*Professor Lieber?*" I whispered.

Thirty

But Tom glanced at Brandt and got a sheepish look on his face.

Bet he wishes he didn't blurt that out, I thought. But *Lieber*? Why Lieber?

Tom glanced toward the kitchen. "Where's Candace? I should give this information to her."

"She's gone," I said. "Kara called and said she and Evan went to the farmhouse, that they spotted Patrick Hoffman there. She and Baca and probably the entire Mercy police force are on the way over there."

"Kara went to that farm?" Tom said. "I told her she had to wait until the crime scene was released by the police, told her that she could get in trouble."

"My brother is with her," Brandt said. "Tell me what Doug has to do with my father's death."

Tom stared hard at Brandt for what seemed like an eternity. "You'll find out anyway. A microchip that I am assuming your father implanted in a cat led me to information stored on the Internet. The two professors were working together to create VanLieber Raw Pet Food. I've got formulas, expenses, everything right here." Tom held up the printouts again.

Brandt looked dumbfounded. "Doug and my father? Working together?"

"That's right," Tom said. "But the money for this business plan seemed to have dried up, and from what I can tell, Professor Lieber had put up a pretty penny."

"He killed my father over money? Is that what you're saying?" All the color had drained from Brandt's face.

Neither Tom nor I said anything for several seconds.

Finally I spoke. "We can't be sure of that. What about your mother? She's with Lieber now, right?" I looked at Tom. "Shouldn't we warn her?"

"I'm switching from geek mode to cop mode. Lieber doesn't know he's a suspect. We don't want to set him off." Tom looked at Brandt. "Can you call your mother, play it cool, ask her what she and Doug are doing? Where they are?"

Brandt nodded and pulled his cell phone from his pocket. His hand was shaking when he tapped a few digits. When he said, "Mom?" his voice wavered.

I could hear her every strident word. "What's wrong, Brandt? I can tell you're upset."

"I'm fine," he said, sounding calmer now. "I was just checking in. What are you and Doug up to?"

This time I couldn't hear her.

After a few seconds, Brandt said, "He didn't say where he was going?"

I heard her loud "No" this time.

I raised my eyebrows, questioning this outburst.

Brandt put the phone on speaker then.

She said, "So I'm stuck here without a car. Where did he have to go in such a big hurry?"

"You got me," Brandt said.

Tom made a motion with his hand to keep her talking.

"Um, any favorite places you guys have found in town?" Brandt asked.

"No. And that coroner lady phoned. The death certificate has been issued and I can pick it up. *If* I had a car."

"Did you call Doug after he left?" Brandt asked.

"I tried. He's not answering, and that's not like him. He got a phone call and he was out of here. And what am I supposed to do now?"

"I can come over and take you to see the coroner," Brandt said.

"Would you?" she said. "That would be great. The sooner we get the death certificate, the sooner this mess can be settled. That farm belongs to you and Evan. If we sell it, he'll have enough for tuition."

"Um . . . I thought Doug said he'd help with that," Brandt said.

"Until about a month ago, I thought so, too. But all of sudden he says Evan should work his way through school. Anyway, we can talk when you get here. Thank you so much, sweetheart."

She disconnected before Brandt had a chance to say good-bye.

Tom said, "Go stay with your mother, but stall her about this death certificate thing. Create some excuse not to get on the road. There's a killer loose, and the police will want to know exactly where you are. And if Professor Lieber returns, stay cool and call me." Tom rattled off his number, and Brandt added it to his phone.

"But what about Evan? You think he'll be okay?" Brandt said. "Was Evan the one who called Doug and he's gone to that farm, too?"

"If Lieber's on his way there, he'll be met by the entire Mercy police force. We'll make contact with them and make sure they know what the microchip revealed."

Brandt seemed hesitant, but he finally left with my urging after I told him he had to take care of his mother.

"I hope Brandt doesn't take a detour to that farm to play big brother," I said to Tom as we stood in the foyer.

"I think he'll do what we said," Tom said. "Now call Candace."

But she didn't answer, and when I called Mercy PD, B.J. put me on hold—probably because lots was happening and he thought I called to chat with Candace.

"Come on, come on," I said into my phone.

"Forget it. Let's go," Tom said. "B.J. probably has more than he can handle right now."

Since Candace had used my van, we took Tom's Prius. It was a lot peppier than my vehicle, anyway. We made the drive to the farm in less than ten minutes, and the whole time I kept trying to phone Candace. But she was obviously too busy to answer.

The tree-lined road was crowded with police and emergency vehicles for the third time in a week. Tom took my hand when we got out of the car and led me to where Morris was standing.

"That's far enough," he said. Seemed his job was to make sure no one got past him.

But when we explained why we had come, that we had important information, he radioed Candace. Soon I saw her running down the driveway toward us.

I could read a hint of panic in her eyes. "Hoffman's got them, both Evan and Kara. We're waiting on a county SWAT unit."

"Oh my God. They're *hostages*?" I said.

"Yup. Saw a rifle of some kind. But we don't know what Hoffman wants until we make contact. And right now that's dangerous without major backup. We need help on this one."

"He's not working alone," I said. "Tom, can you explain what you learned from the microchip?"

I wouldn't have made sense if I tried to repeat the Pledge of Allegiance right now. My heart was hammering. John's daughter was in that house with a cruel, desperate man, and I suddenly realized I felt as responsible for her as John once did. And just as worried as her biological mother would have been if she were standing in my shoes this minute. And where was Douglas Lieber? Was he in that house, too?

"I didn't see that coming," Candace was saying in response to Tom's explanation. "Had my sights set on Hoffman as the only bad guy."

Tom went on to tell Candace about Lieber getting a phone call and taking off.

"C-could Lieber be in there, too?" I said. My voice was tremulous.

"We won't know until SWAT gets here," she said. "But Deputy Dufner only saw three people in the house when he used his binoculars. Once Hoffman figured out we were here, he started staying low and away from the windows."

I gripped Candace's upper arm. "Please help her."

Candace nodded solemnly. "I will. Promise. You and Tom wait in your car. And make sure you make room for SWAT to roll in."

We both nodded, and Tom put his arm around me as we headed back to his car. But then I saw what was probably Evan's rental as well as Kara's car parked not far from the driveway. "Her gun," I said. "Maybe she has it with her."

"Ah, the gun. I warned her about that, too," Tom said. "If she is armed, we need to tell Candace and the rest of the officers. She told me she knows how to shoot, but I'm guessing that means she's had occasional target practice."

"Let's have a look in her car if Morris gives the okay."

Morris said he was waiting for SWAT to brief them and couldn't leave his position, that they were minutes away. But we could look in Kara's car.

I wasn't sure whether I was happy or upset to see that gun sitting in her glove compartment. Tom took it and checked the chamber.

"Not even loaded," he said. "Wouldn't have done her any good. We'll just keep this safe." He carried the gun flat against his thigh as we returned to the Prius. "Don't want anyone going nuts if they see me with a gun. Those SWAT guys are pretty intense."

He set it on my lap when we climbed back in the car. I held up my hands, not wanting to touch the thing.

"It's not loaded. You need to get over your fear of weapons. I can teach you how to shoot when this whole thing is over. For now, just hold it. Get used to it."

My heart wouldn't quit pounding, especially now that I had a gun in my lap. Those two in that house had to get out alive. They *had* to.

"Come on, Jillian. Just touch the gun," Tom said.

It felt heavy on my lap, heavier than it looked. I put a

hand on top of it. No big deal, I thought. Just a hunk of metal.

A few seconds later the SWAT truck rumbled by us. It came to an abrupt stop right in front of Morris.

"Thank God," I whispered.

But then something caught my eye in the woods beyond the ditch we'd parked next to. A white cat was trying to climb a tree, its hair standing on end with fear. But it couldn't seem to do what all cats are good at—climb that tree.

"I have to help that cat." I opened the door and headed for the woods. The ditch was deeper than I thought, and I nearly tripped but managed to keep my footing.

Why hadn't I realized that some of the cats that had been released probably came back here? This was where they'd been fed, after all. We weren't close to the house, so it wasn't like trying to help a cat in trouble was dangerous.

"Jillian," called Tom. "Come back."

I turned and saw that he was following me, and following lots faster than he should have been. He'd scare the cat before I could rescue it. The cat fell down after yet another attempt to climb the tree. What was wrong with it? Weak from hunger, too?

Then something happened behind me; I heard Tom swear—very loudly. I spun and saw him lying in the ditch. I looked back at the cat and figured Tom needed my help more than the frightened white fur ball did.

But when I started back toward where he was groaning in pain, an arm reached around me from behind.

Not again.

Thirty-one

B ut this person wasn't Patrick Hoffman, as I'd feared. No, this person wasn't nearly as strong. I gave my would-be attacker an elbow to the gut with all my might.

I heard a grunt as the assailant let go. I even heard him fall.

I didn't even realize I had the gun with me. But what I did realize was that I'd dropped it when I'd elbowed the guy.

I whirled and saw Douglas Lieber scramble for the weapon. He got to it before I did. Then he stood and pointed it at me.

"You and your little police buddy have been more trouble than I ever needed. I'd shoot you right here, but I need leverage now that your friend in the ditch has seen me. You're coming with me."

I glanced back and saw Tom grimacing in pain and trying to crawl toward us. But those fifteen feet between us might as well have been a mile, and Tom knew that. He began shouting for Morris's help.

Panic flitted across Lieber's face. He said, "Come with me now." He waved the gun back toward the thicker woods.

I didn't move. "I'm not going anywhere."

"Come on, idiot. Or you're dead," he said.

I held up my hands, stepped toward him. "You set this all up, even made it look like activists were the culprits, didn't you? Set all those poor cats loose."

His eyes hardened. "What if I did? You come with me, Jillian. *Now*."

"No," I said, taking another step closer. "I want you to look at me when you kill me—like you looked at the professor while he drank the strychnine. You must have slipped it into his drink. What did you do, tell him you'd come over to talk?" I took another step forward.

"I've killed two people, why not one more?" He squeezed the trigger at the same moment I kneed him hard between the legs. He collapsed, but he still held that gun and pointed it up at me. It didn't seem to register with him that it wasn't loaded, and he tried to fire it again. But the empty gun only clicked.

Two scary-looking black-clad SWAT officers were upon us all of a sudden, demanding that Lieber drop his weapon.

"It's not even loaded," I said.

Lieber complied, but not before giving me a venomous look.

I checked behind me, where Tom was being tended to by Morris. "Can I go to my friend?" I said as the officers laid Lieber on his stomach and pulled his hands behind him for the handcuffs.

"You're sure you're okay, ma'am?" one of them said.

"I'm fine." I was beginning to understand why Candace said she loved her work. Kicking butt felt good. But I was worried about Tom.

The poor cat that started this whole thing had finally made it up to a low branch. I stopped on the way back to Tom and held my hand up. It rubbed against my fingers, and I said, "You stay there. I'm coming back for you."

Then I hurried to where Tom lay. One of the paramedics was already at his side, and Morris was standing nearby, looking a little pasty. When I checked out Tom's ankle, I saw why. Definitely broken, and sickening to look at.

I rested a palm against his cheek.

"You are a fool for cats," he said, trying to laugh.

"I am so sorry." I looked at the paramedic—I remembered meeting her once; her name was Diane. "Will he be okay?"

She was putting an air splint on Tom that resembled a boot. "He'll be fine—after about six weeks."

The SWAT officers were now taking Lieber to their truck. I stared up at Morris. "What about Kara and Evan?"

"As soon as that jerk in the house saw that SWAT was here, he gave up. They should be bringing him out soon," he said.

"But the hostages? They're okay?" I said.

"The paramedics are checking them out, too. But no shots were fired, and that's how we like these things to end," Morris said.

I felt so relieved that tears stung my eyes. "Thank God."

Tom took my hand. "It's okay now, but no thanks to me."

"You gave me that gun. Best defense I could have had—even without bullets," I said.

He seemed confused, and I realized he probably hadn't seen what had gone down between Lieber and me—or he was in too much pain to remember. I said, "Tell you later."

I heard shouts coming from the driveway and saw Candace and two more SWAT officers leading Patrick Hoffman toward a waiting squad car.

He yelled, "I never killed anyone," a couple of times, and then I overheard him say, "Give me a deal and I'll tell you everything Lieber did."

Candace yelled, "You have the right to shut up, dirtbag," and shoved Hoffman in the back.

Two terrible men were soon carted off in separate squad cars. Meanwhile, a stretcher had arrived for Tom and I had to get out of the way.

"I never thought of myself as clumsy before," Tom said as they wheeled him toward the ambulance.

"Can I go with him?" I asked.

"You can follow, but not ride. Liability issues," Diane said.

Tom said, "My keys are still in the car. But you should wait, talk to Kara and Evan. They need you more than I do right now."

I hurried to his side before they put him in the ambulance and kissed his lips. "Feel better," I said.

As they drove off with Tom, sirens blasting, a ridiculous thought flashed through my mind: *How long before Lydia knows about that kiss?*

After I rescued the white cat, who was declawed and thus not very good at climbing trees, Deputy Dufner said he'd take it to the sanctuary. I thanked him profusely and then waited in the Prius for a good thirty minutes. Finally Kara and Evan came walking down the driveway accompanied by Chief Baca. Evan was on his cell phone. Kara was as pale as new snow.

I got out of the car, and Morris the gatekeeper didn't stop me this time. I ran to her, my arms wide.

We hugged long and hard, and she whispered, "Thank you, Jillian," into my neck. "Thank you for being so good to me."

Then I reached out and pulled Evan in and embraced him, too. No words were necessary.

Baca smiled at me. "They're free to go. I have their statements. But I'll be calling them in to sign formal statements later."

"We're parked down that way." Kara pointed toward where I'd already visited her car earlier. No way was she driving out right now. The SWAT vehicle was still in the way.

"We'll take Tom's Prius and head for the Pink House first," I said. "Evan, you've got a mother and brother waiting for you, and Brandt knows enough about these events to be sick with worry."

"I already called them," he said. "But they both need to see me to believe I'm all right."

On the drive, the two of them were pretty quiet at first and got quieter when I told them that Tom was injured.

I was eager to get to the hospital once we dropped Evan off.

"Will Tom be okay?" Evan finally asked.

"Yes. He'll be fine once they set his ankle. But I'm worried about the two of you. Weren't you scared to death in there?" I said.

Evan said, "I wouldn't want to repeat that experience, but Patrick isn't the worst bad guy in all this. He told us everything Lieber did to my dad, said he thought they were partners. All Hoffman was supposed to do was look for any evidence that might have been left behind at the farm. Evidence connecting Lieber to my father's plans. But then we showed up. I am pissed off—no, *more* than pissed off. I'd like about fifteen minutes alone with Douglas Lieber."

"Don't worry. He's in jail, and he'll pay for what he did to your father. Just chill tonight, okay?" I said. "You've been through a rough time." Evan took a deep breath but didn't say anything.

We rode in silence again until I dropped Evan off at the Pink House. Brandt must have been waiting at the window, because he raced out the door and grabbed his brother to him for dear life.

Dear life. Yes, indeed. "We need to head to the hospital, but could you check my cat cam, Kara? Chablis can't get to her family, and she's probably pouting."

I pulled my phone from my pocket and handed it to her. She pulled up the video feed, and for the first time since she'd come out of that farmhouse, I saw her smile.

She said, "I don't see Chablis. It looks like there's catnip scattered all over the living room floor. Syrah and Merlot are totally doped and acting stupid." She laughed.

I silently blessed my cats for their wonderful power to heal.

Thirty-two

Mercy didn't have a real hospital, just an emergency clinic, and after a call to Billy Cranor, I learned that Tom had been taken to the county hospital about thirty minutes north—and very close to Lydia Monk's office.

If the Mercy grapevine was active, I feared Lydia already knew about Tom's accident. By the time we got to the hospital, sure enough, she was waiting in the emergency room. I thought I didn't need protection anymore, but maybe I was wrong.

She wore bright pink skinny jeans and a matching scoop-neck T-shirt. Her bleached hair was held back with rhinestone clips, and she had on the biggest hoop earrings I'd ever seen. I introduced her to Kara, but I was surprised and happy when Kara put an arm around my shoulder and said, "Jillian's my stepmother."

All at once my fear that Lydia knew about Tom and me was forgotten.

"Wicked stepmother?" Lydia said, eyeing me with loathing.

Oh, she knew about the kiss, all right. Otherwise she would have pretended to be the reasonable Lydia, not the crazy one.

Kara said, "Not in the least. What's your problem, Ms. Monk?"

"*She's* my problem." Lydia pointed at me, and I saw little rhinestones embedded in the polish on her nails. "Tom

Stewart loves me and only me. But she thinks she can come between us. Showing up here is just another excuse to get close to him."

Kara turned to look at me, staving off a smile. "Why didn't I know about this love affair?"

Lydia said, "Because—"

But Candace's arrival interrupted Lydia. "How's our guy doing?" she said.

"*Our* guy is waiting for the surgeon," Lydia said. "Or so I've been told."

"He hasn't been asking for you, Ms. Monk?" Kara said sarcastically.

"I'm sure he has," she said.

"I need to talk to him before he goes under," Candace said. "Hope he's not too messed up on painkillers to tell me what he found out about Lieber. I want to verify Hoffman's story." She took me by the wrist. "Come on. Let's go, Jillian."

Lydia started to follow, but Candace turned and said, "Stay away."

Lydia started to protest, but Kara came up to her and somehow managed to distract her.

Candace flashed her badge at the registration desk, told the receptionist why she was here, and then the magic double doors opened, allowing us in to see Tom.

We were directed to the last cubicle on the left. Tom looked sleepy, but thank goodness the pain so evident on his face earlier was gone.

"I did a good job on this ankle, huh?" Tom said. "They can't fix it without surgery."

"I am so sorry," I said, taking his hand. "This is all my fault."

"No," he said, squeezing my hand. "I wasn't careful in that ditch."

"Tell me about what you found on the microchip," Candace said. "I've heard some of it from Hoffman. Did Lieber have a big enough reason to murder two people over cat food?"

"Lieber poured several hundred thousand dollars into the research, maybe even his life savings," Tom said. "There were notes—rambling, copious notes—on VanKleet's site, and some of them indicated that they'd run out of money and that Lieber was 'losing confidence.'"

"No wonder VanKleet was robbing food, milk and meat. Even the farm could be in foreclosure, for all we know," I said.

"Nope," Tom said. "VanKleet called it his 'research facility' and paid cash. I'm not sure Lieber was aware that's how most of the money disappeared." Tom sounded hoarse, like his mouth was drying up.

"Do you need water?" I asked.

"No water until after the surgery. Man, I cannot believe I did this to myself," he said.

I wanted to apologize again, but instead I squeezed his hand.

Two young men in blue scrubs arrived, and one of them said, "We're taking you to surgery. The doctor will speak with you upstairs about what he plans to do to repair the ankle. Your friends and family can wait in the surgical waiting area. It's a lot nicer than down here."

I bent and kissed Tom briefly, then said, "See you on the other side."

"You better be there," he said. "And do me a favor? Don't call my mother until I'm out of the operating room?"

"She won't like that," I said.

"Believe me, it's better that way."

Candace and I left them to their hospital business and went back to the waiting area.

Lydia was gone when we went to pick up Kara for the trip upstairs.

"Where is she?" I said.

"She had to leave," Kara said.

"Are you a magician?" I said.

"Let's just say that public officials don't like journalists all that much," Kara answered. "I told her she might not appreciate what I'd write about her if she didn't leave."

"Way to go," Candace said, offering her knuckles for a fist bump.

The surgical waiting room was indeed much nicer than the ER. Free coffee, vending machines and comfortable chairs made waiting and worrying a little easier.

I bought a bag of Fritos and a Coke; Candace went for chocolate, but Kara stuck with coffee. Once we'd all had enough to eat and drink for a while, I settled against the sofa cushions and said, "I need answers, and I know you guys have them."

"What do you want to know?" Candace said.

"This alliance between Hoffman and Evan. Did Lieber arrange that?" I asked.

Kara raised her hand halfway. "I know this one. Yes. Lieber somehow figured out—probably through the professor—that Evan blew the whistle on the college lab. He was furious and afraid that Evan might have even more to say about his father if Evan stayed on campus. Patrick said that right after the professor was fired, Lieber approached him to make sure Evan made friends with Rosemary and her crowd. I guess Lieber had that group of kids eating out of his hand."

"He took advantage of Evan's drinking problem?" I said.

"Took advantage?" Kara said. "Lieber got Evan drunk the night he passed out in front of the dorm. It was all a total setup."

Candace said, "I made a call to Rosemary to confirm that Lieber was behind the protest that sent Evan to jail. She said she was sorry she didn't tell us, but that Professor Lieber was too awesome to rat out. He cared about the earth." Candace rolled her eyes. "A murderer can't really care about anyone or anything but himself."

"No wonder Lieber bailed Evan out of jail," Kara said. "Lieber didn't want Evan to talk to his mother before he filled his head with who knows what. And Patrick? That dude was such a puppet."

"Sounds like you almost like Patrick," I said.

"I had to make friends with him when he caught us outside the house," Kara said. "That's what you're supposed to do with a kidnapper. Make them like you. So he became my friend Patrick. And Patrick wasn't about to take the fall for Lieber."

I smiled. "Bet you turned on the charm."

"I had to. Evan was so angry at how Patrick had betrayed him, I had to play it cool, keep him from getting all agitated and escalating the situation. Evan's smart enough to figure out the game I was playing."

I sipped on my Coke and wished for a big steak dinner. The Frito meal wasn't very satisfying. "And exactly how did Patrick get you into that house, anyway?"

"A very large gun," Candace replied. "Loaded, too, unlike Kara's."

Kara flushed. "How did you know it wasn't loaded?"

"We can save that for another day," I said. "Hoffman didn't waste a minute once he got hold of you and Evan. Sarah said Lieber got a call, and that's how he ended up on the property. Pretty stupid move for such a smart guy like Lieber to show up on the property."

"My take on Lieber is that he's a control freak. When Hoffman called saying you two were hanging around, Lieber must have panicked and decided he had to take care of the problem himself. Or be close enough that he could tell if Hoffman was taking care of the problem." Candace looked at Kara. "He might have killed both of you, even taken out Hoffman and set it up to look like Hoffman was the lone bad guy. You got lucky."

"Why did you and Evan decide to go there in the first place?" I asked.

"The notebook. We thought we could find it and solve everything," Kara said. "But Patrick told us that Lieber took any evidence of his relationship to VanKleet with him the day he killed the professor."

"And probably destroyed everything the minute he got the chance," Candace said. "Guess you didn't think we knew how to search a house, huh?"

"I was so focused on gathering evidence myself—for the book—that I put both Evan and me in danger. We made a dumb move," Kara said.

"Do you trust me now?" Candace said.

"Absolutely," Kara said. "I trust both of you—and, believe me, I haven't trusted anyone in a very long time. It feels good to know that you guys had my back."

I reached over and squeezed her hand. "I will always have your back." I looked at Candace, who seemed more relaxed than I'd seen her in days. Bet she loved taking Hoffman in.

"I heard Hoffman shouting that he didn't kill anyone," I said, looking at Candace. "That's apparently true, because Lieber told me right to my face that he killed two people. Tom probably heard him, too, though I'm not sure he remembers."

She said, "Good. When Lieber clams up—and I'm sure he will—we've got you to talk about that admission. Hoffman told us he bought the strychnine from Rufus but he gave it to Lieber. He said Rufus had no idea what it was for, but Lieber offered about twice what it was worth. Rufus couldn't refuse with business down. When Lieber went into the house to visit the so-called lab VanKleet had created in the farmhouse, he had the poison with him."

"Lieber was the one who rang the doorbell during Van-Kleet's call to Robin about getting more cow's milk," I said.

"That's right. I forgot about that. Anyway, I believe that when Lieber saw that filthy place and realized what he'd feared—that it was no research lab at all— he decided to use the poison. He was mad as hell and made sure VanKleet paid a horrible price for wasting his money."

"But Lieber seemed like such an intelligent person," I said. "How could he have fallen for what VanKleet was selling?"

"There may have been some good research at first," Kara said. "According to what both Brandt and Evan told me, their father was a genius until he started skipping his meds."

I swished what little was left in my Coke can. "And that's what brought Lieber down. He refused to give up on VanKleet until he was flat broke. I can see that. Being book smart doesn't mean you're people smart."

Kara and Candace nodded their agreement.

"Poor Rufus Bowen," I said. "I feel like I set events in motion. He got worried that the strychnine could be traced back to him, and instead of coming to you, he called Hoffman."

"Right," Kara said. "When you started asking questions, Patrick told me that Rufus called him immediately and they set up a meeting. Lieber was waiting for him, not Patrick. He also said that Lieber ordered him to scare you. Patrick heard talk when he visited Belle's Beans that you and Candace were tight, so he made a phone call to Candace's house, too."

"He was hanging around town?" I said. "And Belle didn't notice him?"

"Guess she missed him. He claims he got familiar with the town on Lieber's orders," Candace said. "Lieber had something on Hoffman, but we don't know what that is yet. I'm betting that Hoffman shouldn't have been hired as a campus cop. Probably had an arrest in his past. When Lieber finds out that Hoffman has spilled everything, he'll be telling us what a bad guy Hoffman is."

Candace said, "Lieber's going down, but Patrick Hoffman's not making any sweet deal where he gets off scot-free. Even if he didn't kill anyone, he knew everything. And I saw what he did to Jillian."

"You collected evidence," I said. "I'm thinking of that ski-mask fiber. Will it be used to convict Hoffman?"

"I doubt it," Candace said. "Confessions and guilty pleas are the best evidence we can get. But don't think for one minute I'll ever stop collecting anything I find that's even remotely connected to a crime. You never know what might come in handy."

"Then there's poor Sarah," I said. "She sure knows how to pick them."

Kara looked at me. "Make sure I choose someone exactly like my dad, okay?"

"There will never be another John. But you can come close." I put my hand over hers.

We sat in the waiting room for another two hours before the surgeon, Dr. Ellis, came to talk to us. She was a tall, commanding woman and told us about the screws and the bone repairs she had to make on Tom's ankle. But as long as he was okay, that's all that mattered. He would have to remain overnight but could go home tomorrow afternoon.

"Can I stay with him?" I asked.

"You'd do better to get some rest yourself. He'll be well sedated and probably need your help a lot more tomorrow," she said.

"She's right," Candace said.

I reluctantly agreed and was allowed to see Tom once he was brought to his hospital room. But he didn't wake up when I kissed his cheek, and I could tell he'd never remember I was here. I tiptoed out, and Kara and I took the van while Candace drove the Prius back to Mercy.

Once we reached town, Candace called me on her cell and said she'd rather stay at my place one more night. But she was stopping off for food. A cheeseburger for her, a chicken sandwich for me, and as it turned out, even Kara was hungry. But her chicken sandwich had to be grilled, not fried.

Kara and I came in the back and were immediately met by three cats. I knelt for a petting session and praised Chablis for her help in solving the mystery. But soon she was racing down the basement stairs, no doubt to take up her vigil outside Dame Wiggins's door.

"What will Chablis do without Dame Wiggins?" I said as I poured dry food into the nearly empty cat bowl.

Syrah and Merlot appreciated fresh kibble and began eating.

"*That's* what I forgot to tell you," Kara said, smiling.

I took a bottled water out of the pantry and tossed one to Kara. "What did you forget?"

"Dame Wiggins," she said. "When Evan and I met at the farmhouse, he told me that his father's cat was named Dame Wiggins and that he hoped to find her at that shelter where the cats were taken. I told him you had her, and he got so excited."

"He wants her?" I said.

She was swigging her water but nodded yes.

"No wonder the professor chose her shoulder to implant that microchip," I said. "I thought he just realized she was the most mellow cat on the planet. Obviously he was entrusting valuable information to a good friend."

"Cats are like people to you, aren't they?" Kara said.

"They've helped me more than I could ever tell you," I said, glancing fondly down on Syrah and Merlot.

Candace arrived a few seconds later with the bags of fast food. I swear it was the best chicken sandwich I ever ate.

Thirty-three

Tom still had trouble driving even six weeks after the double murders in Mercy had been solved. But he could hold kittens while I drove down Robin West's bumpy driveway. Jack was waiting on the porch for our arrival and actually started jumping up and down with excitement before we even got out of the car.

The two cats that had come to Robin's barn had been scanned and examined a few weeks earlier. Shawn convinced Robin that grown outdoor cats such as the ones that had shown up on her farm might do better to remain outdoor cats.

She was ready to give up on the idea of an indoor cat completely. But when Jack found out I had kittens that needed good homes—which I let slip accidentally on purpose—he did not stop asking his mother about them. She liked cats, so that wasn't the issue. She worried about the mess in her house—the cat hair, the litter and the possibility of damage to her furniture. So I worked on her pretty hard, telling her Jack needed the responsibility, not to mention the chance at having two great friends. She finally caved.

Jack had come to my house and chosen the two tabbies, and that's what we dropped off with him. I don't think I'd ever seen a happier kid. He didn't even seem to notice when we left.

But there were two more kittens that needed a home,

and off we went on our second mission—the trip to Candace's apartment building. We weren't taking the kittens to Candace, however. She wasn't home enough, she said.

Even though I'd tried to convince Kara that she could stay with me, she'd rented an apartment in Candace's building. I could understand that. She needed her own space. I carried the kittens because Tom had to practically hop up the small stoop and limp down the hall that led to Kara's new apartment. She and Tom had spent time together in the last six weeks. She was working for him while he was off his feet. Tom said she was a quick study and could now install an alarm almost as well as he could.

I knocked on her door, and she answered right away. I held out the kittens, and she smiled from ear to ear.

"They are so precious," she said, taking them from me.

She let us in—her apartment was almost as bare as Candace's, but she at least had a few easy chairs and a sofa. Tom hopped over and sat down on the sofa.

I pulled out a quilt from my big shoulder bag, exactly like the one I'd also given to Jack's new babies. She sat in one of the chairs, the quilt on her lap, and the kittens immediately sat down and looked up at her with their cute little whiskers twitching. The calico looked more like Wiggins every day, and the orange and white one was a real clown.

"I talked to Evan just yesterday," Kara said, not taking her eyes off the kittens. "He is so glad to have Dame Wiggins with him. It eases the pain a little to have something of his father's. He really loved his dad, even though he knows he was a troubled man."

I sat next to Tom. "He didn't deserve to be murdered, and I hope this book you're writing will address that. Is that why you decided to stay in Mercy? To write the book?" I asked. I'd been afraid to ask that question ever since Kara told me she was staying, but Tom had encouraged me to ask.

"I needed a job, and I found it here, but I also need family. That's you, Jillian. You're the reason I'm staying."

I smiled and felt tears sting behind my eyes. "Wow. Thank you. That means so much to me." I never thought I'd have children, but now I had a daughter, one who had so much of John in her.

Tom turned and gave me an "I told you so" look.

"And I also needed an investment," she said. "I've been clinging to what Dad left me like it would keep me connected to him," she said. "But that's crazy. He would have wanted me to do something with all that money."

"What's the investment plan?" I asked, blinking enough to stave off the tears.

"The farm," she said. "Professor VanKleet's farm. Evan will benefit from the sale, and he needs the money for school. And I saw potential there. But that house has to go. It was too darn creepy, and falling down to boot. You want to help me design a little house where these two little kids can keep me company?" She wiggled her finger in front of the kittens, and one of them batted at it.

"I guess I could," I said.

"You *know* you could," Tom said. "You've got style. Share it with Kara." He reached over and lifted my chin and gave me a small kiss.

"Keep it clean, you two," Kara said with a laugh.

There was a knock on the door, and Kara called, "Come in."

Candace walked in carrying a brown bag. She was wearing her uniform. "Hey, everyone." She saw the kittens, came over and picked one up. She held the calico up to her face. "Aren't you the cutest thing?" She rubbed her nose against the kitten and then gave it back to Kara. "Did you tell them your plan?"

Kara said, "I did. And they don't want me to leave town on the next train."

"There are no trains in Mercy, but you knew that," Candace said.

"Just good people." Then I added, "And family."

Candace pulled a bottle of champagne out of her bag. "I'm officially off duty, so this is okay."

I smiled. "Time for a celebration. New homes for kittens, and a new home for Kara."

Tom reached for my hand, and I tried again not to cry at the thought of how lucky I was to have these three people and my three wonderful cats in my life.